M000235415

THE NORTHPORT STORIES

SHEILA EVANS (1934-2022) taught high school English in California before forging a second career writing stories, novels, and a memoir. Soon after moving to Yachats, Oregon, Evans began to portray her new surroundings in her fiction, including the novel *Maggie's Rags* and the story collection *Northport: Stories of the Coast*, the latter of which was a finalist for the Oregon Book Award.

DAN DEWEESE is the author of the novels *Gielgud* and *You Don't Love This Man*, and the story collection *Disorder*. His fiction has appeared in publications including *Tin House*, *New England Review*, and *The Normal School*, and his essays and criticism have appeared in *Oregon Humanities*, *Propeller*, *Democracy in Education*, and elsewhere.

THE NORTHPORT STORIES

SHEILA EVANS

Introduction by
DAN DEWEESE

NORTHWEST
COLLECTION
Portland, Oregon

THIS IS A NORTHWEST COLLECTION TITLE
PUBLISHED BY PROPELLER BOOKS
4325 NORTHEAST DAVIS STREET, PORTLAND, OR 97213
www.propellerbooks.com

The stories in this book previously appeared, in alternate form, in *Northport: Stories of the Coast* by Sheila Evans, published by Central Oregon Coast Writer's Co-Op, 1998.

Cover photographs by Sheila Evans.
Cover and interior design by Context.

ISBN 978-1-95559-301-4

THE NORTHWEST COLLECTION is a series of titles that represent the rich literary history of the Pacific Northwest, published in well-designed editions featuring introductions and insights from contemporary writers.

CONTENTS

INTRODUCTION

DEWEESE INTRODUCTION TK. Ereptat ut inia quidel-
labo. Ihitiam raepel magnihic tet offic tem repeliquatio con pror
a qui andaesequi ditiorum dolorepe sumquia que cullicipsunt
quatur? Quia acculparum voluptas cum consequo comnim volorum is ex evelis ut quiant, que magniati doloressit ut hilles sus
ipsuntemo cone core, sequiae peditaquis es rem qui blacipi tatur?
   Lupta derit apel event, conecto tatio. Nam dit quia nonsectori
saped que pro et volor simost et esequia ndamus dolessed quodiatur? Qui volorem recaecae doles debit omnihil eria dellam
lam expliamusda velecerum rerferum eum volore, qui alignis
sunturit, corrum, eum iuntibeate commolo riassum, nescian
dipisit eseribus apient.
   Ci diatectur acium voluptaquas aborro magnihilibus nit eicto
tem quas andem netur as consernam, voluptur? Quibus velibus,
erem erchillaut vellatus quam evelecae odit ant delendae ommos
et fugit explab intiunt acia voluptatur? Quidusdae et ommo est
distiae nis vollam, illupta volupie nihicia nimi, ulparia ipitibusam

quost, sum hiciis que occum int liquas repellori apiet endus sum et que ipsandipiet quia quo ea dolupta dipsa aut eum nobit repedigni consequatur molores remos dolescid et verferitati te deles eos et oditiis de et quam fuga. Et fuga. Xim as militi temquam quodit optaspe llaborumquam que seruptae volore laborem sit doluptat ent que con porehent acea vollaut que culpa ipsum int.

Ximus molorep udicaboribea volorum etur aut illabo. Solorep tatent int omnitatur, susdandis eos discill enestrum diti ut molum earum rentibus minimol orrori dolupti beaquam, unti dolorepuda vitae veratis re lab invelit, eum rempore volles et ratquis non cullorit faceseque offic to tende pro demquam lauda corio volectiasin esciet volupta es poribus aut que venducitat hillaci llessequo dolorehent, od ea volorem imus, sitat et quia velecum non consequam arum idicatur atibus saperume secatur eseque poreiun deribus et maionsed eatet litisti dolupti quia nulland ignam, ut idus am, sus natiorpor mi, num iumquas sitaquis ex eos destinv eribus sedi cus sime aut ligenih illauta volorem poriate volorum quianis eliqui sequam quam fugitas accullicat.

Tiscimet eos am, vit hiciae es eaqui dolum acepudam volorum non nis dolupta estrupt aturior as mi, quiatibus nest magnatistis et, quiatius vel inusdam quasimust laut dem. Udiciat et assint officit ionsequam volecus cus dignitatur?

Parum volupis dolupta ssimenda consersperum voluptaquam que nusam fugiand uciust qui ommo maxim aut ani optus audiorectur, quid et pliciam idusdae et aut am eum quas arcipsa vel id moluptas es sequatur re, cullabo ratur, nes as et, totatqui nis maio incius estecerrum quid quidelendem ut excesciur molupta epudam, et enem es est mos excerun duntiorecte veriam fugia praecul leniet doluptat que paribus unt lacescit mos sinit qui custrundae minume cum ut ma que solupta quiaepe rercilibus, ad mi, quodionsed mo odia il inihil ipsapissunt, natem quoditia quo odignit, exeris magniento tem harcipsam ipsam latem quatum fugit poribus dolore consenetusam nulluptatus mod maxim atem il ipsum ligention rem lam, autenit re aut ab in re di andandipsam dolor aut aut esciunt fuga. Odio. Nequi sa cusae porro blaceratur anducipis dellab ipitata tibusda cusdae et quiat etur, quam qui venempo restia dem quo te magnis ma poritis sequias andus molore inctus, quiam volupta tquatum eum aut et es endebitatur rem aut il maio con nobis vendis et magnat vid ent eossit, sitior audaeriaeped et aspicat que doloribus.

On et modisci tatus. Naturias est acestibus eum ut arcipic to explia sed ut dolum rehendem inctiis ciusantiam, consequi delis etur repelliquo voles ari autempori dusciusame nes dolupta simos discideribus aperum consed utem lat autas ent labo. Nam que volorem cor sa dolorporum es aut quidus.

Sollenis velis duntiatem quia perro dest et adiatiorit aut et quam ne voluptatium as audae pliquis es aut la voluptatia non eum illuptatem repudiosam et et dolupti ossinis numquisquam inulpar itatem ius ducia dento consequi coris renis audi blab in poribus quia con con rem suntias perumenda eossime ntorerum autat res etur ad que eostiis solest qui odis parum voloribus ma ea cullorem ex et quo min consend enihit a sunti dolo occus aboris is denisseque consequid ullecatem harum ut quisqui re nos aliquia volorpo rumetur rero volo voluptaes dit re atur aut aute plistium, odi cuptur?

Volum qui duciet eriatec erupturia voluptatum voluptur? Totam, cus sum incimus, conempel modit et qui apide quistecepre acipsa id quatem quunt laborep udipidignam, abore dolut re eliquos et, si dolor aut volorei cipsum quis ut re sitiae. Inciandit rendam qui invelit atemper uptatur res atemporion nimilit atiae. Susae volore, consequos duntoria solo quisto volum core verum, tem vel mos quia consequatur siminum aut ium cus, ut quis que que veligna turerciis mo moluptium quis eaquid quodi consequiae eveni re num es quunt volorrum as sectibus si ut intotae nus ut ut hicae si cus auditiisit enias sima dent.

Undant esciur seris si omnimpor sitiis porumquodit que consequo evernam voluptis dolent, ullam aute elibus dolorat empores equibus dolor antio beatior estion recabo. Volupid quaeressit, aut et omnias moluptatet ut vention cus.

Beri recae. Soluptassi optatempori il im ea debissit et que dio volorio nempor magnit, velloreperia quam et lis re volutas perum suntiusam lame pa non perest oditemo luptatiunt lacienestrum re, cupta eum ressimpor audaero con ressimaiosam aut licilli ciditas moditatur, qui omnis prati quam fuga. Et optatet delis et erum arumquo doloria auda voluptin cupic totae. Et offic temposs imusaperi asperibus eatis eatio vitate natur sequo veriorrum ressit occatur sitatus, odiatum volorita quiaesci bea conserc ipsaepe rchilit, il im aut aut quas moloreiur mo quiat que ne ped et fuga. Parum, et, cullacc uptatinvero tet renderia quo officatus, vel magnimporem iur serestis doluptatur maionse rchiciet, nectectatus sin cumquiaestis dolum venit ipiendunt dit, cuptatiume aut velitatint que venia doles none acepra que pe exerum inimusamus, sequam alicimp oratque ped que volupta spitatur simusanis aliat aborion sequaepudit eatur adit magniet ut et idelecte et fugitis reptat ut prepedi gnihillibus aut erio tet, cusanim posanti onsende stisci sitati doloreperum qui veliqui am rem hilicim iniminu stemquae aut ulliquam eos ania susdantur, iusaerion repratia dolorro vitatur aut accustiis aliquas pellibea pror sit, et magnia voluptatur as cum quod quam sent aute paruntum entia pa qui remquibus.

Orepera que que alitatio. Ebit mod moles nos vellect otatur?

Bistotatem reium nobitae natem asintistium sum, sam harciatur alita ditae et molut fuga. Tum aditias ne maio blaborum di renimoluptam doluptatem et acimilit, sequaest rerem voluptas ius in nis ex evereium evenis iditationsed que nempore, andam faccus di reste volendi tiusaped quost optur, qui diti id qui deribus aperis nis sin ere libusanda nobis delentur? Quidessimus, comni omnis qui aut ex enditam aceatium explautem et elignis cone voluptis quosa niam voleseque nobitatem que dolupta doluptur, totatus reiunt ullaut estibus reici ut ut mo berum adi nita necestrum, cum quat.

Gia sit, quo ideles aut que vellat voluptur auda dolum ipiderovid quis ab int.

Ehent quam et iscilibus aspedio. Nam vollita verum nimi, cum ipsandiate ex eum fuga. Nam rempedi psandame porepernam vitatisim faceaqui dollorest quatur si cusdantia quiam quis rem niat.

Et harit lab ipsunt optat quosti to tem nossit deseque debitatur, ni odigenditiam aut aut od eostis ilitatus, occupta spelici llatis dolum que prerit ipsam quostio rectur rest acerum quunt volesti doles andandignis aliam, volupis es ducil enimus ilibusa ndelest, quis si id ulpa dolupta perum et abo. Hendi doluptatis aute ipsum fugiatum est, voluptam il ma non reiunt.

El illore poribeatiur atecusdam harum facessus, consequam aut exercium inciumquo tor similiquati quis eate nulla verum facculpa comni utem eatem re pa inia consequam, solupta nus ea volupta sum sam in reium ium cuptati dolore sitatecea volorit aerferum ut eum natet, officab oreriam dolo etur? Cia doluptatur? Qui rempore nditatquam estio officiis si comnimilis et resto eum a dolorep taturi blaborrore si corepe nonsequibus.

Ant facest, quatia consequibus esciant ectenit alibus denem ex ellaute ctotae nestore hendebis endelles et odi blam quia quas ad ut ium nis adi des necti te nis essi vero eost verum facepe volorae velitatur, od unto ipsum consequidis enis dus maiorem cum venectetum dolor aute eliquat litis solori sedit autem. Faccaerit re comnient.

Pudanis et ut mo digniti istorepra veligendis suntia sit re nes poratquis et, tem. Nam, quia duciatem aliquundant, simus audi ut ditae ad utatemquat alique ditiam quidunti inulpa quam que nimolestrum volupti officia volorrum nonessum doloren tiorehe ndaecti con ex enimpeditiae cor maio. Necersped que expedit iumquamet vel is disi odipsam, sa consed ut ex es invelendus est es volupta conetur, quiscia nimus, sitatur sam, a illuptat ped quodist, sum fugia dolorep erchict iossendit vellabo. Piet qui ut ullest ipsus rerchilit endi rem andaest runtur alis ut offici rerisi volorerspid ea peritat ere se sequam is si alicide dolest is dit fugias dunt.

Apel et od mosam apissit, aut restiat eos ut id quodi siminicturio. Dit accae pos ni offic tem quistiis rat alitem sam nonsequ atetur? Epedis mosamus, voloreprat labo. Pudam as amet pero discidebit abo. Nam repeliquas sam quist dellore voloribus ma aute velitios il entus at quidust, to quibero vitiis suntionseque sum quos moluptatur, quia et perae nihicimi, nonsece archiciae. Et volupti orempor ibusae nus, testibu stiatum verum ditiatur andandit re earum facerci dolorios eosandi suntioratium exerspis re voluptatur recat.

Pudanis et ut mo digniti istorepra veligendis suntia sit re nes poratquis et, tem. Nam, quia duciatem aliquundant, simus audi ut ditae ad utatemquat alique ditiam quidunti inulpa quam que nimolestrum volupti officia volorrum nonessum doloren tiorehe ndaecti con ex enimpeditiae cor maio. Necersped que expedit iumquamet vel is disi odipsam, sa consed ut ex es invelendus est es volupta conetur, quiscia nimus, sitatur sam, a illuptat ped quodist, sum fugia dolorep erchict iossendit vellabo.

Apel et od mosam apissit, aut restiat eos ut id quodi siminicturio. Dit accae pos ni offic tem quistiis rat alitem sam nonsequ atetur? Epedis mosamus, voloreprat labo. Pudam as amet pero discidebit abo. Nam repeliquas sam quist dellore voloribus ma aute velitios il entus at quidust, to quibero vitiis suntionseque sum quos moluptatur, quia et perae nihicimi, nonsece archiciae. Et volupti orempor ibusae nus, testibu stiatum verum ditiatur andandit re earum facerci dolorios eosandi suntioratium exerspis re voluptatur recat.

—DAN DEWEESE

THE NORTHPORT STORIES

GREEN MOON

I HAVEN'T seen Denise, my only child, since her split from number three. Husbands, well, not exactly—she's been married only once. The first several were live-ins, but they each lasted longer than her one fling at matrimony. Denise is easier on her men when there's an element of impermanence, of unpredictability. I know how this works because I've had live-ins, too, and have been married three times. What kind of women are Denise and I, with our multiple failures? Are we poor judges of character? Unreasonable and demanding? Torn between freedom and security? I don't know.

I retreat from my own questions while also retreating from log truck exhaust on 101. I'm waiting at the curb in front of the Suprette for the bus from Bend that's bringing Denise back to me. Clutching a bunch of orange dahlias with heads like little mops, a portable welcome mat, I rehearse the terms of a truce, a sort of I-won't-bring-it-up-if-you-don't that will smooth us through what could be a prickly visit.

Another log truck grinds by, jake-braking for the descent out of town. The kind of thing Rudy would do. I glance into the cab for his hawk-like profile, although I know he's long gone. Rudy had been my second husband, a brawny, silent man brought home to compensate for husband number one, Felton. Felton is Denise's father, a learned but benign bumbler, an elementary school teacher. I'd no doubt brought him home to compensate for my father, a hard-driving overachiever. And as long as we're counting, the last one, Tony, husband number three, twelve years my junior, he'd been brought home to...well, who knows. Shit happens.

SHIT HAPPENS. That's one of the sayings you run into in Melody's Gift Shoppe. Amusing, maybe, when Oliver North first said it, but now I find it as irritating as most of Melody's merchandise: double-billed baseball caps printed with *I'm their leader, which way did they go?* or plastic vomit or acrylic ice cubes with flies. The sorts of things Tony enjoyed. He'd watched *Evening at the Improv* over and over just to get the jokes down pat.

Again I pace out and peer into the distance for the bus. Feeling silly with my flowers, I think I could go home to wait. Denise knows the short-cut to the cabin that's been in my family since 1904. The one thing, besides Denise, I've held onto through my divorces. Felton had had a claim because he had put money into it—new roof, a real kitchen, wrap-around deck. But I'd traded him for my share of our house in Eugene. Just my dumb luck the beach house with its wooded acres above the bay is worth more now than what I left then. My one smart move: a pure accident.

The bus, the bus, finally. It screeches to a stop by a barrel of nasturtiums gone to weeds. I scan the windows before the door hisses open, and I know when Denise is in the aisle the same way I'd know the wind is blowing across a field. There's a movement, a bending, a turning. She does that, she turns heads. I'm wickedly proud of her; and I'm worried. She has no idea how short-lived this dewy point of perfection is. She thinks it's permanent, she'll go on and on. I know differently. But this is the kind of thing you don't tell your daughter. Besides, I've never had much luck telling her anything.

"Mom!" she cries, and drops her backpack so we can embrace. Her straight blond hair is waist length, and she manages it like a veil. She's wearing a green dress the color of moss, the perfect shade to bring out the creaminess of her skin and the gold glints in her eyes. It's very short, with a complicated peek-a-boo laced-up arrangement in front. She's also wearing sandals, the kind with laces twining up her legs. She's forgotten that nobody wears such things in Northport, where the wind is directly off the Aleutians. Denise is as out of place here as an Amazonian butterfly.

"I'm so glad to be home, you can't believe!" she gushes. I'm taken aback, because she's never lived in Northport. Felton, Denise, and I—when we'd been a family—had used the cabin only for holidays. "Lemme get the rest of my things," she says. "Where's your car?"

The bus driver has opened the luggage compartment and is stacking boxes by the barrel. "What is all this?" I say, but I know.

"Mom, it's all my stuff. I gotta get outta Bend, everywhere I go I see Randy, even if he's not there—you know what I mean? I need a fresh start, neutral turf. We'll be together, you and me, make a new family. Won't that be fun?"

We stand there, a two-person island in a sea of boxes. I kick myself for not having brought the car. But she'd always traveled light before, hedging her bets, and I'd planned to walk home by way of the short-cut. Down Seaview Terrace, through Thayer's cabins so she could see the retriever puppies, then across the field with the path mowed in it. A quick review of the town, and a way to provide a few minutes of sideways adjustment without that frontal awkwardness our intimacy seems to generate. Instead, I have to leave her there to sprint home for the car. I'm irritated at my lack of foresight. I should have known.

But when I drive back, I become irritated at her. She's talking to two guys I've seen hanging around the Drift-In. And I recognize the signs. She faces into the wind so it molds the dress to her legs, and flips her long hair back with a practiced, graceful hand. She slants her smile to bring out her dimples and arches her back, inclining into supple posture.

"Oh, Mom," she purrs, "these guys'll give us a hand. This is my mom, you guys, she lives out there on the point." Her voice has a new timbre, a layer of butter she's added for these unimpressive men she doesn't even know.

One of them is smoothly good looking, like a guy from a beer commercial. The other has a cloud of bushy hair and an earring. Men like these no longer interest me, nor I them. We are almost of a different species, and I dismiss them except for what they're doing to Denise. She is paying them in gold for their tinfoil attention.

Smooth and Bushy load Denise's baggage into the car while she coos encouragement. Watching her operate, I'm aware of my own contradictions: at first I'd wanted to walk home to dilute her attention, but now I'm disappointed at its loss. I do not know what we want from each other, or how we are to get along.

In the car, away from the men, she slumps. I'm a bit shocked and made shy when she dissolves into moist dependency. "I'm so glad to be here, Mom," she blubbers. "I can't tell you. When I got down, really down, I thought of you. We were always close, you and me."

I reach over and pat her knee. "Yes, honey, close. We've been through a lot. We'll be each other's best friend." I turn to smile at her and she's twisting her mouth around to bite her lip. She's done this since she was a baby, and I am touched.

"We'll be a new family. Things have a way of working out for us," I murmur, and pat her knee again.

She draws back—this is too much. "Well, sure," she snaps. "No biggie. I know I can make it here. You do."

"Yes, but I work part-time at the bookstore."

"These motels, they must need help. Restaurants hire all the time. Besides, I could take a course on something. How to do hair, or teach aerobics. Computers. I can live in the Annex, you won't even know I'm there." The Annex had been Felton's achievement. It had originated as a tool shed, but he'd converted it to a guest house with the help of handyman books on plumbing, wiring, carpentry.

"But Denise, I've already rented it out to a writer. He's working on his...masterpiece." I italicize the word with my voice, to show that my perception of the project is tinged with healthy skepticism. "It's a drama about Alzheimer's—*The Green Moon*, he calls it. This old couple, the man says the moon is green and his wife goes along with it, to humor him, but he really thinks he's humoring her. It's quite good, I guess." Hearing myself babble, I stop.

Denise slumps again. I kick myself for rambling, which I suspect is a diversionary tactic. Denise wants reassurance, not a story. At least I think that's what she wants. I try another tack. "You'll have your old room, of course. All your stuff's there, your agates, the driftwood mobile. You can pick new curtains, a new spread. How about some new paint?" When her mouth turns down, I rephrase it, "Well, redecorate, how's that? Get rid of that flimsy wicker for some oak or brass."

She sniffs and I hand her a Kleenex. "You still got those felt wall hangings I made in sixth grade?" she asks.

"Oh, yeah. And your stuffed animals, the puppets, your salt and pepper shaker collection—"

She laughs. "And the music box with the pink ballerina. Mom, you're hauling around a shrine to arrested development."

I draw myself up, throw her a look. But she's biting her lip again so I say gently, "You can go through it, get rid of whatever. I did put the ballerina out, I just had to. No harm in that."

Now she pats my knee, as if I'm the one who needs solutions. "No biggie. I'll just unpack bare essentials, use the boxes to clear out that old crap. I'm sorry, Mom, but I gotta have some space."

Crap. Crap. In a cold spirit of retaliation—I'm not proud of this—I lob Randy into the mix, like a grenade. But I'm unprepared for my direct hit, for the way she explodes. Denise jerks up straight and launches into angry stories of hassles over where to eat out, and Randy's non-stop beer drinking. Which she could have handled, she says, but not his playing around. She happened onto that by accident. Seemed that the car was always out of gas; she had to keep tanking it up. "Mileage was poor, it needed a tune up...but then she started keeping track on the odometer.

"On this thing here?" I tap the dashboard. Cars are not my long suit.

"Yes, Mother." She's as exasperated with me now as she is with Randy, doesn't even notice my cabin's new window boxes and shutters. When we enter, lugging boxes, she doesn't comment on my new front door.

"So I finally asked him," she says (we're in her room now, unpacking and repacking layers of her life, the pink ballerina in, the acrylic nail kit out), "where he went that he had to drive thirty miles every Tuesday and Saturday. He gave me a bunch of shit about being a control freak, you know, the usual stuff guys say. Then, Mom, this is kind of awful, but funny, too. I borrowed Linda's pickup and I followed him on a Saturday out to Redmond. I watched him meet Susan Parker—yeah, my friend from work. They leave her apartment all lovey-dovey, and go to this oak-beamed fake English pub, the kind of place he'd been ragging on me about as too expensive. I waited for them to come out, then followed them back to her place. They were in there two hours—two hours, Mom. What're they doing for two hours? Only one thing, if I know Randy."

By an unspoken signal we leave boxes and migrate to the kitchen where I put on the teakettle. "Then," she continues, "the next Saturday I borrowed Linda's pickup again. I waited for Randy across the street from that pub thing. After they parked and went in, I Karo-syrupped the gas tank."

"Oh, no, Denise—"

"Yeah, Mom, I did. I flipped the gas cap and dumped in a quart of syrup. I figured it's quicker than sugar and easier to dump. Randy loved that Audi, he loved his plates, that HAUDY AUDI thing he made up. You know how he always parked it way out so he wouldn't get a ding."

I pour tea, imagining it's Karo syrup. "Denise, that car wasn't even paid for yet."

"Oh, Mom, you sound just like Dad. That's what he'd say, something about the money, the cost, the repair. Randy loved that car more than he did me. It was the best way to get him, to payback. Well, anyway, he made it home that day, but then the car started acting up, finally quit on him out on the highway—ha! on his way to Redmond. After I told him what I did—why do it if he doesn't know?—we had this humongous fight, I mean yelling and throwing stuff. He smashed all my oil lamps, Mom, he took them out on the balcony and heaved them into the parking lot. And my records, my Steve Miller Band—you can't get them anymore, and my Madonna tapes. And my dishes, Mom, my dishes you gave me. They're all smashed." She glares at me, and I feel a traitorous shiver of sympathy for Randy.

"Still, Denise, to take it out on the car, that nice car—"

"Mom, you just don't get it! I'm telling you, you never knew a guy like Randy."

"But you picked him, Denise. He was your choice." I'm taken aback by my comment. It has a confrontational edge that I don't like. I'm usually not this direct with Denise because sooner or later I will pay for it. She will use it against me, point out that I've been no role model, that my character is less than perfect, my choices less than sensible when it comes to men. I am a flawed person. For me to have snagged three husbands is a fluke; I'm not that good. That's how Tony put it.

But Denise ignores the challenge. She gets up to pace around the kitchen Felton remodeled for us. She is more suitably dressed now—sweatshirt, jeans, sneakers. She pauses at the window to search for answers in the sea. As sometimes happens in the fall, the sea is flat as a platter. A mere ruffle of surf whispers ashore, as if worn out by a hectic summer.

She glances at the Annex, about a hundred feet back from the cabin. A movement at the window: the writer is taking a break from his work. She says slowly, "Yeah, I picked Randy, and I know why. He was exciting, dangerous. My statement to Dad. I know Dad's a good guy, but he's too safe." She turns to me. "So why'd you pick Dad?"

I smile into my cup, pour more tea, glance at the clock and run a quick calculation of meal preparation time...then I stop.

This is what I always do with Denise. I hide, dodge her questions. They are inconvenient, risky, would lead me into exposing too much of myself. But maybe we can connect if I level with her. She is biting her lip again, and looks so young. Yes, there is a connection, and if we are to be a family, I must admit to the doubt and chaos that run so deep. I must admit that I've had trouble when it comes to men.

I take a deep breath. "I met your dad in the bookstore. He was chuckling into a Pogo book, he loved Pogo. Still does, I bet. Yeah, he was safe, with his pink cheeks, his glasses. He was already going bald and a little pudgy around the middle. He was soft and easy as an armchair. A way out."

"Out of what?"

"Life, I guess." I sigh. "And I sure got it. Your dad and I were married twenty years and I spent it asleep, or dead. Numb, anyway."

I glance at her for any hint of derision, judgmental superiority. But she is listening intently, almost as if I have something to say, as if I am not her mother. "I remember counting down how many days till Friday, grocery-shopping day, and dividing that number into the bananas I had left. If I came out with zero, it was a good week. Mark of a successful week: to have no bananas left. Can you believe it? I thought I could pull it off, just sit there... like a banana. But then I started getting weird. I thought I had a temperature, or was getting cancer. I woke up at night drenched in sweat, not able to breathe. I was dying, and I'd never lived."

"I remember once Dad had to take you to the emergency room when you thought you had appendicitis."

"And asthma, and heart attacks. Then I left your dad after you took off with that cowboy we had in to clean the carpets."

"Okay, okay, I don't want to hear about it."

"I went back to the bookstore and never had another attack of anything. No heart murmurs, no cancer scares. But I was right where I started. That's progress, isn't it?" I chuckle, to defuse bringing up her carpet cleaner, and to show I see the irony in my own story. "Say, you want a glass of wine? I usually have one about now. I'm baking pork chops with apples and sauerkraut—you used to like that." I know this is a shameless derailing of our conversation, but I don't want to push my luck.

To my relief, Denise allows it. She relaxes her mouth and stretches. "Wine? No, too many additives. And I don't eat meat anymore. I wrote you that. How 'bout that book I sent you, John Robbins' *Diet for a New America*, did you read it? Well, no biggle. Just stick a potato in the oven. Potato and yogurt... no yogurt? That's okay. Just a potato and salad."

She drifts off, and I immediately review what I've said, turning it this way, that way, as you would an outfit you suspect is unbecoming. I pour myself wine while I cook, feeling anxious. I've given her too much, too clear a look into her father and me. As if I've handed a loaded gun to a toddler. I shout some meaningless conversation at her until I realize she's absorbed in arranging her things.

I usually eat in the living room with the TV, but this will be a formal occasion calling for a suitable amount of trouble. So I set the table with woven Indian place mats, and my family's silver that's as old as the cabin, and the orange dahlias that are holding up well despite their travels. I've begun to feel the wine and I have to work hard to maintain my crispness in the face of her cold sobriety.

"You used to like wine," I say, then regret the accusatory edge to my voice. I think I detect condescension, a bit of "ah ha!" in her eyes, and I suffer a blue spark of depression. But we go on with our meal: I cut up my chop, she slices open her potato for a grind of pepper, even salt, which surprises me, so pure had I supposed her. Then after dinner she brings out a couple of joints.

"You're so careful with your diet," I chide, "then you do this to your body."

Denise explains that pot is more healthy than wine, which is hard on the liver. And it's better than animal flesh, which is hard on the animal. Marijuana, in contrast, is a vacation for the body and the mind, with a long honored history going back to Stone Age peoples. So we take our vacations out to the deck where we watch the sun disappear into the ocean.

We light up and pass the joint back and forth with careful fingers. I don't want to do this, but I owe her for the wine. Maybe it will loosen us up, cut through our evasion tactics. I cough and sputter, the smoke is harsh. That's because this is good shit, she tells me.

Lights have twinkled on in the Annex, and we see the writer at his kitchen window, busy with his dinner. "He has grant money," I rasp. "Not much, but those right-brain thinkers don't need much." I laugh loudly, and too long.

"Oh, he wears a beard." She laughs, too.

"And a haircut like Saint Francis, like an acorn cap. Sometimes I give him a trim."

"You cut his hair? How sexy! Why, Mom, you've got the hots for him, haven't you?"

"No, Denise," I say tartly, then laugh. "See, it's a trade-off. I cut his hair and he does the recycling, separates papers, cans, bottles, makes the dump trip. He does have nice hair, though. Thick, straight, black with some gray. And nice chocolate brown eyes."

Denise giggles. "Oh, Chocolate Man," she calls. "Come out, come out, wherever you are."

"Hush!" I hiss, then dissolve in laughter. Distances have begun to telescope, then blur. My legs are much too short to carry me around, and if stand up I'm sure I can walk under the deck railing. I am so small I'll fall through cracks in the decking and disappear into the sand below. The whole idea is hilarious, and I have a laughing fit while Denise smiles indulgently.

"Look at those clouds," she murmurs. "Isn't that the writer up there stretched out in a bathtub with his beard poking up? Or is it a hard-on?" I roar at this sally, collapsing my short body into a knot of merriment.

"Oh, I see an aircraft carrier," I gasp, "with a castle for a superstructure," which strikes me as entirely logical. Now a breeze has elongated the writer's shape into a dinosaur, a Tyrannosaurus Rex pulling a train. She sees it, too. This is the most meaningful fun I've ever had with Denise, and she is the most dear, the most understanding, the best person, friend, daughter in the world, which is a wonderful rosy place.

The letdown is so gradual I hardly notice it. But the sky grows too dark for bathtubs or castles, and I grow too big and stiff for slipping through cracks and under railings. We droop back into the house for ice cream and wash it down with a gallon of milk. Denise imposes no self-restrictions on dairy items.

Reluctantly we resume our personalities—the frog story in reverse. I feel my warts, warps and miscues retake me. Time to turn in. It's been a long day and I'm exhausted.

Denise snoozes so late I peek in, to make sure she's okay. She sleeps on her side, pillowing her cheek on a hand, her knees curled up. Just as she'd slept as a child. She *is* a child, vulnerability nested into a knot of blankets. I almost expect to see her clutching a teddy bear, so tender has she become. Squaring my shoulders, I draw a deep strengthening breath: I'm going to be this girl's protection, stand between her and the rest of the world. At the same time, I'm glad she's asleep so I can drink juice and coffee alone—I'm headachy and parched as the Gobi Desert—and have a look at the paper. But I've finished it down to the want ads, which I read with an eye to her predicament, before she appears.

She's been reading, too, and emerges with a Victoria Holt paperback. To mark her place she has doubled back the spine and I long to snap, "Don't do that to your book," but I bite my tongue.

"How do you live without yogurt?" she grouses. 'I bet you don't do tofu, either." She's wearing a tee shirt that reads *I Love Oral Sex, It's the Phone Bill I Hate*, and a pair of bikini underpants.

"Denise, get away from that window. The writer's up, I've heard his printer. And there are always people on the beach right out there. You want coffee or tea?"

"Tea with honey." She stretches. "Your writer, when can I meet him?"

"I don't know. Mostly he keeps to himself. It's a wonder he didn't come out last night, the way we serenaded him."

She turns away from the window. "He's probably a fusty old guy, in there hiding his eyes."

I, too, am hiding my eyes as I put the kettle on. I'm uncomfortably aware of the smooth, uncomplicated body of youth. No bags or sags, no wrinkles in inopportune places. I harbor an unworthy thought, a flash, a hope that Denise keeps herself together until she's made a suitable match. Got her money's worth, so to speak. I would never say this to her, but I don't have to. She already knows how a woman is valued.

After tea and toast, Denise puts on cutoffs, a sweatshirt, and sneakers and goes for a run on the beach. Her hair is plaited into a braid that swings down her back as she jogs off. There's a movement at the writer's window. Andrew, my tenant, is watching Denise, too.

I wonder if Denise is right. Am I a bit gone on Andrew? He does remind me of Rudy, the same look of a hawk only half-tamed. I dreamed of Rudy last night. He's the one I still dream about, although our marriage was short-lived. I was crazy about Rudy, even after I realized his strong manly silences meant only that he didn't have anything to say, apart from a remark about the ball game or that we were out of Coors—in his Arkansas twang, he pronounced it *Curs*.

It was a wonder Rudy could talk at all, such a muscular tongue he had. Nothing put him off, coarse hairs, the body's natural secretions or odors. Such control, so generous, the dedications—he never got fooled into blind alleys, mistaken flaps or folds as Felton had been wont to do. When Felton could make himself function at all, that is. Rudy pursued his goal—my pleasure—with a single-mindedness I couldn't escape even when I was angry or depressed or determined to withhold. After he'd done me, he'd do himself with deep thrusts and unalterable rhythms that produced a different kind of spine-tingling release. Then he'd get up and bring us glasses of ice water and we'd gulp them down, slaking the thirst. Once, right after he left and I still talked about such things, I told a girlfriend about Rudy. "I know what you mean," she'd said. "Sometimes I'd trade it all for a really good fuck."

I'd been appalled. That wasn't what I'd meant at all. Or was it?

Of course not. Rudy had been more than sex. He'd been a delicious protective animal to cuddle with. He'd been dark and hairy, with a soft springy mat across his chest, an animal's pelt. I'd sheltered with him, my caveman, my buttress against the world. Only trouble was he drew women like a picnic draws ants and I began watching him, I began carrying around jealous caution like a load of stones, and I set out on a campaign of vindictive eating that made me pack on thirty-seven pounds before he jumped in his truck and split. But, Lord, the Godmother who gives out good genes had been kind to Rudy.

He'd had glittery brown eyes that burned with fire behind inky lashes. A little like Andrew's, the writer.

In self-defense, I haul out the torpedo-shaped vacuum cleaner and go over the rug. We dragged in sand last night, I can't remember how. I'm still troubling over my dream when Denise comes in with more sand. She's flushed with air and sun. "Guess who I met on the beach!" she gushes. "Jeb! Yeah, the guy who helped with my stuff yesterday. The good-looking one. Mom, I asked him for dinner. Let's have a dinner party. You, me, Jeb, the writer—the four of us. Won't that be fun?"

"Fun? When?"

"Tonight. Don't have a tizzy. I already stopped in to invite your Andrew. He was delighted. Don't you ever ask him for dinner? Let's do an Oregon thing, native stuff." She gallops off on her horse of a plan to check the tide chart thumbtacked above the phone. "At low tide I'll pick mussels. Yeah, I eat seafood. Somehow a fish seems less alive than a cow or a pig. We can have chanterelles—the woods must be full of them now. There's still some blackberries, too. Remember how we used to pick blackberries for cobbler?"

I should tell her it was her father who knew chanterelles from amanitas. I should tell her that I never did anything so useful with my time at the cabin as learn mushrooms. Something's dawned on me: I've been too hard on Felton. He was better than I gave him credit for being.

While Denise prances around I notice her cutoffs are so short only the thready crotch seam holds them together. But she has strong, smooth legs—she should flaunt them. I know why she does, too: she's compensating for being flat-chested. Poor Denise. She gets this from me. The women in Felton's family had been plump little birds with shelves of bosom. But not me.

After she showers, we take the car to the Suprette, because there will be too much to carry home on foot. I must wait for a lighter trip to impress her with the pleasures of the short-cut: Thayer's puppies, Stella's kittens, Lucille deNiro's flower garden, which had supplied the orange dahlias I'd met Denise with. Denise browses in Melody's tourist trap while I do the shopping. Chanterelles are eight dollars a pound, but I buy a few anyway to secretly substitute for whatever Denise brings in. A salmon roast, as well; I don't know about those mussels out there on our rocks. This is what I've always done: I short-stop Denise's rashness. But I don't mind, I tell myself. I don't mind. To prove it, I add salad material, french bread, vanilla ice cream, wine, designer coffee beans, and a quart of yogurt. I stagger out rich in food but down to my last dime. I've blown my whole week's food allowance.

Yes, this is for her, for Denise, whom I see through Melody's window trying on straw hats, laughing with Melody. And it will be a good party. I will gladly give up my nap for it. I've taken a nap since my days with Felton. Then, it was something to do, it broke up the days. Now, it's habit. But I will give up my nap so Denise can have this party. It's the least I can do for her. After all, I'm the reason she drifts, has a flat chest, needs a man so much.

It's a tiresome afternoon, though, mucking around in the kitchen. I set the table with my fussy best. The dahlias are now slimy-stemmed and dropping petals, but in soft light, they'll look fine. I get out new orange candles for the crystal holders, and polish the glass.

Soon Denise comes in with blackberries so heavy and ripe they release a crush of juice on the countertop. They also release a swarm of small spiders that scamper away for shelter. I collect them from their hiding places for a trip back outside, and I think of Felton when he was grouting in those tiles. They are handmade, created by Lois, my neighbor who does ceramics. The splashboard trim is decorated with images of tide pool creatures: sea stars, urchins, barnacles. I'm impressed again with Felton's thoughtfulness and I'd like to thank him in our once-a-year communication (a Christmas card exchange) but it would upset his current wife.

Again Denise returns from a foray. She has mushrooms, and they look okay, like little fluted ears, but as soon as she leaves, swinging a pail for the mussels, I substitute mine from the store. Lucky for us I have the salmon, because we have miscalculated low tide. The sea has reclaimed the best mussel beds, and Denise brings in only a dozen or so that I scrub and debeard while she has a tub soak. I've developed a crimp in my neck, and it doesn't get any better when I vacuum again. Sand getting in here is a new problem.

Denise emerges from her bath in a cloud of fragrant steam. She's wearing my robe and is toweling her hair. This is the second hair-wash in less than two days. The word adolescent occurs to me. I'm annoyed, and I know the bathroom is festooned with wet flapping things she's rinsed out, which is why she's wearing my bathrobe. And there are probably long blond hairs in the tub. I'll have to check, because having company see a messy bathroom is a sign of loss of control. I do not want to seem out of control.

I've just relaxed into my afternoon cup of tea when Denise sits down and gives me a long look: another exchange of confidences. I hone my psychic attention, wanting to be open, inviting. But she says, "You know, I can see a line under your chin where your makeup leaves off."

"Yeah?" I rub my naked neck.

"Yes, and when did you quit putting a rinse on your hair?"

"I don't know. A while back."

"Why?"

I sigh and clear my throat. "I thought it was time. I didn't want to look odd. There's a woman here in town, she must be in her seventies, she dyes her hair ketchup red. I don't want to get silly like that." I give a self-denigrating chuckle. "Don't I look okay?"

She continues her unblinking gaze and I smooth my tweed hair. "About your eye makeup," she says, "you should quit on that shiny white stuff on your lids. It accentuated your wrinkles. And don't draw on half-moon eyebrows like a Kewpie doll's." I notice she does nothing with her brows—they are full and bushy, not one hair tweezered. She wears layers of black mascara, and eye shadow in odd smoky tones, and a row of earrings up her right ear. I understand that wearing two earrings, one in each lobe, as I do, is passé.

I feel testy, snappish. "Well, I'm sorry, Denise. I'm not as young as I used to be. Remember, when I was your age, you were six years old."

She leans over to put her arms around me. "I'm sorry, Mom. You look great, really, for your age. And I know you missed your nap."

Yes, I missed my nap. If I hadn't been too sleepy to get up and put in my diaphragm a nap-time a number of years ago, she might not be here now. However, I will never tell her this. I will always keep up a bit of fiction.

For our dinner party, Denise has borrowed my purple and gold caftan that is slit up the sides to mid-thigh, and has replaced her stud earrings with my gold hoops. She has also helped herself to my perfume. I realize I've begun a hard-hearted tally. It's difficult not to, because I've grown accustomed to the use of my things. But, ah, god, it's Denise, and she looks and smells wonderful as she glides around serving goblets of the pale bubbly non-alcoholic wine Andrew has brought.

It's a warm, still evening, and the sun is setting in furious apricot colors. The three of us—Jeb hasn't arrived yet—take our wine out to the deck. When Denise sits down, the slits in her skirt fall open to reveal her smooth legs. Andrew squirms a bit. He is turned out nicely in a crisp red shirt, gray pants, and cowboy boots with stitching as elaborate as that on a Mexican wedding dress. He leans forward with a smile to listen to Denise, and I'm pleased. Like a cat that has brought in a mouse to gift its mistress.

Seems Andrew, too, is a vegetarian, a fact he discloses with a shy sort of righteous satisfaction. They discover they've both lived in Bend, so Denise tells Bend stories, but omits mentioning Randy. Andrew's time there coincided with a more pure era in the town's history, when it was full of true artisans, not ski bums flocking to Mount Bachelor. He tells of a tourist asking if he had Indian blood—this was during his wood-carving period—and Andrew's chocolate eyes shine with the pride of being mistaken for an Indian. He and Denise talk of hot tubs and spas and rolfing. They've both been rolfed, which they preferred to reiki. I gather that rolfing involves an exfoliation of psychic layers, but I'm not sure.

They don't even notice when I leave to check on dinner, but why should they? I have nothing to add here. I don't know Bend well, or much about spas and hot tubs, and nothing at all of rolfing.

Now is when I miss Tony, the most recent of my husbands. Tony had been a storyteller. He could tell a clean or dirty story about anything, anytime. He'd been great at parties, the nucleus of an admiring circle, in which I'd been included. He'd hitchhiked across Europe, barged down the Rhine, dived in the Sea of Cortez. But he didn't talk only at parties. When we were alone, he talked just to me. In the car we made a game of watching for exotic license plates. Once, on spotting one from Maine, Tony's native state, Tony told me how difficult it was to be a Mainer if your parents had not been born there—his were from Boston. "If the cat had kittens in the oven, would you call them biscuits?" was how a guy in Lubec put it. Tony worked there on a fishing boat.

But if Tony were here now, I'd be listening to the same old stories. Smuggling rubles out of Cairo under his tongue. Chasing an Italian pickpocket through Rome on a bicycle. Meeting his old college roommate on the beach at Cabo. After a while, you want more than stories.

"Mom," says Denise coming into the kitchen, "Jeb's here."

Her young man is Bushy, not Smooth. He has walked up from town and seated himself outside with Andrew. "Isn't he good-looking?" Denise whispers gleefully.

"Well, no. I thought it was the other one."

"Come outside and meet him. You'll see what I mean."

I do, too. Jeb seems slightly foreign, as if he has strided in from another country on his rope sandals. His hair is tied back with a black ribbon, and his cotton shirt and pants look homemade. His frame is strung with wiry, useful muscles, not Rudy's show-off kind. His eyes arrest—they are long and wrap-around, as if he could see off to the sides. They're slightly triangular in shape, with no hoods, and give him a look of strange intensity.

Jeb leaps up as I appear and presents me with a string bag. "Mrs...ur," he mumbles.

"Graham. Allison Graham, but call me Ally."

"Ally, this is for you. Homemade porter. Takes a real connoisseur to appreciate the flavor. But after this, regular beer tastes like water." He smiles, showing large, businesslike teeth. "Drink at room temperature."

Denise announces a dislike for beer, so I fill two water glasses with dark foamy liquid for Jeb and me, and we toast ourselves. I discover the stuff has a real kick, so before it paralyzes me, I hurry away to get dinner on.

Later, over his salmon, Jeb says, "Ally, you've been coming

here your whole life?"

We have just finished a litany of complaints about changes on the coast—traffic, congestion, pollution. The usual.

"Yes, and my father, and his father, too. They came on horseback down the Northport Canyon. Forest so dense they used the river bed as a road. Mail delivered on horseback, down the beach from Newberry at low tide." I'm looking at the mussels. Steamed open, the meat resembles the female genitalia, a long slit between fleshy folds. A few stray hairs still cling, adding to the illusion. Quickly passing the bread, I add, "Back then, the salmon were so thick you could walk on their backs crossing the river. And game—bear, elk, deer. The birds, oh—ducks, herons, and thousands of whistling swans darkening the sky. They wintered on a pond north of here."

"What pond?"

"It's gone now, filled in. That whole area leveled and graded for condos." I shake my head. "And clearcuts—"

"Mom, don't get started, please."

I glance at Denise, trying to gauge if I've gotten too shrill. I can't tell anymore: I've lived alone too long, have gotten used to being uncensored. Then Jeb says, 'This is a spiritual place with the trees, the river, the ocean. Shame to ruin it."

"Yes, but do you live in a wood house?" says Andrew. "Everyone complains about cutting down trees, but we all use wood."

"Forestry practices are wrong," I announce loudly. "These clearcuts! The hills look like plucked chickens. There's got to be a respect for old growth and biodiversity. We need select cutting, even a return to horse logging. A limit on state land logging, a tax credit for keeping private land in trees." I set down my fork. "And an end to log exports."

"Well." Andrew takes a few of the obscene mussels and squirts lemon on them. I look away.

"Yes," says Jeb, then turns to Andrew. "So you're a writer."

"Trying to be. How about you? You in the arts game?" He looks at Jeb's hands. We all look. He has short blunt fingers and his nails are rough, broken.

"Not at the moment. I'm doing cement work for the Pueblo Motel. Pays pretty good."

Denise asks eagerly, "Are they hiring? Maybe you can help me get on there."

"What can you do?"

"Oh, anything. Whatever."

The discussion turns to the coast economy, which we pronounce dead except for the influx of California retirees, and we tell of our financial sacrifices to live here. Denise does not mention Randy, nor I my two-days-a-week at the bookstore.

The moon sails up behind a wild sky of stratocumulus clouds. The three of them go out on the deck to admire it while I prepare dessert: berries and ice cream. Jeb appears at my elbow, and I think it's to help carry dishes. But he says earnestly, his wrap around eyes wide, "Ally, I hope that logging talk didn't upset you."

"The clearcuts do upset me."

"But you looked distraught. I hope this doesn't upset you either, but if you're not on a hormone replacement program, you ought to consider it."

"What?"

"My mother got real unsettled, panicky, when she went through that change-of-life business. All she had to do, though, was add a herbal drink a couple of times a day."

"Herbal drink?"

"Yeah, natural ingredients rich in estrogen. Ginseng or a little dong quai. You get them at the health food store. Made all the difference in my mom's hot flashes, her anxiety attacks."

I look carefully into those long eyes and all I see is sincere concern, what a sensitive son would feel for his addled mother. "Well, thanks, Jeb, for the tip. I'll keep it in mind. Here, you take these bowls out. Coffee's almost ready. Do you drink coffee? You're not watching your caffeine? It won't keep you awake?" I know it will keep me awake, but I will spend a restless night anyway, reliving this party. I am angry and embarrassed and the word I want to shout is *Whippersnapper!* straight from the affronted heart of my grandmother's behavior code. *You young whippersnapper! You uppity pup! Keep some respect about you, boy!* I want to bark.

After Jeb leaves, I stand there staring out at them on the deck. Denise has lit the army surplus spotlight to illuminate the surf. Tony installed it, one of his last projects before he disappeared to chase new adventures that would make him a hit at parties. I don't know if I can join them. Those three are as accessible to me as teenagers in the mall, and as unappealing. Jeb and Andrew, they are the new kinds of men. I see Jeb as the product of encounter groups, of consciousness-raising sessions, full of tenderness for people that he views, from his elevated position, as flawed. I wonder how well he'll age, dragging around such baggage. Andrew is an opportunistic dilettante, eking out an irresponsible existence with grants, SSI checks, stipends, wisps of windfalls. Moreover, his beard annoys me: it's affected, sissified.

But Denise, my daughter Denise, that brave girl, that poor girl having to make do with these types! But: she is her own person, not an extension of me. We are a lot alike, but when she cuts herself, I do not bleed—although I run for a bandage. Through the kitchen glass I watch this clever girl finesse these guys, a glance here, a smile there, such a touch she has. I cannot detect any sign, omen, slight favoring that foretells the future. I'd like to arrange some dramatic climax, some suitable way out for Denise. I'd like to have Randy call from Bend and say, "Honey, I can't get along without you, please come back." I'd help her pack, put her back on the bus. Or maybe Felton would take his daughter under his wing, arrange an entry level job in Eugene, a teacher's aide in some nice kindergarten. But I'm as likely to see these things happen as I am to see Andrew's green moon.

Denise and I will have to go through it. Sooner or later I'll stumble over cowboy boots or rope sandals in the hall. I'll awake to giggling in her room. There will be three of us for breakfast, a stiff affair. But it won't work for long. Soon this slippery girl will come to me and say apologetically, sadly, "You know how it is, Mom. We need our space. We're not deserting you, we're just getting our own digs. You understand, don't you?"

And I will. I'll return to careful, small pleasures, a happiness that requires strategy. Walking on the beach, admiring my own footprints. Sleeping in late, then eating cold spaghetti for breakfast. Listening to the rain in the hood over the stove, curling into a quilt with a book, something I've read before with no unpleasant surprises.

I'll be here, though, when Denise comes back to me again. She'll be back. She's not like me yet. She's not willing to concede that a little is enough.

GREEN MOON

Lois figured someday she'd run into Connie and Tom in Northport. It could happen in the coffeehouse. Tom had liked the ambiance there, the rough-hewn open-beamed ceiling, creeping charlies trailing under skylights, casual mismatched oak tables and chairs. He'd sat for hours over tiny cups of espresso arguing politics with Jim Larson or Emmett Robinson while the people with him, especially Lois, grew bored and retreated to the loft to read used paperbacks.

So Lois always found herself keeping up a façade there, a forced although pleasant demeanor while sipping coffee. *Well-adjusted dilettante at play.* Or *counter-culture artist relating to mammon.* Something lofty, wryly skeptical, showing her own ironic sense of how pretentious she could be.

But it was in the Suprette that Lois caught a glimpse of Connie pushing a rickety cart down a cluttered aisle. Lois's heart thudded with adrenaline; a painful rush prickled the backs of her hands. Playing cat-and-mouse, Lois trailed Connie around the deli case and up the pet food aisle, allowing time to compose herself before meeting Connie at the checkstand. Then Lois said in a hearty voice both aggressive and embarrassed, "Well, hello there, stranger."

Connie's face creased in a wide smile, and Lois was struck again by her light green eyes, the clear pale tint of old Coke bottles. Connie was very tan, almost leathery, the skin on her face and neck lined and dry. Too much sun, thought Lois, then remembered that Connie and Tom had bought a vacation condo on a golf course near Reno. Lois had hated golf.

"Lois!" exclaimed Connie. "I wondered if I'd run into you. Knew you were still around."

"Oh, yeah, doing business at the usual stand. Stella and I bought a house down the street across from the park. Are you alone? Tom with you?" Lois turned to peer through windows plastered with ads for weekly specials, searching the parking lot beyond. She wondered why, because long ago she'd lost track of the kind of car Tom was driving.

Connie said quickly, too quickly, "No, I'm alone. Tom sent me over to talk to the renters in the Seaview Drive house. Neighbors have been calling, complaining of loud music, too much noise."

Lois felt a flash of irritation for Tom. Just like him to dump unpleasant chores on someone else. But she laughed nervously and said, "Lucky you." Then to Eileen, the checker ringing up Connie's total, "We don't have bad renters here, do we, Eileen?" She was taken aback, such a transparent ploy to enlist Eileen on her side, a juvenile power-play shenanigan she thought she'd gotten beyond.

To her relief Eileen replied, "City of saints, that's us."

Connie's turn to chuckle nervously. "Wish you'd convince Tom of that. He's talking of selling the house, but I say to hang on. It's a good investment." She compressed her lips, as if regretting this slip that exposed a gap in their solidarity.

Lois said, "If you decide to sell, let me know. I'd like to buy it back and fix it up. Sentimental attachment, I guess." She grinned wryly.

Lois had been Tom's first wife, and the Seaview Drive house their first home on the coast before they'd moved to Salem for Tom's job. They'd divorced a few years back, and Connie, once Lois's best friend, had married Tom.

"Come by the house for a cup of tea or something," said Lois. "I never get to really talk to you. Come, please."

"That wouldn't interrupt your work? Or Stella's?" Connie faltered, looked away.

"No, Stella's not home. Stop by," Lois urged, almost meaning it.

The house Lois shared with Stella had started as a beach cabin, but over the years it had gone through multiple renovations. One of the best had been adding a foundation; the worst, building a half-bath that jutted into the garage, rendering it incapable of housing a car. "Nothing to code," Lois explained blithely on the tour she led Connie through. "But that's the way it used to be, in the good old days."

She went on, "This house is like an Indian Ocean seashell, convoluted, rooms that wrap around rooms that open onto more rooms. See here? A one-way mirror so our interior bedroom still has an ocean view through the living room, but people outside can't see in."

"Clever," Connie chirped, glancing quickly at furniture, at snapshots of Lois and Stella stuck in the frame of a dresser mirror. Then, with an almost audible sigh of relief, she turned to look out the mirror-window. "Oh, nice yard, nice flowers. Someone does serious gardening."

"Stella. Well, Stella does the heavy stuff, pick and shovel, wheelbarrowing. I plan the flowers, the design—well, the landscaping." Lois italicized the word to show she properly demeaned her role in the garden. She and Tom had fought over yardwork. He'd complained that she'd spend fifty bucks on bulbs, then never water or weed. "Why bother?" he'd roar. "Why waste money if you're not going to follow through?"

Connie murmured, "You're an artist, Lois, your pottery, so wonderful. You were always clever."

"Yeah, I still throw a pot now and then. Pop it in the kiln. Got two kilns, electric for bisquing, gas for glazing." Lois always got gruff, almost surly, when someone commented on her artistry. "Studio's out back. Had to fight City Hall to keep it there. Some nonsense about zoning. You should have seen Stella take them on. A real tiger. But I don't pollute, make noise or cause traffic. Earns me a buck or two, enough to pay the cable bill. Plus I do a little subbing for the art teacher up at the high school." She wrinkled her nose to show her opinion of *that*, then went on, "We don't need much here. We actually prefer the simple life. Now the boys are out of school, no more support money to them. You probably hear more from them than I do."

"Not really. I'm afraid they're mad at both you and Tom."

Lois said, "They've got the right, I guess. Doing okay, though. Paul's a security guard in a fishing-village-turned-boutique in Puget Sound. Wears a beeper, roars around in a black Dodge Polaris with a light clamped on top, static on the radio. Eddie's living in some commune outside Deadwood. But they don't call them communes anymore. Now it's 'extended family.'" She laughed sourly. "You'd think that given their pursuits, they'd loosen up and forgive me for the split. Maybe someday."

They migrated to the kitchen. Lois asked from behind the refrigerator, "You want a beer? No? How about a wine cooler?" She loaded a tray with glasses, ice, club soda, and a bottle of pale yellow wine with a showy floral label. "Let's go out on the deck. Hardly any wind today."

Outside they settled in a pair of Adirondack chairs painted forest green. There was also a wrought-iron table sprouting a green-striped umbrella from its navel. Lois tilted the canvas to shade their faces and discreetly studied Connie. In the greenish light her tan took on a muddy tinge, the skin on her face dry as parchment. But she was still attractive, so attractive. And those eyes, those eerie green eyes.

Lois thought to ask about Connie's daughter, Lynn. Connie's face lit up. "Lynn, yes, doing great. Married an attorney, has a house not far from ours. I'm a grandma now. Lynn's got a toddler. You should see Tom fussing over little Michelle, he dotes on her..." Connie trailed off, then added, "Well, fathers and daughters, that sort of thing."

Lois felt a jab of jealousy, not for herself but for the boys. They'd needed so much from Tom, and had gotten so little.

Back then Tom hadn't liked complications, interruptions, baggage that slowed him down. Lois said more sharply than she intended, "Tom wanted a girl, now he's got one. Better late than never." She took a gulp of wine to staunch the old fire of competition. It always had been a competition, herself and the boys on one side, Connie and her blond cupcake of a daughter on the other.

Lois had been a first year art teacher in a wild Salem junior high when she and Tom first met Connie. They'd met A.J. too, but Connie's husband had always been a shadowy figure in their foursome. The kind of guy who was there, but...not really. After he died of cancer, Lois tried to recall him as a person, apart from a counterweight to Connie, but came up with only a fuzzy outline of a man. It had always been Connie.

Connie and A.J. had been Tom and Lois's neighbors in a stark new cookie-cutter subdivision at a time when everyone was ravenous for friends, and eagerly starting out on new careers. Everyone but Connie, that is, who'd stayed home, content to be a housewife. Connie was there in her cheerful kitchen, ready to pour Lois a cup of coffee or a glass of wine when school let out in the afternoon. Connie listened to Lois's horror stories of clay modeling in a seventh-period class of forty thirteen-year-olds. Lois had ordered twelve tons of clay in September, and by Christmas it had vanished, stuck to ceilings, to walls, under desks, in lockers, in books, in kids' hair, on everyone's clothes. Connie cooed sympathetically while Lois described her latest embarrassment. How she'd sat on a clay snake that had been coiled on her chair. How the air rained clay balls every time she turned her back. How the assigned pinch pots sprouted grotesque breasts and penises.

But by the time the clay ran out, Lois had wised up. She put aside her impractical philosophy about the sanctity of art and self expression. She'd isolated ringleaders, instituted iron-clad class rules, seating charts, point systems, and regular parent conferences. In short, she retreated behind a gang-buster mentality, and it worked.

So Lois no longer needed Connie to calm her down, but they went on being friends. Saturday nights, after bedding down the kids in sleeping bags, the two couples played spades in alternating kitchens. They'd split a six-pack of beer, Tom and A.J. drinking two each while Lois and Connie made do with one. These evenings followed a formula: Tom and A.J. always partnered, always won. Tom was aggressive and loved to shoot the moon, which made Lois angry. Around eleven or so, or when the score reached 500, the women made coffee and served up some gooey dessert, always a new one. Their version of shoot the moon.

Or Connie's. Connie won the dessert competition hands down. But Connie had made a career out of being a housewife, Lois told herself. Connie had the time and dedication, thought nothing of dumping a whole pound of butter into a shortcake crust. However, Lois had to admit that when Connie wanted to, she could cut back. When A.J. had a lean month down at the used car lot where he worked, Connie could put together a great mock apple pie from Ritz crackers, with a powered milk topping. "Wasn't that good?" Tom would murmur later. "She's a real artist, isn't she? Think you could make that thing?"

"No, I don't. Why should I? It's just to save money, and with me working, we're doing okay."

"If you could manage like her, you could quit and stay home and cook, too."

"Why would I want to do that!" Lois would bark.

But not even Tom's untempered admiration could sour Lois on Connie. Lois loved going into Connie's well-ordered home, so clean, charming, hospitable. Lois admired the beige gingham wallpaper under decoupage hangings Connie had done herself. She was in awe of frilly curtains Connie had run up from dime-store material, with matching pull-down blinds stiffened with iron-on pellon. At Connie's, all the pieces came together, in trendy blues and beiges. Life was the way life ought to be, right down to her daughter Lynn's perfect school papers displayed under fruit-shaped refrigerator magnets.

At her own house, in contrast, Lois was uncomfortably aware that something was amiss, especially with Paul and Eddie. Both of her sons were loners, underachievers, given to violent fights that rocked the house and broke holes in plaster walls. Lois thought they'd get along better, maybe even become friends with each other and Tom, too, when Tom bought the ski boat. At least Connie and A.J. had liked water skiing, hanging onto the tow line for miles, going nowhere with great noise, commotion, and expense. To indulge their new taste for water sports, they camped together at Shasta. They boated, fished, and swam in the rust-colored rim of water around the lake's edge.

"Do you suppose it's a lot of trouble, a hairdo like hers?" Tom asked wistfully, admiring Connie's pageboy that made her look like Julie Christie in *Darling*. Both Connie and Lynn tanned well, turned a nice cafe au lait, while Lois, Paul and Eddie burned, freckled, and peeled. Paul and Eddie spent most of their time glowering from a picnic table in the shade, and this worried Lois.

But not too much. After all, Connie was there, Connie, whose magic presence soothed them all. With her around, Lois couldn't properly worry about a lot of things.

One day in camp Lois happened to notice A.J. giving Connie a rough caress. Lois watched them amble off, noted they were gone a half hour or so. A firewood hunt...a picking of wild flowers for the table...but no. When they sauntered back, a smarmy smudged look about them, she noticed pine needles stuck to their clothes. Why, they've been rolling around on the forest floor like a pair of teenagers, Lois thought, shocked. And Connie had liked it. A revelation, a jarring one. Lois and Tom gave up sex on vacations due to tactical problems of sharing the tent with the boys. Which secretly relieved Lois. But now she shot a look at Tom crouched over a tangle of fish lines and lures, and she realized that Tom knew what they'd been up to, too, and was jealous.

That was when Lois understood that both of them had fallen

in love with Connie.

Lois got up to readjust the green umbrella. The wine, which they drank without soda, had tinted the day a rosy hue. Or maybe it just seemed rosy from a contrast with the green of the deck furniture. Lois was unused to either wine in the afternoon or a day in the sun.

Connie sighed. "I see why you like it here, Lois. So beautiful, the ocean, mountains, the trees."

"Sometimes I get claustrophobic. The town's very small. Then I read some Ann Beattie, the angst of the seventies, and I feel better." Lois laughed. "I fit right in here, I've got my share of quirks. Ever notice how people resemble their houses? Me and my convoluted clam shell. The guy down the street, see how his paint's peeling, gutters mossy? Just like him. He's dog-eared, ragged, yellow teeth edged with tartar. And that house over there? Hedge trimmed so sharp you'd cut your hand on it, rigid flower beds, lawn like a carpet. Like him, so uptight—do people still say that? I can't imagine him nude."

Connie giggled. "I'd hate to have you analyze Tom and me by our house. You know Tom. Firewood's stacked so tight you almost can't get a piece of it out." She traced the pineapple pattern in Stella's cut glass crystal. "Nice stuff."

"Stella's family's crystal. The sterling, too. All came down to her, plus a little income. Nice for her and me, too, because I just walked away from Tom. Which was nice for you."

Connie shuffled and recrossed her smooth legs. She wore spaghetti strap sandals, as out of place on the coast as a string bikini. Her legs and feet were tan, her toenails painted coral pink. "Why did you do that?" Connie asked. "Just bolt? I'm not accusing you, I'm just asking. One day you were there, the next gone. I never really knew why."

Lois was so mellow she considered telling Connie the whole story, but thought better of it. Connie was not capable of understanding Lois's sexual experiment, her fling.

Wesley Smith taught woodshop, out in the barn set aside for crafts at Lois's school. The crafts teachers stuck together, a reaction to their assigned status as outcasts from the main intellectual stream of teachers. Woodshop, mechanical drawing, photography, sewing/cooking (girls got one semester of each, taught by the same person), art—teachers of these subjects ate lunch at a splintered table in their outpost, and one day Wesley moved across from Lois. He began to flirt outrageously.

"The way you eat a banana makes me almost come in my pants," he murmured in her ear one day.

Lois flushed with embarrassment. And with pleasure.

She began sprucing up. She entertained crazy ideas about plastic surgery to straighten her nose. She had always hated her nose. Maybe a face lift. Liposuction. Instead, she went on a diet and lost twelve pounds, which entitled her to new clothes. She had her hair cut short, not into the pageboy that Tom admired so excessively on Connie, but into something called a wedge—to minimize her jaw, which bothered her almost as much as her nose. She experimented with makeup and tints.

"Your hair's never the same color twice," Tom said sourly, watching her struggle with hot rollers and hair sprays. But out in the barn at school Wesley leered appreciatively.

On that memorable day, the day it all began to unravel, Wesley sidled up to murmur, "There's a school board meeting tonight. Why don't you go to it? Afterward we can grab a cup of coffee. Or something."

Or something. Lois's nerves raced, she flushed, she tingled with understanding. That night she cruised off to the meeting shaved, showered, oiled, and powdered. She was also wearing her diaphragm. And she wondered why. She hadn't been attracted to Wesley before he started his campaign, had actually mistrusted him because he was a known player, the butt of in-jokes.

But there she was, on a hard folding chair, staring at the back of Wesley's neck, pretending to listen to board members babble about the budget crunch. She doodled the alphabet, first in block letters, then in cursive, down the margin of her agenda, which was horribly long. Each item was crushed to death under a barrage of meaningless details. She toyed with sneaking out and going home, but knew she would not.

During an intermission, out in a dark corridor, Wesley muttered in her ear, "You leave now, drive down to the library. When I circle by, follow me out to my place."

She waited in the shadowy library parking lot, all nerves, craning for a look in the rearview mirror to apply yet another coat of mascara or check her hair by a quick flash of dash light. She half hoped he wouldn't show, asked herself aloud, "What the hell am I doing?" But when his lemon yellow Honda Civic glided up, she drew a deep breath and pulled out after him.

She turned in behind him at his complex, a nondescript cement block of condos off a frontage road. She rolled down her window to ask, "Where should I park?"

"In any space not numbered."

"Aren't people going to see my car? Shouldn't I sort of keep out of sight?"

He laughed. "Are you kidding? They call this building Interlocutory Court. No one cares who's parked where. As long as you're not in their spot."

Wesley lived in a cave of an apartment in the basement. It was furnished haphazardly, with the kind of things Lois and Tom had discarded years earlier. A chrome dinette set, a flowered couch, spindly Danish modern tables. A giant poster of a Polynesian girl, eerily lit by the glow of an empty aquarium, dominated the living room. Smiling demurely, the girl wore only her long black hair and a crown of orchids.

"You want a cup of coffee or a beer?" Wesley asked, helping her off with her coat. "Oh, no, nothing."

"I know what you want, babe," he muttered, running his hands up her arms, knotting them behind her neck and drawing her face toward his. She closed her eyes against his kiss, but not before spotting a couple of stray nose hairs. She thought wildly, as he pulled her toward the open door to the bedroom, that a lone wolf like Wesley had no one to look out for him, to tell him it was time for a trim, a shampoo, a tidying-up.

As a frame holds a picture, the bedroom held an enormous waterbed with mussed sheets printed with rainbows. On that bed Wesley assaulted her, raped her. At least so it seemed to Lois as she gritted her teeth. After all, this was what she'd come for, wasn't it? It was some sort of test. Or punishment.

Assault it was, though. The unexpected pain of his entry, because she was nervous, and dry as a fist. The easing around, as if he were tracing zeros in her. The quickening pace, the battering ram he made of his short purplish penis. The final deep thrust as he spent himself. She felt wetness seep beneath her and wondered if it was blood. Then she began to rage. Lone wolf or not, the least he could have done was make the bed!

An anxiety attack almost paralyzed her on the way home. What if the station wagon quit out here, so far from the school board meeting? But listening to it purr, Lois realized it wouldn't let her down. Tom took the greatest pains with its maintenance because this vehicle's primary function was to tow the boat over the Siskiyous so the boat could tow them around Lake Shasta. So much towing! So much circling and going nowhere! So pointless.

Of course Tom maintained her, too, in an aloof, casual way. He'd become established as an architect and the family no longer needed Lois's paycheck. She could quit, stay home and do what Connie did. Weed, make pastries, sew her own curtains, shellac decoupage designs onto interesting pieces of wood. But she'd gone on working, pursuing her "career," pursuing something that led her to coming home full of another man's semen. Surely Tom would smell it on her, this alien sex. The ache between her legs increased, as if Wesley had stretched something delicate. Lois pictured a thin membrane, tight as a water balloon, spider-webbed with red veins.

Unnecessary and painful. That described Wesley's appetite, his activities.

A waste of time. That described her whole life.

Tomorrow it would go on, and the next day, and the next.

Wesley smirking at work, Tom sighing at home. Each wanting from her something she could not supply. And Connie, sweet Connie so sure of herself, having learned, or not having had to learn at all because it was instinctual, what Lois could not even imagine, had no notion of. Lois slowed the station wagon in front of Connie's yard, nursery-nurtured, tamed and trimmed. She thought of Connie in the kitchen finishing the dishes, emptying the sink basket of debris, wiping her hands on a towel carefully coordinated with her decorating scheme, then spreading it to dry. She'd take a quick look around, checking for loose ends, spots, bits of fluff, anything that dared be out of order. Then she'd click off the light, her universe squared away.

Lois ached. She throbbed. Her new skin-tight size-ten jeans cut into her waist. For this she'd given up butter and ice cream and Connie's cherry cheesecake. Now she'd have to give up Connie, too. She drummed the heels of her hands on the steering wheel, angry and frustrated.

Lois thought about the day she and Connie had driven out to the country to look for barn siding. How excited Connie had gotten discovering a derelict barn peeling the exact faded red she'd envisioned against her wallpaper, then how coy she'd been with the farmer, wheedling from him a few slats. She'd sanded and sealed the old surface, then applied the decal of the sheep with their frantic black faces turned toward the viewer like flowers. How carefully she'd brushed on the many coats of varnish that preserved her treasure from A.J.'s cigarette smoke—the smoke that was killing him.

Once, when Lois told Stella about sitting there in front of Connie's that night, Stella asked patiently, for she'd heard it all before, "Did you like it, this decoupage stuff?"

Lois barked a laugh. "Lord, no. I thought it was tacky. But see, I was sitting out there feeling so bad, so degraded, and I'd done it to myself. I couldn't go in there anymore. I'd forfeited Connie—so safe, so secure, so sure of herself. And of her decoupage."

"That's when you turned the car around and drove to the

coast."

"Yeah, made a U-turn right there, shone the lights into Connie's dark kitchen, the shrine to a way of life I should have fit into and didn't. I never went home again. Called Tom, talked to the boys, called the school and quit. That was the price I had to pay, like in some board game when you get the go-to-jail card."

But Lois only put it like that when she was down, when she wallowed in remorse. During those times she wailed about what she'd done to the boys. It was people like her, she told Stella, who were bringing the country to its knees. She was the cancer destroying the nuclear family. "You can't undo the family just because it doesn't fit anymore," she'd moan.

Stella would shrug, murmur, "Yes, of course. But maybe not. Who knows?"

Lois got up to collapse the green umbrella. The sun had dipped behind wind-slanted cypress trees that ruffled in the afternoon breeze. The wine had turned bitter, and Connie drained the dregs from her glass into the bark dust of a planter. She stretched and said, "Let's not wait so long to get together. I'd like us always to be friends. Next time I'm over, I'll stop by. And you stop, too, when you're in Salem. You've never seen the new place."

Lois laughed and began stacking glasses on the tray. She avoided Connie's eyes while saying, "Oh, no, I can't do that. I never get out of town, anyway. You come see me, though, please."

"Say, Lois, I almost forgot. I brought you some things. I thought if I ran into you—well, truthfully, I was looking for you. Come out to the car with me."

Connie and Tom no longer needed sinewy boat-towing vehicles, so Connie now drove a sleek, gunmetal Ford Probe. It was as curvy as Connie used to be at Lake Shasta, in her little two-piece suits. Lois remembered one see-through crocheted number with bits of lining in strategic locations that made Tom's eyes pop. Lois realized, not for the first time, that she had done them all an enormous favor by removing herself from a competition she never could have won.

Connie opened the passenger door and pulled out a box. "Baby pictures of the boys, old report cards, things they made for you. Here, their handprints from kindergarten, and a mobile Eddie made out of driftwood. Oh, the leaf collections. And Paul's papier mâché piñata, some Cub Scout badges. Well, you go through it all. Whatever." Connie folded down the flaps on the box and handed over the dry shells of Lois's previous existence. "One more thing, I hope you don't mind. It's this, from me to you." Connie unwrapped a bundle and Lois saw nestled in tissue the faded red barn siding of the sheep decoupage. "I had an idea you liked this, and since we've done the new place in contemporary, it doesn't fit anymore. You hang it somewhere and think of me."

"Well," sighed Lois, taken aback. She was at once horrified and delighted. Connie placed the piece of siding on the box in Lois's arms and Lois looked down at the sheep. They gazed up at her with eyes as glassy and cat-like as Connie's own.

Lois wanted to laugh, felt whole and light and free. Hang this ridiculous thing? She would just as soon hang a velvet painting of a bullfighter. Or a poster of a naked Polynesian girl.

The Ford Probe slid away, and Lois felt as if something that once hurt dreadfully had been amputated, leaving her in peace, except for an occasional ghost pain in the missing limb. Life had been so puzzling back then, so bittersweet, so mixed up. She wanted to sob with exasperation, but at the same time to laugh with relief at her narrow escape. She would hang this thing, this decoupage. She would put it somewhere to mark a milestone in her life. Like doctors hang diplomas, or merchants their first dollar. Or primitives show off scalps, or foreskins.

ON EDGE, ON THE PACIFIC RIM

I'VE COME back to my old hometown on the Pacific Rim. It's a small town anchored on a shelf of basalt that geologists call a "sea terrace." How do I know this? Jeremy used to talk about such things last summer as we stood gazing out at the surf. I loved listening to Jeremy. He was generous with words, scattering them before me as I do crumbs for the gulls.

When I grew up here, this town was boom or bust, depending on logging or fishing. Now it's full of retirees, four hundred of them, the most people this town has ever had, and they're a natty, self-satisfied bunch. Despite what some of my friends say, though, I think we're lucky to have them. They save us from being a rural slum. Such things happen to little towns like this. Tell you the truth, when I was growing up in a lumber camp north of here, that's what this town was. A rural slum.

Tourists shouldn't judge us by what they see on 101, which supports our middle like a spine. When they get off the highway they find our lawn decor has upgraded from plastic pink flamingos to iron deer and stone lions, or at least to wooden butterflies fastened on new cedar sidings stained fashionable marine hues. We present our best face to visitors coming in from the south, dropping down from the Cape into our postcard scenery. From that angle, no one notices the beach shacks where young people like me live, the twenty-somethings working for minimum wage, cooking and cleaning and clerking in shops, motels, and restaurants. Also invisible: clear-cuts marching like razor burns down our hills.

The heart of town is a tic-tac-toe cross-hatch of illogical streets, as if drawn by a child with thick crayons. These improbable lanes are lined with shoe-box-sized cottages in pastel colors, outlined with patches of old-fashioned flowers: pansies, daisies, geraniums, sweet peas, hollyhocks. The Northport River meanders through, and it doesn't hurry much, not even in storm-driven high tides. There used to be fish in it. I remember fish in it, salmon, bass, perch.

Our retirees have built rich new houses up on the hill to catch the view, which is cabins like mine and then the Pacific Ocean. These new houses are engineering marvels of redwood and glass, but they're on streets too steep for their owners to walk into town. So Buicks, Beemers and Volvos are driven down to collect pension checks, issues of *Modern Maturity* and *Consumer Reports*, *Wall Street Journal*, *Land's End* catalogs.

The post office—that's where I meet this juggernaut (also one of Jeremy's words) of well-off newcomers that powers our economy. They're really nice, too. They don't mean to block the doorway, talking to gray-haired friends about real estate values, social security benefits, stock market fluctuations. It's just that I'm in a hurry, hoping in vain for some sign, a letter, a card, anything, from Jeremy.

Fall is the time to come. The wind dies then. Also, aspens and alders pale to gold, and dogwood turns its big pointy leaves blood-red. Tourists have discovered this season, so it's not as restful as it used to be. I've noticed the change up at the Quarter Deck, where I waitress. Tips are good, but lately I want to hide from life, not engage it. So this new season of bustle and prosperity doesn't agree with me any more than the old sluggish hard times that once drove me out.

Downtown shops perch along 101 like birds on a wire. And there's enough wires. All our utilities (except up on the hill, where they buried conduit) are strung on poles canted crazily, guyed this way and that against the wind. So we're living under a kind of net, a weaving of power and cable and telephone lines, like trapped animals. They hum, too, those tense wires, when the wind blows. It's nerve-wracking listening to them. Like getting a low dose of radioactivity, or having a mosquito trapped in your bedroom.

Inventory—one each: tavern/pool hall, laundromat, market, bookstore, hardware store, fly shop, lapidary supply store, beauty parlor, nursery, video rental. Two each: gas stations (Chevron, Texaco), churches (Presbyterian, Methodist), bakeries (Italian, mainstream), banks (both are wheelchair accessible, neither chains down pens). Seven real estate offices. Eight restaurants (counting the ice cream parlor). Eleven motels (twelve counting the RV park). Seventeen gift shops, full of wood and woven geegaws from third-world countries. I've discovered that you can spell collectibles with either an *a* or an *i*, and there really is a myrtlewood tree they cut down to make into salad bowls. But they've cut too many because these bowls are spendy as hell.

We have no school, dry cleaner, drugstore, lumberyard, auto supply, Sears or Penney's or Ward's, doctor, dentist, vet, hospital, or funeral home. So you can live here only if you and your pets are healthy and have achieved certain milestones but are not yet anticipating that Last Great Adventure. We have no neon (city ordinance bans it), and no plate-glass windows. Our trendy shops sport Dutch double doors and country-style windows with many small panes. I remember the last plate glass I saw myself in. It was outside the clinic in Salem, and, as I threaded through chanting protesters, I caught a glimpse of how terrible I looked. I'm glad there's no plate glass here. I don't need anything bigger than my dresser mirror to show me how pale, how bloodless I am. Bev chides me, "Come on, Cheyenne, snap out of it. No biggie. Get on with it, willya?"

Easy for her. She's a veteran, been to that clinic three times already.

The double front doors of the Quarter Deck are diagonal

wood planks with porthole windows. Bev, she's the hostess, and is supposed to keep the glass clean in between greeting and seating guests. She clears her throat in this phony theatrical way when she wants to call my attention to someone, usually a fox or a freak. One day she hurrumped at me, and for a split second I thought it was Jeremy she was tucking into a booth. In shock, I almost dumped plates of fish and chips on my people. But it wasn't Jeremy, it was just another blond curly guy, good-looking in a generically vanilla way, duded-up in denim and Dockers. But I kept sneaking peeks, the way this guy's hair tumbled over the left side of his forehead, the curve of his cheek. I remembered that last time when Jeremy fanned the bills out on the table and said, "Come on, Cheyenne, it's just not going to happen, that's all."

"It's already happened," I said.

"Listen, kiddo," he hissed through clenched teeth, "take what you can get now, don't hassle me. Besides, how do I know this kid's mine?"

Well, that's true. How does any man know? "But what if it's a girl, a little blond girl with blue eyes," I said. "Maybe she'd have curly hair, with a widow's peak like yours. Would you like that? Someone to share your hairline with?"

That nasty laugh haunts me. "You don't get blond and curly out of straight black, don't you know that?"

Later Bev said, "You shoulda slapped him." She looked up from gluing on her acrylic nails. "Or held out for more money. Besides, they have ways to tell that now—blood tests, DNA or whatever. But you did the right thing. Get it over with."

"But Bev, if my mom had done what I did, I wouldn't be here now."

"Times change. It was easier to raise a kid alone back then. Trust me."

Trust me. Everyone says that. Who to trust is a modern problem. Growing up, I trusted the people who lived in my row of shacks up by the mill. If my mother was busy or sick or asleep,

I could go to the neighbors for company. We were cheese-rind apple-core poor, but we shared what we had. All the women were family, all the men my uncles, related or not. That's what my mother called them when they stayed overnight: my uncles.

Our houses were as alike as doug firs. All shabby, falling down, repaired with materials other people had thrown away. Scrap iron, weathered plywood, mismatched curling shingles. Maintenance the same: paint halfway around, then switch colors or quit; patch in odd-sized windows, leave the raw wood to warp; begin a side-room, then desert the project.

Our yards were interesting messes of bedsprings, old refrigerators, plumbing fixtures, remnants of good ideas gone bad. And cars. Usually one running, one on blocks (the project), and several being parted out. Yes, everybody had a weedy yard full of rusty beat-up cars and dogs with gray muzzles and scrawny cats and goats and sheep and lots of chickens flapping around underfoot. Why would Jeremy, who knew about sea terraces and juggernauts, want someone who came from that?

Now it's all gone, the mill, the row houses, the junk. The people who lived there—Pacific Rim Joads, I admit, but real people, more real than the ones I know now—drifted away like flotsam and Jetsam on the spring tide. A few found timber jobs in other places where the mill whistle blows at eight and noon and five like a call to prayer in Mecca. Most, however, demoted themselves to the fish processing plant that makes cat food up in Newberry, or to the fruit crops around Hood River. My mother and I migrated there, and in the heat we weren't used to she dried up like an apple granny doll before she died.

Then I decided to come back here, to live by the ocean. I got off the Greyhound bus in front of the Suprette, trudged down Marine Drive with my backpack to admire the surf, the river, the mountain backdrop, and I was home. *Home.* Like walking into a painting a rich guy like Jeremy would hang over his sofa. Who'd want to live anywhere else?

But there'd been changes. Even my old mill neighborhood

had been "developed," steamrolled into a ring of condos around a golf course. The greens are machine-manicured and sprayed with pesticides and fertilizers that run off into a pond. Once there'd been ducks, geese, herons, whistling swans, kingfishers, even eagles around that pond. Now the water is clotted with thick green algae and nothing goes near it. But the Quarter Deck gets a lot of dinner trade off those golfers.

Now I live in town, within walking distance of the restaurant. I rent a little cabin, one of a set where fishermen used to stay for eight dollars a night during smelt runs, back when the smelt ran. In our row there are five cabins squatting under peaky little roofs like dunce caps. Bev lives on one side and on the other there's an old guy who wears a Greek fisherman's cap when he pedals his bicycle around town. I don't know the other two tenants, except one is a part-time bartender at the Pueblo, and the other does firewood and odd jobs. He roars around in a big Dodge power-wagon, his claim to fame a "Volunteer Fireman" tag next to his license. (Jesus, do we love fires! It's a real bloodthirst, a deep need for horror and excitement. We relish fires, explosions, RVs going over at the top of the Cape, surfers swept under. The bloodier, the better.)

The walls between our cabins are thin, uninsulated. Even the rubber drapes I bought at the Thrift Shop don't help much with drafts. They flow through my two rooms like an undertow. An unhealthy place to raise a baby.

The old man next door spends his time in a fog. Some days he thinks I'm his daughter and complains to me about things that happened in his family. Other days he regards me suspiciously. I'm a burglar about to break in and steal...but what's he got that anyone would want, I wonder. The few times I've looked in his room, I've identified in the chaos cracked and dirty dishes, a box of fruit jars, a saggy threadbare green sofa under an army blanket, stacks of papers and magazines, an empty birdcage, a set-up ironing board, a plastic bag of clothes (I've seen him pedal it back and forth to the laundromat), a plastic bag of plastic (religiously he recycles on his bicycle), an enormous TV sprouting rabbit ears (his TV must be broken, because I never hear it), and his old balloon-tired Schwinn. Everything seems to be where it is because that's where it landed. As messy as the end of a love affair.

Now Bev, she's another story. She's seeing a married guy she met up at the Quarter Deck (like I met Jeremy) who loves opera, so she's trying to love it, too. Through our paper partitions, I listen to it with her. And her *amore* likes Italian food, so she's learning to cook Italian. Sharing her garlic and onions, I'm right there with Bev while she cooks pasta al dente, and I listen to Mimi, Puccini's *La Bohème*, dying of tuberculosis.

I remember Jeremy wrapping himself in a blanket in the mornings, and I rejoiced in secret discoveries. The constellation of strawberry moles on his stomach, the arrow of golden hair pointing to his groin. I knew his body as well as I know this town. I remember him saying, "Don't worry about it, it's okay. Trust me." And I did, I trusted him.

To drown out Bev and her lover boy going at it next door, I listen to noise on the cracked boom box I bought at the Thrift Shop. All my stuff came from there. Spindly Danish modern couch with mismatched cushions, scarred blond coffee table, dresser with drawers that slide in at crazy angles, round cloudy mirror, chrome and Formica dinette. Last summer we had a spell of hot weather and the naugahyde on the chairs got as sticky as warm blood.

Yeah, I know, to Jeremy, my cabin was a foreign country—a place to visit, not to live. Or maybe it was like camping out. A quaint experience, interesting for a while.

Trouble is, the wires hum, the fifteen wires that connect my cabin to the pole outside. Why are there so many wires when I've got only three outlets? My rooms are a mass of extension cords running everywhere like snakes. So why do those wires hum?

In autumn, the wind dies, and the wires kind of shut up. That's when we celebrate the sea's bounty with a Smelt Fry. The last few years, though, I hear they've had to substitute frozen herring from Canada for the smelt because smelt don't run anymore.

I'm helping out, frying these little bits no bigger than goldfish in the tanks at Ben Franklin's. Bev talked me into this. "It'll be fun. We can scout around for guys." Then she got all tied up with her new man. So here I am, dredging fish in flour, me and a blue haired crew of women. They're retired from up the hill, come down to do their civic bit.

"Oh, Cheyenne, honey, do it like this, see?" says one woman with blue eye shadow that matches her hair. She demonstrates, then hurries off to annoy the cole slaw crew.

So I'm standing here, nails full of goo, hair full of greasy smoke, when I see this little girl toddle by. She's an angel with blond curls and blue eyes round as marbles. She's wearing a frothy pink dress, lace trimmed pink socks, and white, white shoes. Her mother, also blond, talks to someone while keeping an eye on the baby.

"Hi there, sweetie," I coo, dropping my fish into the plate of flour. I rush around the counter toward the child. She turns shy when I bend down. "What's your name, sweetheart?" I murmur, and hold out a fishy hand.

The child turns away, throws her arms around her mother's legs and peers at me over a pink ruffled shoulder. "She's Kimberly," says her mother. "Can you say 'hi,' Kimmy, hon?

Kimmy says nothing, looks at me as if I'm the real fish at this shindig. "I have a little girl at home just like you," I say. "Her name's Angela."

"Oh, really," says the mother. "Kimmy's fourteen months, just walking real good."

"Yes, exactly Angie's age. She's walking, too. She walked at eight months, talks quite a bit now. Of course, I'm the only one who understands her. Her daddy says she and I have a secret language."

The mother laughs a little too loudly. "Yes, I know what you mean. Come on, Kimmy. Let's get a balloon, hon."

"My Angela, well, we read to her a lot. Then she pretends to read to us. She wants us to sit down, and she holds the book and we can hear punctuation, where the paragraphs are. It's a riot. We don't let her watch TV. Don't you think TV is bad for kids?"

The woman picks up the child and backs off. "Yes, yes, definitely. TV is not the thing, no. So nice to...well, nice you've got Angela and all—"

"You live around here? No? Well, we live up on the hill, in that big gray house with the round window. See it? You can see it from here. At Christmas, Jeremy—he's my husband—Jeremy outlines a big star in white lights against the mountain, for Angela."

The woman hurries to get away, but I go on, "We had a birthday party for Angela, the whole family came, Grandma, Grandpa, aunts and uncles. Angie's the only baby, so she's a star herself."

"Wonderful." The woman rushes away.

I watch them scurry off, then go back to breading my little fish babies. My own words hum in my head louder than the wires. My cheeks burn, my heart thumps, my hands tremble. What's the matter with me! I'm losing it, I'm closer to the edge than I thought...I didn't know I was so close.

Later, walking home from this hateful Smelt Fry, I think it's time to go. Move on to some less pretty place out of the wind and away from the wires. So easy. All I have to do is load the backpack I came with, then tell Bev and the old guy to have at my junk.

But I can't go. I stride by my cabin and head out to the surf. I stand on the cliff edge and watch waves advance and retreat, a regular rhythm, as close to eternal as I can get. Here: this is beyond my ability to affect with right or wrong. This doesn't feel lack, or pain, or change. This doesn't listen to the shriek of chainsaws or the hum of wires. Nothing makes any difference to the ocean. So heartless that I take heart.

CANOE

MARCY HAS done little driving during the almost four decades of her marriage to Howard. She admits to herself that staying home has been more the result of her passive nature than anything Howard has said or done. But to others, she blames her lack of driving skills on his constant criticism. Easier to turn the wheel over to him, she says, than listen to him gripe. So now, at the age of fifty-nine, she's had less on-the-road time than your average sixteen-year-old.

She stares out the windshield at the undulations of 101 northbound, gripping the wheel with white-knuckled intensity. But even at that, she isn't as tense as Howard in the passenger seat. He inhales sharply and presses his foot to an imaginary brake pedal when she inches out from behind a giant RV to check for passing room. She loses her nerve and eases back in line, rotating her shoulders with relief. "No sense in rushing," she chirps at him with false brightness. "We might be just a teeny bit late, but we'll get there in one piece."

Howard sighs heavily. "Thing is, you shoulda got 'round this yahoo back when you had a passing lane."

"I didn't think I was close enough. No point in breaking the speed limit just to pass someone."

"And you didn't turn around to check behind you, either."

Marcy replies, "I looked in the rearview mirror. That's good enough."

"Is not. You shoulda turned around."

"Now Howard, we've been through this before. I'm driving the way they say to in the DMV booklet."

"Okay, okay. Big deal. Just stay outta the bike path, willya?"

"I'm not in it," she snaps. After a glance at him, though, she wishes she hadn't been so sharp. He is huddled in a tight knot under his seat belt, looking gray and old and tired.

But her irritation flares again when he says, "Listen, I've had years of defensive driving seminars, and right now you're following a billboard down the highway. You can't see a thing the way you're sticking behind this RV." He stretches over to honk the horn, but she pushes his hand away.

"Howard, remember what the doctor said? You've got to relax if you don't want another heart attack." Then she adds in a soothing tone, "Easy does it, dear, easy does it."

"One thing to say it, another to do it," he says testily.

"And the boys will come home any time you want them. Help you cut and stack firewood. Do the yard work. Finish painting the garage."

That's what he'd been doing when he'd staggered in three months earlier, complaining of indigestion, of pains in his left arm. He'd panicked and gone over the head of their old family doctor in Northport ("Might as well go to the vet," he'd groused) to consult a specialist in Newberry who'd immediately put him in intensive care.

Marcy had been shocked to see him lie there wired to machines, so ashen, so shrunken, so vulnerable. He'd never seemed quite human before: he'd been the strong one, the engine driving their partnership. He wasn't a big man, barely an inch or so taller than she, but he'd been a powerhouse of restless and, to her, uncomfortable energy.

Marcy had always been slow-moving, contemplative. (Howard's mother had once, perhaps accurately, termed it "lazy.") She could spend hours by herself, mulling over the plots to movies or odd bits of conversation or fragments of dreams, while Howard cleaned out the garage and washed both cars.

She could dawdle away the whole morning reading the paper in her bathrobe while he mowed, edged, and watered the lawn. "Aren't you dressed yet?" he'd snap coming in to gulp glasses of water, his sweaty T-shirt clinging to his wiry frame. He exuded energy and thrived on exertion while she got up only to add thick socks under her slippers to keep her feet warm. Yes, the formula had been Howard the doer, Marcy the dreamer.

But now here he is, too ill to drive. First the heart attack, then the mysterious lump pushing up from under his ribs that had sent him running to another specialist. And suddenly everything they read, everything they saw on TV or heard in conversation reverberated with the dread word, *cancer*. So today Marcy is driving Howard to Newberry to get the biopsy report, for which Howard's ribs had been split apart. *Cut up like a chicken* is how she thought of it.

Howard says dourly, "I know the boys would paint the garage, but I'd rather do it myself. Quick and dirty is the way they paint. You gotta have your heart in it to do a good job."

"Yes, dear," Marcy murmurs, mentally siding, as usual, with the boys. How important can it be, watching for brush strokes in the paint on a garage? Does it really matter?

The hum of the Volvo's tires takes on a higher pitch as they break onto the bridge span. As she usually does, Marcy looks down, scanning the fretwork of boat docks below, searching for sailboat masts. There are few sailors in the bay, nothing like there used to be on Lake Mead near where they'd lived before moving to the coast. Sometimes Howard and Marcy say something to each other about their sailing days, but only occasionally. And of course they never bring up the Steins.

Twenty years earlier, when they were living in a Las Vegas suburb, Howard bought a Catalina 27 and they joined the Lake Mead Sailing Club. Howard had always wanted a boat, and he thought it would wedge him into a strata of the business world he'd not been able to penetrate. He sold security devices, everything from electric fencing to burglar alarms. He also thought the boys would love sailing, but they'd hated it, spent their time sulking, smoking pot in the bushes with other turned-off teenagers who longed for speedboats and water skis. Finally Howard gave up, left them home during club events.

Marcy also hated sailing. When the wind blew, the boat keeled over at frightening angles; when it didn't, they sat there for hours, the unforgiving desert sun frying her thin skin. Races—which, of course, Howard loved—were the worst. To her they were a chaos of boats milling around the start buoy, lunging and weaving like demented water bugs. Her heart throbbed with panic at the start gun. Then Howard would scream orders in his incomprehensible jargon: "You're luffing, point her up! Can't you read the tell-tales?" "Crank on more jib!" "Ease off the main sheet!" "Tighten the boom vang!" When that ordeal was over, there were shocking, embarrassingly angry scenes in the committee room over protest flags. Races were disasters from start to beyond finish. Way beyond.

Finally, when she'd entangled the spinnaker with the jib after letting it droop into the water, Marcy was permitted—no, she was ordered in dire terms—to wait out the races in the air-conditioned clubhouse. There, she read dog-eared water-themed paperbacks. It suited her exactly. She devoured James Jones scuba adventures, Joseph Conrad sea yarns, Frank Yerby swashbucklers, the Captain Horatio Hornblower series.

She was rereading *The African Queen* when Everett Stein wandered in. She knew he was waiting for his wife, Faye, who was off racing her boat, a twin to Howard's. Faye Stein terrified Marcy. She was shrill and competitive, the kind of woman Howard termed a "tough broad." She wore her blond hair cut painfully short and had chunky, muscular legs. Little corks dangled from the ear pieces of her dark glasses and she painted her nose and lips unashamedly with zinc oxide. She exuded self-confidence and could take "knock-down"—the keel coming out of the water far enough to submerge the sail—with the best of them.

However, Everett, with his soft ways and mild eyes, merely

irritated Marcy. Especially that day: she'd wanted the place to herself. And she'd had it, apart from a couple of guys at the bar and a few kids outside on the deck eating slices of watermelon from soggy paper plates. She was looking out the window at them, thinking what a sticky mess—they were spitting seeds at each other—when she realized Everett's gray suede shoes were crossing the room to stand by her chair.

"Are you as bored as I am?" he asked, smiling. He had small, even teeth, like kernels on an ear of baby corn. His eyes were so brown and shiny she caught a reflection of herself in them.

Marcy drew herself up stiffly. She was shy with men. "Why, no," she said. "Actually, this is a good book."

"But you've read it before. I've seen you with it. You know what I think? I think you're as out of place here as I am." He sat down and leaned forward, so close she could smell his aftershave. It was spicy, like cinnamon. "I bet we have a lot in common. You're more aware of your feelings than these people, more sensitive," he said softly.

She leaned back and crossed her legs, a motion he followed with his eyes. She said uncomfortably that she was just like everyone else, the most ordinary kind of person.

"Why aren't you out there, then?" he asked.

"Because I'm too lazy to work so hard in this heat."

"My wife," he said sadly, "is the kind who has to interact with the environment. The total spirituality of the water is beyond her. She wouldn't understand that book you're reading, the ironic clash of personalities in an exotic setting. Africa is so tragic now, so exploited. I suppose the whole world is." He went on in a melancholy way about the disappearance of spirituality, the submersion of life's meaning in the harshness of commercial values.

She was surprised at how easily she could talk to him. She told him about being an only child (he was, too), born late in her parents' lives. He said his father had just died, a hard, stubborn man who had never given Everett his approval. He described the hospital scene when the old man had turned his face to the wall rather than relate to him. He told of his desire for children of his own, so he could reverse the pattern. He hinted at problems with Faye over this issue. His brown eyes shone with grief, with tragedy. He was so lonely, so sad. Marcy could understand this. She ached for him, murmured little cooing sounds.

While he talked, she flicked quick glances over him, so as not to give herself away. His crown of fine, dark hair was brushed straight back as sleekly as the pelt of some cunning animal, an otter perhaps. He smiled and she smiled back, then looked away, shaken. The air in the room took on a slightly charged quality, as if it had been ionized. In the pit of her stomach, Marcy felt the kind of lump she'd get if she were next in line to ride a world-class roller coaster.

She returned abruptly to earth when Howard and a pack of Catalina racers whooped in. On a beery blast, sun-roughened and disheveled, they crowded at the bar. She heard Howard bellow, ordering a round of drinks. Marcy noticed his straw-colored, sweat-soaked hair, dented from the brim of the Aussie-style hat he'd adopted. He glanced over, nodded, waved his clipboard—she knew he was going to protest—while Everett leaned back and crossed his arms. They sat there, silent, marooned in a sea of one-liners, put-downs, belly laughs, general nonsense and hubbub from the bar.

With Howard in the room, Marcy looked at Everett with a new sense of security. She smiled when he leaned in to whisper of mismatched pairs, of harmless pleasures, of stopping to smell the roses. His eyes were beautiful, velvet brown, so dark she could barely make out the irises. Then she dropped her gaze to his forearms, now folded on the table. They were smoothly molded, downy with soft brown hairs. Howard's body hair was tough, bristly. Everett's skin was honey-gold, so delicious looking. She could almost taste his skin, sweet, spicy.

Later, when she and Howard pulled out of the parking lot, Marcy caught a glimpse of Everett trailing behind Faye, hauling a duffel bag of her stuff to their station wagon. He towered over his wife, whose legs were encased like sausages in pink polyester pants. Marcy remembered that Faye's daddy—she had a "daddy," implying munificence, indulgence, and an unbridled up-bringing that wouldn't settle well into marriage—had made a bundle on defense contracts.

Marcy listened to Howard's account of the race with uncharacteristic patience and interest. He was enormously pleased at catching Faye's boat in a wind shadow coming wing-on-wing down the home stretch and had left her rocking in his wake. Marcy was wickedly pleased: Everett would have a cross wife tonight. Faye hated losing even more than Howard did.

Howard's pathologist's office is embedded in a complex of medical buildings north of the Newberry bridge, just beyond the marina and Coast Guard station. Marcy steers the Volvo carefully into one of the parking lots bordering the area. She leans toward Howard slightly, as if he's deaf instead of recovering from surgery, and murmurs in tones suitable for a petulant child, "Here we are, dear, safe and sound."

"Use your turn signal."

"Yes, dear." By this time she has already turned, but she clicks it on anyway, to please him. She points the Volvo toward an empty slot.

"Not this one," he growls. "That Toyota's too close. He'll ding us opening that door."

"I'm trying to get you as close to the door as I can. Besides, I thought you were in a hurry."

"Not that much of a hurry. Dings rust in this climate. How many times have I said you gotta take care of a good paint job... there, pull in that one."

Obediently, she eases into another slot, locks up, and hurries around to help him out. He leans heavily on her, pushing himself up with his good arm. "Sorry about this, old girl," he puffs.

"No problem."

She expects him to let go quickly, to push her away, but he continues his grip even after he's gotten his equilibrium. "This is a hell of a note," he barks hoarsely. She realizes with a start that he's crying.

"There, there, dear," she murmurs, and glances around uncomfortably. She's embarrassed, and ashamed that she is. But no matter how disabled he'd been lately, he'd not allowed himself such dramatics. "This is just a formality, dear, just getting the test results," she says, and pats his back. He is a collection of bones, his spine as sharp as a bread knife. He shakes with sobs. She digs for a Kleenex, and he honks into it.

Soon, though, he clears his throat. "Listen, that stuff we went over last night...you sure you understand how the stock plan works? What's in the safety deposit box? When to send in the IRS coupons?"

"Yes, of course, dear. Don't worry yourself now." She guides him toward the entrance, a pair of smeared glass doors. It opens onto a white hallway that smells oddly of chicken soup and disinfectant. It is lined with gurneys and wheelchairs. They pad along, hushed by the humming echo of unseen machinery—as if wading across the bottom of a long, thin aquarium.

The pathologist's office is painted gray with blue racing stripes at chair height, and furnished with chrome chairs the same colors. Howard settles carefully—lowering himself as if he's balancing a stack of fragile dishes. Marcy sits and begins picking through tattered magazines. *Ford Times, Modern Maturity...* she shuffles them back onto the Formica table. At least the cardiologist had offered *Newsweek* and *Lear*.

Howard leans over to whisper, "Now, no matter what the doc says, don't make a scene."

She recoils slightly. How like him! Pulling her in with one arm, pushing her away with the other. He goes on, "Remember how you went on to the heart guy? You just can't pump these guys for information. They'll tell you only what you should know."

"Howard, you're lecturing me. You can just go in there by yourself. That way for sure I won't embarrass you." She grabs a *Ford Times* and barely looks up when a starched nurse calls him. He lifts himself carefully, balancing his glass spine, and meekly follows her, his authority submerged by her health and position.

Marcy flips through "Autumn Extravaganza," an article about Vermont. The pictures show curving ribbons of road twisting through villages of white-painted houses with window boxes, and spired churches on old-fashioned main streets. Real stores. No malls. It would be fun, seeing places like that. She and Howard had once talked of traveling after the boys were gone. Now perhaps they never would.

Marcy plops the magazine down and wanders to the window. The view is of an interior rectangle of grass, supposedly a courtyard, but the effect is ruined by a row of trash cans lined up by a dumpster. The weather has turned to drizzle, and Marcy catches the moan of foghorns in the bay. Standing there, surrounded by Northwest gloom, she realizes that her affair with Everett twenty years ago, in those passion-lit desert days, had been the high point of her life.

In 1972, Marcy and Howard had already been married eighteen years, and had teenaged sons.

Then Everett appeared. Suddenly she was wild for club events, could barely wait for races on Saturdays so she could talk to him. She saved up things to tell him, bits of her days he'd find interesting or funny. She asked his advice, told him jokes, described her dreams (except the ones featuring him). He believed there was meaning in dreams, and told her his. They complained that their day-to-day lives were dreary and meaningless; their spouses not the kind of people they needed to make them happy. They talked in phrases like getting in touch with their feelings, seeing behind their masks. It was all up-to-date stuff, like she'd read about in self-help books.

Everett always returned to his problems with Faye. She was cold, unreasonable, demanding much but giving little. He couldn't please her no matter what he did, even in small things like the making of a tuna salad. (He did the cooking, as Faye was not at all "domestic.") He felt sorely the lack of children. Marcy wanted to cry for him.

Away from him, Marcy lived on his memory. She'd replay her mental tapes of their conversations over and over. She'd analyze his words, his feelings, his moods. She'd line up questions for next time, squirm with impatience to ask them.

Feverishly, she began dolling up. She got a new hairdo, a shag, and learned to curl it on hot rollers. She bought new clothes, flippy little polyester skirts and tank tops. She wore them with bare little sandals and painted her toenails Hawaiian Fire Red. But not her lips. She did them in an ashy, almost white shade, to emphasize her eyes. (Everett said they were her best feature.) She practiced outlining them with fine black pencil, adding little wings at the outside corners. She pierced her ears for hoop earrings, and daubed on Estee Lauder perfume, despite Howard saying something in it made his eyes burn.

That was about all Howard did say, though. He was blind to the changes in her, having become more absorbed than ever in the boat. He spent his time at the dock in complicated maintenance, sanding, waxing, varnishing. Either that, or racing. Marcy didn't care. She welcomed it, this convenient inattention.

She'd worn out her fantasies of the seduction before it happened. One day, after months of shadow-dancing with him in the clubhouse during races, Everett asked her to go for a ride to see his house. She would understand the climate of his marriage, he said, after seeing his house. It had won awards, had been written up in *Sunset*, but it was no good. She would see.

Of course she'd already seen it. Wearing dark glasses and a scarf, she'd slunk around the neighborhood a couple of times, sniffing out hints of his life with Faye. Once she'd even followed Faye's Corvette into a mall parking lot, had been nervy enough to brush into her coming out of Bullocks. Faye had been loaded down with plastic bags, a shopping binge, she said. She'd lost so much weight on Metrical that she needed a new wardrobe. She showed Marcy a new pair of white hip-hugger bell bottoms with a paisley scarf belt.

Now, with Everett, Marcy stared boldly at his home. It looked like a set of glass cubes strung together on laminated beams, like an upright tic-tac-toe game. It was in a pricy subdivision of five-acre parcels, an area that had supplied Howard with a lot of work. Howard himself had wired the Stein house with silent alarms, pressure sensors, panic buttons. The amount of time he'd spent on it had prompted Marcy to exclaim, "What's in there? Van Gogh paintings? Fabergé eggs?" Howard had murmured vaguely about hiding wires, replacing rugs and slate tiles, some nonsense, almost as if he were being secretive. Not like Howard at all.

"How beautiful," Marcy said, shivering, gaping at Everett's icy home. "It's like a really modern chandelier."

He snorted. "Good way to put it. About as warm and comfortable, too." He stared glumly. "Faye's daddy designed it."

"Umm," Marcy murmured, thinking that Daddy must have paid for it, too. "Well, it is a little...a little cold-looking."

"It's a mausoleum. There's no life. No place for a dog, or even a cat. And I'd like a garden. Can't have a garden. It doesn't fit in with the landscaping theme. So says Faye, anyhow."

Inside, across tiles and thick gray rugs, they tiptoed like conspirators, although Faye was away racing her boat. "Still," whispered Marcy, "it's beautiful."

"It's sterile. I hate this Southwest theme, these cow skulls, the Indian warrior stuff." They stopped and stared out a window the size of a billboard at the rolling desert beyond. "Even the view is dead," he said.

Marcy said slowly, "But there's a special mood to it, don't you think?"

He laughed. "It's like the moon. A moonscape by Salvador Dali." Then he led her down a hall to peek into the bedroom he shared with Faye. Perched on a white dresser, where children's pictures should be, stood Faye's latest sailing trophy.

Later, driving away, they fell silent. Marcy worried that he regretted showing her around. She fretted over something to say. Accidentally, their hands brushed on the seat; she moved hers away, but he reached out. She grasped his fingers, rubbed her thumb across the pulse point on his wrist. He laced his fingers through hers, cleared his throat, shifted in his seat. "Your hand is so warm." He sighed, then said in a stressed voice, "You in a hurry to get back to the clubhouse? There's no wind. That race will take hours."

She tingled with nerves. "Well, no..." She squeezed his fingers again. They were soft, not rough like Howard's.

He turned onto the old highway that had been bypassed by the new interstate. It had deteriorated into auto repair and sheet metal shops, second-hand stores, a derelict trailer park. A fortune teller's shack sat under a home-made sign announcing PALMS READ WHILE YOU WAIT, and Marcy thought wildly, how else?

Her heart raced when he pulled into the entrance of the Headliner Motel. It was a seedy stucco, what people used to call a "motor court," painted aqua and salmon. After a minute of tense silence (an opportunity, she thought, for her to change her mind), he unfolded his long frame and ambled—why did he amble, she seethed, watching him. Why did he not hurry? Was he ambivalent, equivocating? She willed him speed, urgency, as he strolled casually toward a hand-lettered sign that read OFFICE.

His back receded, disappeared. She sat there, tingling, aching, throbbing. For months she'd been ready, wanting this, planning for it. She'd arrived at the club deodorized, lubricated, stray hairs carefully plucked, legs shaved, clad in her best new filmy underwear. God! she burned for him, burned for him, yearned for him. But with him gone, she slumped, she sagged under the weight of her actions.

Without his magical presence she was torn, a part of her asking what in hell she was doing, pulling this trick on...well, Faye hardly counted. If half of what Everett said about her was true, Faye deserved this. Moreover, Faye had never been a real person to Marcy, with her loud voice and pushy ways, with her careless control over masculine things like knots and buoys and racing rules. No, Faye didn't count.

Howard counted. But lately he'd been so off-hand, so distracted, so out of it. Once, when she and Everett planned to sneak off to an evening poetry reading, she'd told Howard to get the boys' supper. "So, where are you going?" Howard asked vaguely. "Is this part of that class you're taking?"

"Yeah, sure, the class," she'd answered. What class? She was taking no class. She could tell him anything, or nothing. Something else: when he'd made overtures, which hadn't been often, she'd said she had cramps. What did he know? Or care?

Then, when all he'd said was, "I'll check the car, make sure you got plenty of gas," she'd been so piqued that she hadn't even taken anything out of the freezer for him. Let him deal with it.

So with new determination that lent her an oddly disembodied freedom, Marcy twisted off her wedding ring and dropped it in her purse. It was a plain gold band dating from hers and Howard's lean start, from the days of eating on a card table and sleeping on a mattress on the floor. Faye—well, Faye flashed a diamond solitaire as big as a kidney bean. But she had that rich daddy.

Everett reappeared, grinning crookedly. Behind him the Pakistani manager leered from the door—it looked like a leer to Marcy. And a leer is what the room deserved. It smelled of moldy shower and rug disinfectant and was done in wild sunset colors. Road noise penetrated the uninsulated walls; a door slammed in the next unit, somewhere a baby cried. (Later Everett explained why he'd picked this shabby place: no one he knew was apt to spot his car here.)

She stood uneasily in the middle of the room, frozen with a new fear—was he going to be able to pull this off? But he turned to her, his brown eyes shiny with love. She buried her nose in his neck, inhaled his scent. "What is that stuff you wear?" she murmured.

"It's called *Canoe*," he said, and they laughed nervously, hysterically. They laughed until they were breathless and flopped on the bed. It was an unheated waterbed, cold as a glacier. They shivered, wrapped themselves together, explored each other shyly. Everett kept his eyes closed, as if in prayer. She found this oddly touching.

But he was so shy! And so slow! Nothing like Howard, who presented a battering ram and beat her with it as if waging an interior war. No, Everett needed much help, and even then, for all her effort, she got something like a poorly preserved pickle all soft and slippery from oozing. Oozing until there was nothing left for her. But she worked, experimented, learned, then congratulated herself for having brought off something Faye hadn't managed to do for years, according to him. Yes, she'd bested Faye, possessor of trophies, diamonds, and glass houses.

Marcy learned to pleasure herself, too. When he'd gone off to run water in the bathroom, so much running of water...what was he doing in there?...she buried her nose in his pillow, inhaled him, conjured him up the way she wished he were, and did for herself. Yes, she learned quite a lot.

She wasn't a bit angry with Everett, either, for the big build-up. She knew little about sex, never talked to her girlfriends about it. Sexual satisfaction seemed like so much pie in the sky, a Chicken Little thing. Mass hysteria. Everyone seeing something that isn't there. You don't want to seem weird so you say you see it, too. That had been sex, for Marcy.

Later, Marcy asked Everett, "What were you and that Pakistani guy laughing about?"

"He asked me if I wanted the room by the hour."

"What did you say?"

"I said yes, start the odometer. I'd pay monthly for a lot of hours. No, just kidding. But what would you say if I had?"

She giggled, then gave him an arch look. She'd been taken for a test drive, and was now headed for his garage.

It went on like that for months, and might have lasted years. Marcy was happy with the routine: an occasional wine-tasting or art gallery; a bookstore visit or a classic movie. A once-a-week tryst, a chance to pleasure Everett, then herself with fantasy games while he was in the bathroom. Yes, it might have gone on if it hadn't been for a really bad nosebleed.

She'd gotten them since childhood. They were triggered by allergies, the reason she and Howard had moved to the desert in the first place. But lately the bleeding had gotten worse, a legacy of the desert building boom. At least Marcy hoped dust in the air, and not something psychic, was causing the bleeding.

The stubborn bloody flow scared Everett. He tried ice, pressure, and various head elevations. Then he rushed her back to Howard at the club. Howard had always known what to do.

When they reached the parking lot, Marcy knew Howard's race was over: Desert Dancer was swabbed out and buttoned up in her slip, as was Rag Top, Faye's boat. Everett let Marcy out at the clubhouse steps, and delicately turned away to wander the docks. Marcy pushed through the club's double redwood doors, clutching a blood-soaked handkerchief to her face.

A rush of cool air full of cigarette smoke swooshed by as she broke the vacuum seal. She quickly surveyed the room. Almost everyone had gone home. The sullen kid who did clean-up stopped in mid-swipe to gawk at her. The slight murmur of conversation stilled. Or so it seemed to her. For Howard was at the bar with Faye, and instantly, Marcy knew.

It was his posture, the way he was bending into her face, the way he pointed his pelvis at her. And Faye was angling back receptively, laughing up into his eyes. Faye had become dangerously sleek, supple. Her hand lay open on the bar, palm up. Marcy remembered reading somewhere how sexy a gesture that was, a sign of acceptance.

"Howard?" Marcy called out. He turned slowly, still wearing what Marcy thought was a greasy smirk.

Howard, her husband whom she'd hidden behind, sheltered with, worn like a coat all her life. She thought of another coat: a Fourth of July fireworks in the park when Howard had spread his coat for her to sit on, his suede jacket. His pride and joy, he'd laid it out on the wet grass for her. They'd been eighteen, just out of high school.

"Howard!" He must not leave her for Faye! Divorce had bled through their crowd like a shot of red dye in a load of white wash, and Marcy had seen what it had done to women like her. Suddenly, these old babies, yes, babies, were out there looking for jobs, when the most they'd ever worked was at the voting booths during elections, or organizing bake sales. Those were Marcy's sole achievements. Somewhere along the line, she'd neglected to prepare herself for real life.

"Oh, Howard..." If he married Faye, they'd have children (by now she knew why Faye and Everett never had), and what a mess that would make for her boys. They were shy boys, introverted like her. They needed Howard, needed to inherit. There was enough, now. But not enough for a second batch.

"Howard, hon...oh, uh, Faye...Howard, I've got one of my nose bleeds. Help me." She marched across the room to anchor herself, wedge herself between them. She could almost smell their musk. These were frighteningly efficient people. They must not be allowed to combine their forces. Their power and authority needed curbing. They needed her and Everett. They needed handicapping, like racers with high-tech boats pitted against the ordinary.

"Howard, let's go home," Marcy said. And so she turned her back on Everett. She turned from fantasy to what was real, her life with Howard.

Marcy sighs and rotates her shoulders, remembering that awful year of weaning Howard from the boat, and from Faye. The same year she turned forty.

She'd worked at it, planned her tactics as if at war. She'd said things like, "If we sold the boat, we'd free up enough capital for the video rental franchise." Then she'd show him her figuring on odd bits of paper.

He'd said, "I know, I know. And these VCRS are going to be big, I can feel it."

"Slip fees go up almost monthly. With what we pay in moorage, you could buy that red Porsche."

He'd gotten up to pace. "I sorta like the silver one better, the convertible. What do you think?"

Of course Marcy knew Faye had a new silver convertible. She'd seen Faye chase around in it, her personalized license plate reading RAG TOP 2. Slouched at her side, under a jaunty canvas hat, was the new guy from the club who raced a Hunter 30.

It was Howard himself who supplied the impetus for his quitting the club. He became the butt of in-jokes when an item about him appeared in the "Bilge Water" section of the newsletter. He had inadvertently used the women's restroom in another marina. He hated cutesy names for the john, and it enraged him when the item coyly asked, "Who knows all about wiring, but not if he's a 'hole' or a 'pole'?" Howard had mastered 'buoys' and 'gulls', 'inboard' and 'outboard,' but being laughed at as a 'hole' made him resign.

They did him a favor, though, nudging him into selling the boat. He got into the video thing just as it boomed, made enough on a string of outlets to retire early. Then they moved from the desert to the Oregon Coast, away from Faye and Everett.

Marcy hears a door close and looks up to see Howard stepping briskly toward her. Spots of color glow in his cheeks and he grins. "Good news. Nothing to worry about. Benign tumor. You're gonna have to put up with me a while longer, old girl."

She rushes to him, feeling light, happy. She makes to put her arms around him, but now, back in charge, he eludes her, pats her down. She chirps, "Oh, honey, I'm so pleased, this is great. I was thinking maybe we could do some traveling, see the East Coast..." She rattles on, making plans, taking stock, assessing the future.

He laughs indulgently. "Whoa. Wait up now, kiddo. First things first. I gotta finish the garage, then there's yard work."

He doesn't need her help getting out to the car. He's so newly complete, so assured that she asks, "You want to drive home, dear?"

"Nah, you go ahead," he says. "Chauffeur me around. You need the practice."

Then, despite his reprieve, or because of it, he nods off after they cross the bridge. He leans against the window and begins breathing deeply, rhythmically. The Volvo whispers along, shutting them together against traffic, construction noise, the rain which is falling in earnest now.

Life has been good, and Marcy is content. But when the mood is on her, when her guard is down, she still thinks of Everett. She once bought a bottle of his after-shave and went around smelling him on her wrists until she couldn't stand it anymore and threw it out. Then a few years back she got an anonymous package from Bullhead City: an embarrassingly religious self-help book, the kind of thing Everett would no doubt have taken up these days. She threw that out, too.

But her defenseless dreams are full of his shy brown eyes, his dark, thick hair (Howard is going bald), his smooth arms. She hears his voice sometimes, in stores or in crowds. She catches his laugh, his shy little throat-clearing, and she looks around wildly, electrified.

She remembers the dimple in his chin that held exactly three drops of Chardonnay. He'd loved good wine, especially Chardonnay. Howard drinks beer, any kind, the greener, the better. She remembers Everett's warm, fragrant skin, his delicate torso with seventeen hairs. She remembers the downy line, like a seam, that joined his navel to his pubic bush, which had been springy, not stiff like a vegetable brush. Howard sleeps nude under his Oregon quilt. To Marcy's cool, incurious, wifely touch, he feels like a raffia mat.

Marcy happens to notice her hands, now resting lightly on the steering wheel, since Howard's criticism is silent. Knobby knuckles, bunchy veins. She pushes up her sweater sleeves to inspect the skin on her arms and sees that it hangs on her like poorly-ironed cloth. Well, she's getting on, no doubt about it. But Everett would be, too. He'd be old enough now to collect Social Security—not that he'd have to, not with what Faye's daddy probably left them. Why, he could be one of these old fogies poking along in an RV.

The thought depresses her. To lift herself from it, she clicks on the turn signal and swoops around a bus-sized Pace Arrow. She glimpses in at the driver, and no, it's not Everett piloting the monster. It's just some old man. A gray old man like a million other gray old men.

AUNT OLIVE'S HOUSE

WHILE DRIVING down to visit David, I'm suddenly gripped by an impulse to look up Aunt Olive's old house in Glendale. Rather, it hits me like a case of the flu. I go hot, then cold. I tremble with fever; I break out in a cold sweat. Succumbing, queasy with both longing and dread, I swing off 1-5 onto San Fernando Road, the old 99 in Burbank where I grew up. Glendale's the next town, but to find my way I've got to start from here.

I'm sick with memories. Memories of growing up in a cheap jack box of a house, in the crosshairs of railroad tracks, junkyard, seedy trailer court, and the defense plant where my father worked during World War II. I'm sick with gray air and tawdry discount stores lining the road, as well as personal defeats, school flops, fits and starts leading nowhere. What am I doing! Either I should know better, or I should handle myself more carefully. The doctor would not be pleased. All that therapy gone to waste.

Then too, seeing David upsets me. He's my older son, now living in San Diego. His life is a study in black and white, and right now it's black. He's bunking in a friend's tool shed, and however grim that is, it's a step up from a month or so ago when he was among the truly homeless, sleeping under bridges, overpasses, in culverts.

With David, I take up self-flagellation, even cannibalism. I chew up parts of myself, my cuticles, the inside of my mouth. I create rough patches of raw flesh that tempt me into even more destruction. I eat and drink too much, talk too long and loud. I want to throw myself, or at least my purse, off high places. When I'm around David, I stay away from balconies, out of skyscrapers.

"What are your plans now, dear," I'll say, firing away. "Have you thought about going back to school? Computer programming isn't so hard to learn, I hear."

David will give me that cold, flat look I've learned to dread, and will reply with pained patience, "I told you my plans, Mom. You don't listen."

"David, living in a cabaña in Costa Rica is not a real plan. It's what you do after you've finished a real plan."

This is his current and favorite "plan": living a simple life in a thatched hut nestled in a tropical bower. Ambling down to tide pools, under tequila sunrise skies, to gather obliging lobsters, then reaching up from his hammock to pluck exotic fruits. David has been telling me such nonsense for years, and I try to listen, to keep a suitable expression on my face, not too accepting, not too rejecting. A fine balance that wears me out a half-hour into my visit.

"Mom, it's a plan to me," he'll say, heaving a deep sigh, running fingers through his shaggy gray hair. David takes after me, and has gone gray prematurely. My younger son Gene is dark like his father. "Trouble with you, Mom, is you never dreamed. You're the one who never had a plan."

I'll flinch and back off then. I'll try to smooth him over with honeyed phrases like "Yes, of course you're right, dear. It's your... uh, plan. Worth a try, yes." Which fools neither of us. He knows when he's got me, when I can't face the result of my genes and upbringing expressing itself with such painful self-delusion.

But I put this expected scenario in the back of my mind and concentrate on San Fernando Road. It hasn't changed—if anything, the traffic is lighter, and moves slower than it did thirty years ago when it was the main artery into L.A. Newer freeways, perennially under some sort of bottleneck repair, have siphoned off the heavy commercial traffic.

Old landmarks stand out like scars. The municipal ballpark where I fell off a bleacher and cracked a tooth that bothered me for years. The Cornel Theatre, now showing films in Spanish, where Eddie Curtis, my high school boyfriend, once ushered. Saturday nights he'd sneak me in the side door, and we'd settle in the dark back row to trade sloppy french kisses during the movie.

There's Thrifty Drug, where I waited for the bus in the shadows, watching carloads of classmates whoop by after football games. And Burcal's Department Store, where the girls with clear skin and good figures bought angora sweaters. Next the import outlet with the giant rattan elephant in the parking lot, where I bought incense to burn in my room to keep my parents from smelling my cigarette smoke. They didn't care if I smoked—it was expected that I'd smoke and drink and swear and lie. And fail at all endeavors. I was, after all, my father's daughter. It was just that he didn't want me filching cigs from his cache.

There's the day-old bakery, still next door to the gym. Used to be Vic Tanney's; now it's Gold's. When I weighed one hundred and eight pounds and thought I was fat, I bought a membership and worked out there. Then I went next door and gorged on stale donuts. Perennially bent on self-destruction.

Here's the dairy. The pungent odor of manure assails me. Unchanged, Jessup's Dairy holds on, resisting urbanization right across from the Southern Pacific switching yards. I remember when the dairy started selling ground beef in addition to milk and cheese. One way or another, you could get a piece of cow.

I develop a headache. Dairy stink. Smog. Exhaust. This horrid road. Everything along it seems the same, but the road itself appears to be dirtier, narrower, as if dried out in this land of no seasons. A beef jerky stretch of road.

I remember the address, or enough of it, from an envelope in my mother's stockpile of old letters. She saved everything. My dad and I spent weeks going through her keepsakes when she died. Opal Avenue, five hundred something. I'll recognize the house, if it's still there. Only saw it that one time, but I've carried around a mental snapshot all these years. The doc would no doubt make something out of that. Out of this whole detour. I turn east on Western Avenue, toward what was once the center of town.

I was young, five or six at the time. But the house made such an impression, I visualized it in school when we read *House of the Seven Gables*, then *Wuthering Heights*. It'll be gone, I tell myself sternly, the house will be gone, bulldozed for development, or it will turn out to be a shabby bungalow, given the way kids remember things. But I barrel along, full steam ahead, as if on a mission.

Deeper into the heart of Glendale, I thread through intersections with three-way stops. I maneuver down four-lane streets with traffic rushing by at an alarming clip. Catch sight of Opal Avenue almost by accident, double back to make a turn.

In culture shock, I cruise slowly. The trees are gone, the big old elms whose interlocking branches had made the street a tunnel. Now it's a canyon hemmed in by walls of apartment buildings. The dominant architecture is pseudo-Spanish, purposefully rough white plaster studded with red bricks like freckles; bleached tile roofs; flimsy wrought-iron staircases and balconies; dusty palms and cactuses. A desert where a forest used to be. I ache with disappointment: sure enough, Aunt Olive's house is gone. Where I guess it should be is now a parking lot, acres of asphalt to accommodate these beehive dwellers.

I sit staring at the expanse of blacktop until a couple of guys working on a car began to stare back. So I pull slowly into traffic at a loss, almost wishing I could tell the doctor how I feel knowing the house is gone. But what had I expected? It'd been more than fifty years since I stepped through that heavy door with its oval of stained glass. I remember as if it were yesterday, the scene in the glass: a translucent dark-green vine trailed around clusters of red and purple grapes. I'd never seen anything so beautiful. Or so ominous.

Just before World War II my parents packed me and their meager belongings out of Kansas, not exactly Dust Bowlers, but close. I remember hearing stories of skies dark at noon with blowing dirt, of non-stop sandblasting winds, of crops that failed or were never planted. We came from country north of the real Dust Bowl, but our problem, the Depression, knew no geographical boundaries. My father was the oldest of twelve, one of those big Irish Catholic families that sent waves of emigrants pulsing westward as railroad work tapered off and farms went bust.

"So you were like the Okies and the Arkies," David would say. He'll listen to these old family stories, which is more than I can say for Gene. Gene sided with his father in the split, and I don't hear from him much.

"Okies, no. Okies traveled in old trucks piled high with mattresses and kids. When an old wreck like that rumbled through town, your grandpa would stand on the curb and stare, hostile as anybody. No, we came in a 1936 Ford sedan. You've seen the pictures."

At the slightest provocation I haul out and inflict on David old curled photos of me standing in front of the car, canvas water bag hung on its bumper. In the background, state line markers. New Mexico. Arizona. California. The old Route 66 headed toward the bonanza of the Southland and my rich aunt Olive in Glendale.

Aunt Olive wasn't really an aunt—she was my mother's aunt's cousin. So the line was thin and the claim small. But the family grapevine had it that she was so well off she had a man-servant, to "do for her." And she had Holdings. A woman with a man-servant and Holdings. Untold riches.

We'd settled in a shabby duplex in Burbank before setting out on the supplicant's pilgrimage to Aunt Olive. Then one day we were on the road, and I remember my father driving round and round blocks of big dark houses. Clearly edgy, he blamed my mother for misdirecting him when we circled the same block twice. He ordered me to sit still in the back seat and quit breathing down his neck. I was wearing a scratchy brown and yellow pinafore and stiff new shoes I was told to keep off the prickly Mexican serape covering the seat. The feel of that pinafore and that serape makes me itch even now.

My dad was a poor driver, tense and nervous behind the wheel. He was given to jackrabbit spurts of speed, screeching stops, and had suffered more than a few rear-enders. My mother added her own brand of excitement by uttering exclamations of alarm. She never learned to drive, but wore out the floorboards on her side of the car with braking maneuvers.

Motoring slowly, we peered into leafy porches, finally found the number, parked, and gazed at the house. It was bigger and darker than the others, daunting in its lifeless quality. Windows with many small panes struggled for space with dusty vines and bushes. I wondered what the servant, the man, had to do. Clearly there was nothing "doing" here.

We marched circumspectly up the flagstone walk. My father pushed the bell, which sounded a whole scale of notes somewhere deep in the house. He cleared his throat, retucked his Sunday shirt. It was a faded blue-check affair smelling of fried foods, cigarette smoke, and sweat.

Here David would interrupt, "You're always so hard on Grandpa. You make him sound like a redneck."

"Not far from it," I'd reply. "His favorite outfit was a T-shirt, one with a vee neck. He'd make a cuff in one sleeve to tuck his smokes in."

"That's stereotyping. What about Grandma? She wearing an apron splotched with chicken blood?" By now David's tone would make me apprehensive, but like a fool, so anxious to tell my story, I'd rush on.

What my mother did wear were printed dresses from Mode O'Day and cotton stockings rolled up to just above her knees. The garters, circles of dimestore elastic she stitched together herself, showed when she sat down, revealing the fish-belly white of her upper legs. That day, on Aunt Olive's porch, she shuffled just behind my father (and it was her relative), clutching her cloth bag, her "pocketbook," as if it were a sack with her life in it. Then a little man that I later associated with Kato, the Green Hornet's houseboy, opened the door.

After a few sentences of embarrassed explanation (the visit was a surprise, since my parents never trusted the telephone; they didn't have one until after I'd married and gone), we were ushered into the sitting room. It was cold and dark, cluttered, high-ceilinged, echoing with the loud tick of an enormous clock. I had an impression of hard plush upholstery, teardrop chandelier, tombstone furniture. No kid had ever been in this room before. My father cleared his throat, squared his shoulders. My mother fiddled with her hanky. They both snapped at me to sit up, sit still, behave. Which I was already doing. Clearly, this was enemy territory.

The aunt's tapping cane sounded on the stairs and my parents stepped forward to place ceremonial pecks on her cheek. I stared. She had quivery white hairs on her chin and was older than my grandma and grandpa put together. White hair also frizzed around her face, which resembled cottage cheese—same color and texture. She tapped to a chair and sat with her legs apart.

My parents mumbled something about the weather, then family news. Kato brought in a wicker tray of coffee and I peered into my mother's cup, remembered hearing earlier, "She's so close with her money she boils the coffee grounds twice." The coffee did look pale. I wanted to ask if Aunt Olive really made jam out of grapefruit rinds and watermelon seeds, also according to my mother. The clock ticked.

The stiff visit wound down. My aunt saw us out, stood leaning on her cane at the majestic door while giving some sort of directions to my father. I was immensely relieved to go. I'd begun to worry we were to move in there. She had room for us in her cold house, but the sidewalks, all buckled and cracked, were no good for skates.

I was dead set on skates for my birthday but wasn't sure I'd get them. I'd already begun to lose faith with adults, eye them suspiciously. Their dangerous bulk and strength, their inappropriate hairs, nasty secretions, their odors, the messes they made. It was war, me on one side, them on another. Don't all kids feel this way? I once asked the doc and he said no, but I never believed him.

My dad steered the Ford out into traffic. We threaded through the strange town to its outskirts, ending up on a sagebrush covered hill far above the last houses. We parked and got out. My father wandered around, taking in the lay of the land. He squatted on his hams, gathered a handful of sand and let it run through his fingers. "Worthless," he said. "Never grow anything here."

Now, here's what I think happened that day: from her Holdings, the aunt offered my father property. That area would soon be subdivided into expensive view lots, but he, the farmer, couldn't see that. To him the soil was thin, stony, arid, not fit to grow corn, wheat, or even potatoes. And with that judgment, he did our family out of a great deal of money. No use denying I held his decision, his shortsightedness, against him. He turned his back on the aunt's offer, and we were affected by it.

"So that was a real turning point," said the doctor. "A time he could have made a difference."

"Well, yes," I said. "Seems to me you get only two or three chances in your life to make a meaningful decision. These are serious events."

"Like when you decided to divorce Lou."

"I didn't decide that. He did. Besides, the marriage was dead, nothing going on except a fight. No air in it."

"Cathy, you are so naive. You think every family except yours gets along peacefully, happily? That at all times there's 'air in it'?"

Yes, I thought that.

"Don't you see you're not allowing people to be human?"

No, I didn't see that. I knew a real family had a sort of mystical connection. That was why I rejected my own parents, and

Lou, too. They, we, didn't connect.

"And you'd be different, better, if your father had taken the aunt's offer?"

Yes, exactly.

I might have been one of those girls, the cheerleaders, the stars in school plays, the ones not afraid, the ones who waited for the bus across the street from Thrifty's. I might have been homeward bound up new streets that twisted around the hill like yin yang curves with names like Starlight Court, Horizon View Summit, Skyline Drive, to split-levels with expanses of glass and open-beamed ceilings and great sweeps of lawn with circular drives. I might have been one of the girls the football players took to the prom.

If my father had chosen differently, he might not have been consumed by drink. Because soon after establishing ourselves in the little box in Lockheed's shadow, almost under its camouflage netting, my father began keeping company with bottles stashed in the garage. He began arguing and slurring and crashing around. He began sleeping in the alley and coming in bruised and red-eyed and trembling. And my mother cringed and stooped under the load of her martyrdom, and complained and wept and accused both him and me of hard-heartedness. "When I die," she'd say in a quivery high-pitched voice, "just throw my body out in the alley and let the dogs eat it. That's all either of you cares for me."

I never go this far when I tell David about HOW MY FATHER THREW AWAY A FORTUNE. I stop right after, "This land is worth less, won't grow potatoes." And I laugh ruefully, carefully, to show how well-balanced and accepting I've become of my parents and their choices.

Doesn't work with David, though. He's apt to say, "You're hard on Grandpa. He didn't know. He was a farmer, not a real-estate developer."

"Yes, that's true. But don't you see the way it turned out, we might just as well have been Okies."

David will frown, rub his forehead as if it ached like mine

does now. "But you used to tell me how tough his father was on him when he was young."

I confess being hard-hearted toward my father is easier when I don't consider his childhood, how cruel and bleak, how dangerous. My mother, in one of her push-pull moods of be-kind-to-him-you-don't-know-how-he-suffered, used to tell me stories.

Liquored up, my grandfather stropped my father till he bled: then, when he wouldn't stand still and take it anymore, the old man chased him down rows of corn with a straight-edged razor. "Why?" I asked my mother, horrified.

"Well, the old man always picked on the fair-skinned ones, worked them hard, beat them. He favored the ones like himself, dark complected, eyes black as buttons. The old devil got it in his head it was your dad who set fire to the curtains, burned the house down. They all knew it was your aunt Lucille, smoking in an upstairs bedroom, but he wouldn't accept that. Lucille was his pet."

These stories shake me badly when I tell them to David. I have to look away from David's blue-eyed stare, from that ir-ritating knowing expression. He doesn't really know, not really. He can't know something that's beyond me, can he?

"Geez!" David would mutter. "Talk about screwed up! How did the rest of the kids turn out? How's Lucille?"

"Haven't got the faintest. Haven't seen her for years. She didn't come to your great-grandpa's funeral, neither did a few of the others. There were enough of the brothers, though, to make up six pallbearers."

I could see David thinking this family background is why I don't get along with men, why I didn't get along with his father. I know David discusses this sort of thing at his AA meetings.

Not true, anyway, that I didn't get along with his father. When David and Gene were little, Lou and I had a relationship that worked. Lou went off every day and I stayed home. If you call that a relationship. I guess I related better with Marilyn de Walt, who lived next door and came over to drink coffee every morning after her husband left. We sat there complaining about the housework that never got done while our kids ran amok making even bigger messes. But I muddled along. At four o'clock the boys turned on the TV to watch *The Three Stooges*, then *Superman*, while I rushed around throwing some order into the place, getting ready for Lou, who arrived at five. He liked to nap for twenty minutes on the den couch, so we had to be quiet. Then we had to be quiet while he listened to the news and ate. Lou frowned when the gravy got cold; when the boys' table manners failed them; when the menu lacked complexity. He would not allow one-dish meals such as soups, casseroles, stews. I was to maintain firm control over the dinner hour. Everything that happened then was my fault.

"But did you communicate with Lou?" the doctor asked.

"Sure. Oh yeah, we communicated." Once in a while Lou demanded that the two of us sit at the table while he lectured me about how life should be in his home. He'd come from one of those split-levels up the hill and he knew. He'd been a "catch," and I'd been lucky to get him. Such was the thinking in certain quarters.

For openers, Lou would say, "At least on Sundays you could set the table with that damask my folks gave us."

"Yes, but it's hard to iron."

"Just dampen it, fold it up in a plastic bag, and the next day press it. My mother never had any trouble. Call her and ask how she organized. There were three of us kids, remember, and you've only got to manage two. Anyway, she'd be glad to hear from you. Also about the ironing, when you finish my shirts, make sure you get them on the hanger straight. Otherwise, they don't look sharp. And I want to look sharp. The big boss is scouting a replacement for Mel, and I want it to be me. Don't you want me to move up? Well, all right now, when do you iron?"

"Whenever I can."

"Why not when the boys go down for their naps? That way you can concentrate. If a thing's worth doing, it's worth doing right."

What he didn't know was that when the boys napped, so did I. I was always sleepy, always tired back then, despite all that coffee Marilyn and I drank when our husbands left in the morning. To tell the truth, I didn't know where my time went. The days melted away, bled into each other with no edges. "Cathy," the doctor once said sternly, "you're admitting you lost control of your life."

Yes, yes I did. Couldn't make a choice back then, couldn't make a decision.

"Did it frighten you, being out of control?"

Yes, it did.

"Must you be in control? Don't you find being in control stressful? Couldn't you just concentrate on pleasing Lou, let him be boss?"

No, I couldn't.

"Don't you wish for Lou back? Wouldn't you like to turn the reins over, quit being in control?"

Control! Control! What was it with him and control? With all men and control? Do they want you to be in control, or not?

Not able to tell the doc anything real for fear he'd use it against me, I distracted him with fantasy. I told him I wanted to see a remake of *King Kong*. This time a gigantic muscular woman would rescue a helpless little man, cradle him in her powerful fist. I'd change the ending. Forget the Empire State Building caper. Instead I'd have her maroon him in a padded cell full of little kids, then become lofty and aloof, cold and critical. High point of the day: The Three Stooges.

I finally quit my sessions with the doc. Not because of this no-win situation over control, but because he made me face an uncomfortable truth: the resentment and anger I'd felt for my own parents had taken root and gone underground. All my relationships had been poisoned, distorted, as if my garden were infested with nematodes. And yes, David had been right; he'd known this all along. But I couldn't accept it. Not then, anyway. I wanted the doctor to listen, not deal out useless knowledge.

I come to the end of Glenoaks Boulevard and turn left on Verdugo Road, routing myself by the swimming pool where I'd met Lou.

I'd worked there my first summer out of high school, handing out towels and locker keys to nine-to-twelve-year-olds who swarmed in like gnats from the surrounding neighborhood. In that bunch Lou stood out like a hawk. He'd just mustered out of the army, had been in Korea. I found this out later. He came alone every day, lay down on his Peter Max towel, leaned on his elbows and brooded. His dark face closed like a fist while he stared at the junior shenanigans raging around him.

If he'd fallen all over me, I'd have scorned him. But I had no defense against his rejection. I went for him, mounted a major self-correction campaign; lost weight, bought a membership to that gym I drove by a few minutes ago, worked on my tan, and decided black mascara had more impact on my pale lashes than brown. He started paying attention. One day after my shift, we went to Bob's Drive In in Toluca Lake, sat there and talked for hours. Soon we were parking behind Hansen Dam for long necking sessions while Jackie Gleason's *Music for Lovers Only* played on his car radio.

By Christmas we'd decided to get married, to run off to Las Vegas for a quickie ceremony. Lou's mother had a fit, which delighted Lou (marrying me, I discovered later, had more to do with exacting revenge on her than it did with love for me). She pleaded for a real wedding. Lou shook his head, his face dark with that look I'd later learn to dread. At least a reception, his mother urged. It would be at their house. His parents could meet mine, for the first time.

Well, they tried, my folks. My mother dolled up in a new powder-blue taffeta with wide bat-wing sleeves and shoulder pads, and a full, swishy skirt, the most playful outfit I ever saw her in. But my father outshone her in a bright blue suit from Robert Hall, in a hard-finished synthetic, which he wore with a brown print sport-shirt imbued with his personal aroma. He was nervous, did a lot of throat-clearing and shoulder-squaring until the champagne bar worked its treacherous magic on him.

The doc interrupted, "So why did you serve champagne? You knew his problem with alcohol."

"It was Lou's folks," I answered. "They arranged the whole thing. We were just sort of guests—"

"They were welcoming you into their family and you didn't have enough faith in them to communicate your father's problem?"

No, I did not. They were strangers to me. Anyway, I thought my father could pull it off, at least for an afternoon. I should have known better.

He was fine for a while; alcohol always peeled him away in layers. First the introverted, nervous man with trembling hands relaxed into a witty conversationalist. I heard him begin to tell jokes in the Irish brogue he'd perfected. Then he went on to stories that illustrated his ironic twist on life.

"But he didn't stay in this stage long, is that it?"

Yes, exactly. Soon he was louder, and sprinkling his speech with profanity. The noisy braggart stage. My mother wrung her hands when he started slurring his words. Then the stories turned nasty, how he'd cheated the lumberman at Glickman Brothers Hardware—"out-Jewed a Kike" was how he put it. Fast as I could, I steered him outside for a smoke. I was walking him around, getting some air into him, when I noticed a sheen of gray on his cheeks that he'd missed shaving. He was old. My father was an old man.

"Go on, Cathy," the doctor urged.

He started crying, saying things like he hadn't been a good father, how sorry he was, wished he'd done better for me. Then he gave me a pin, a scrolly gold *C*. It had belonged to my grandmother—she was Catherine, too.

The doctor murmured, "You're wearing that pin now."

I told him I always wore it to our sessions.

"Why is that?"

I rubbed the pin on my lapel. "I don't know. Well, yes, I do. It connects me to my family, what was best in them."

"What was best, Cathy?"

I took a while to answer, then said, "My mother's steadfastness, her dedication. My father's wit—those Irish jokes were funny. His depth. He was deep. Shallow people don't suffer like he did."

"So he touched you, presenting this heirloom."

I said of course it had touched me. Giving me a little pin, in this rich house full of the right stuff, crystal, china, lace. All Lou's people with perfect teeth and manners, degrees after their names. And my father had only this one little thing, and he gave it to me like it was his soul, a piece of it, all he had left. "He was kind of blubbering, and he stepped into the bushes," I said. "And I had this awful flash he was going to urinate, but it was to blow his nose through his fingers, farmer-style. Just then Lou's mother and sister appeared in the doorway in their sleek dresses. Lou's mother said—I heard her say this—'Water finds its own level,' and turned away. And behind her, there was my mother in that weird get-up like a cheerleader's costume, and my dad in that neon suit, but with no handkerchief."

"But Lou married you, not your parents."

"Yeah, but he knew then I was my father's daughter. We'd never make it."

Past Verdugo Plunge I continue north to Montrose Avenue, turn left, and arrive at the area of the aunt's Holdings. (The man servant, Kato, inherited the entire estate, and what a storm of satisfied gossip that generated!) I drive slowly along twisty streets, stunned. What I'd thought such richness now seems cluttered, narrow; the houses shabby, small, pinched-in with RVs and pickups. Lou and his current wife live not far from here in a house like one of these, where, I'm sure, Sunday dinner is under control and is served on the damask.

I'm flushed with unexpected satisfaction thinking of Lou in his split-level. I'd once dreaded seeing this area, for fear I'd covet, or regret, or otherwise tear myself apart. Because what my father turned down so long ago could have finally been mine if I'd played my cards...well, not right, but differently. I see now, though, that I've been pardoned—I've been released from this kind of padded cell. I don't have to try to live here, and I'm as relieved as if I'd just gotten a clean bill of health, the pain proven to be indigestion, the lump benign.

At the top of the road I park and walk out into a vacant lot to view the valley below. Through the smog I pick out where Highland Avenue intersects Brand Boulevard, both built wide enough for streetcars. A few edifices reach presumptuously into the gray air: the Alex Theatre's Alhambra-like towers, the art-deco fussy fingers of City Hall, the post office, the courthouse—1930s WPA attempts at majesty. But true majesty lies in a giant Robinson's department store anchoring a new mall south of what used to be the city's heart.

On the east edge of town Forest Lawn Cemetery maintains a sweep of greenery polka-dotted with white grave markers. It means nothing to me, though, since my parents are buried with the Catholics farther out in the valley, in Van Nuys. I admit that once, at this point, I might have been sappy enough or phony enough to say, "Then, thinking of them, I cried, blurring the scene with tears and love for my people. I cried for what could have been and never was..." Blah, blah, blah.

I'm more honest now, and I feel this is an improvement, this is progress. The truth is that when I got that call from the Burbank police telling me my father had been found dead in his garage, I was relieved. He'd been a weight I didn't want to carry after my mother died. Another truth: I was glad when my hair turned white, because then it was a different color from his. I'd hated looking like him.

On Sundays, duty days, I'd call and ask, "Are you coming over? I've got a roast for dinner, and there's a game on tonight," and hold my breath—then let it out, relieved, when he'd mumble about being too busy, about having to putter or paint or repair things around the house. "And there's the garden," he'd say.

"Your mother's roses need pruning, and it's time to divide the iris."

I pictured him alone in his smoky living room, a ballgame droning in the background. I knew he never went anywhere, too befuddled and afraid to drive. He was still up to his old trick of drinking in the garage, a ploy now unnecessary with both my mother and me gone.

So the proper place had been the garage. He'd spent most of his time out there. He didn't fumble it, either—he got it right. Stuffed rags in cracks, ran the hose from the exhaust into the car, turned on the ignition, and settled back to breathe—with enough gas in the tank that the coroner guessed the engine ran all day before a neighbor walking a dog in the alley heard it. Given these circumstances, the Van Nuys Catholics had been kind to accept him, although I understand they're getting more liberal about such things. And my mother was already there.

Yes, he did the proper thing for a man in his condition, with his background and proclivities. I was glad to be rid of him. Such hard-heartedness. Such honesty. Maybe therapy pays off in ways you don't expect.

I plod through the dirt back to my car and, against the threat of heat on I-5 southbound, take off my jacket pinned with the gold *C*. What a farce, that line of malarkey I'd fed the doc about this pin. My father never gave me so much as the sound of his voice, unless in a lie, or hoarse with anger, or slippery with contempt. I bought this gilt thing myself in a garage sale. I can almost hear the doc saying, "So why do you have to tell me a lie, Cathy? What does your father's lack of love mean to you?"

Well, I can't answer that. Not yet. Maybe never.

I open the car door, then sit and stare at the debris I shake from my shoes. Gray-beige sand, meaningless, dead. My father was right: this land is worthless to people like us. We can't grow our lives here. I see that my father and I were or rather are a lot alike. I have achieved a green connection with my blood. Freighted with this knowledge, I spin a U and head back down the hill.

David—I've got to tell David about this. For the first time, I see he's the one who will sympathize. I rip a cuticle down to the quick, suck at the blood, and begin chewing.

SHAG RUG

Dick waited in the garage for Barbara's storm of housecleaning to abate. She knocked herself out before an evening of company, and the place looked great when she was finished. But he felt a little sour about his banishment. He disliked having his routine disrupted—he napped in the afternoon—and knew he was wasting time sorting through his fishing tackle. It'd been years since he'd used it. Why bother? No fish left in the Northport River. Even tide pools around the inlet had been picked clean of urchins, sea stars, even snails. Tourists! They'd swipe anything.

After an interval of silence—surely she'd stowed the damned machine—he opened the kitchen door. Yes, the coast was clear. Just inside, he exchanged his shoes for his slippers, sentinels kept there to guard his shag rug from careless sand and street debris. Being vigilant paid off. He glanced into his tidy living room, and savored the newly vacuumed and raked rug. Not a footprint marred its loops standing erect and even, smooth as his manicured lawn outside.

He congratulated himself for having picked a wife who knew how to care for things. Thanks to her, no one would guess the age of that rug. The only details giving away its age were the length of its loops–trend now was to a short almost flat weave and the rug's color. Antique gold had died a sudden violent death in the late seventies. True, Barb was nagging him for new carpeting—she said she hated the color now—but Dick was not sorry he'd jerked it up when they'd sold the San Jose house to relocate to the coast.

He chuckled to himself imagining how the new owners of his former house had reacted discovering the rug missing. But maybe they hadn't reacted at all. Immigrant South East Asians, they probably didn't know any better. They'd fit right in with the neighborhood though. It had turned "yellow" overnight, every house crammed with thirty or forty people, ten more in the garage.

The racial turning had been so sudden that he and Barb hadn't noticed it until their dog had gone missing. After a futile search for it, Dick had discovered that no one on their block spoke English anymore. Then there'd been stories in the paper about missing pets, about one culture impinging on another—a fancy way of saying the new people flooding in believed a dog's place was in the fire, not curled up next to it. So Dick had pulled out, with his rug. Well, the new people had to learn; might as well start with a real estate lesson about wall-to-wall carpeting.

Dick washed up in the company bathroom, en wiped down the sink. He dried his hands on the bath mat to save Barb's hintcy little hand towel. Pausing in front of the mirror, he slipped a comb through his hair. He approved of his hair, still thick and wavy, a becoming silver. Matched his eyes. Strong sensible color for a strong sensible face.

Then in the kitchen he called out, "Good-looking dessert, hon." The pie cooling on the counter was cherry, his favorite, if she'd used enough sugar. He rubbed his hands together in anticipation. Kind of an evening he liked: sensible friends enjoying pie and coffee with good talk. Wouldn't cost a penny, either, beyond the pie ingredients. Sacrificing his nap seemed a small inconvenience.

The Robinsons arrived late, which was not like them. Dick had settled into a TV program about America's empty victory in the Gulf, a point he liked to make himself, when Ann and Emmett crunched up the gravel driveway and knocked. Dick was interested in the program and considered keeping it on tuned low, but thought better of it.

"Howdy, howdy. You get all the way over here without being mugged?" Dick joked, his standard quip. Ann and Emmett lived just one block over on Marine Terrace, and the last person to get mugged in Northport had been an Indian in the 1800s.

Emmett chucked, then focused on the fading TV. "Reason we're late, I started watching that same program. Those Arabs..." He pronounced it *A-rabs*, long first syllable. "I dunno about them, even the good ones."

"Now, Emmett," murmured Ann, "don't get started. And please don't turn it back on for us," she added quickly when Dick looked back at the TV. She settled into the same corded armchair she always sat in.

"Yes, please, called Barb from the kitchen where she was slicing pie and making coffee, "don't turn it back on. I don't want to hear anymore about that awful war, or any news. It's all so upsetting."

While they ate their dessert, they discussed the same list of topics they covered every time. Dick began by bemoaning the proliferation of gays and lesbians, and condemned their increasing aggressiveness. He'd just read about a Queer Nation's parade in Eugene that had turned ugly. At the end of his comments, he aimed his fork at Emmett and exclaimed, There they are, tying up police forces that should be out solving crimes and protecting taxpayers. Something ought to be done about those people, is all."

He was taken aback when Barb piped up in her baby-doll voice, "Yes, Dick, but look at Stella and Lois right here town. The most peaceful people, and nice. Artistic, too. Those beautiful pots Lois makes...that's one right there."

They all looked at a brown asymmetrical jug filled with straw flowers on the coffee table. Dick said, "It's lopsided."

Barb said sharply. "That's the way it's supposed to look, sort of oriental."

"I like it," said Ann. "Nice texture, and pretty the way you're using it."

Just like women to back each other up, thought Dick. He felt slightly nettled and threw a look at Barb. He hadn't known the origin of the pot, or that Barb was so crazy about those lesbians, He wondered what other nonsense she'd come out with...maybe even something about Alicia, and he didn't want that, for sure.

But Dick relaxed when Emmett said, "Good ice cream. Is it Häagen Dazs?"

Perfect, a change of topic, and he could tell about what a bargain it'd been. "Yes, from the Suprette. It was marked wrong. almost half-priced. That young clerk they've got closing up, the one with the long hair, she didn't even know the difference."

Barb said in a low dead voice, "Dick got her all flustered with some nonsense about how people steal from stores and she just rung it up."

Dick threw her another look, but she had her face turned. He said, "That clerk, Eileen, isn't it? she told us you can't steal from stores because it's all computerized." He laughed. "Computerized! That makes it easier."

"Oh, computers," sighed Ann. The bane of modern existence." She told a computer horror story of sitting in a plane on a Chicago runway for five hours because of a New York power brownout. Emmett corrected a few details, then took over the telling just before the conclusion. Dick listened, approving of the way Emmett and Ann operated together. Their thinking dovetailed, as it should in a strong marriage. Like his did with Barb's. Barb, how good she was, how right for him! He had a fleeting image of her coming out of the shower, stepping daintily down the hall wrapped in her towel, her skin pink and moist, her hair curling in tendrils around her face. He enveloped her in warmth. She felt his look and turned to him with a perplexed expression. Well, he'd explain later, after the company left.

Talk droned on. Dick relaxed into it, feeling warm and lazy. He stretched his legs into a comfortable sprawl and gazed into the artificial fire, enjoying the cozy red and orange glow from the light bulb behind the revolving cylinder. Emmett brought up the antics down at city hall, he called it "silly hall" to Ann's delight, and they all agreed that the new council was crazy. Then they compared their tax bills, which had just come in the mail, and concurred that their hard-earned money was misspent on fighting drug wars in hopeless urban jungles when their own town needed to upgrade services, fix potholes, improve restroom facilities, and plant something besides geraniums and nasturtiums in the barrels downtown. Dick joined in at the right places, but his responses grew fuzzy, those big city faraway problems surreal and blurred—things happening in a distant country he'd once lived in but would never visit again.

He snapped to attention, though, when Ann said, "Isn't that a new picture of Alicia?" She was looking at a flattering portrait of Dick and Barb's only child, who lived in Portland with her husband.

Dick stiffened. If Barb was going to let the cat out of the bag, it would be now. He relaxed when all she said was, "Yes, it was done for Dick's birthday in August. It's good of her, I think." Then she talked of Portland, how congested, how sewn up in gridlock, how complicated life was there.

Soon Barb, in a ritual of conclusion, clattered the dessert plates away to the kitchen. Ann and Emmett stretched and rose to slip on their coats. Dick followed Emmett out to the yard and together they admired the sky glittering with mica, the moon a fingernail paring. Barb and Ann joined them, Ann clutching one of Barb's personalized recipe cards. How good to have a wife who inspired others to ask for recipes, thought Dick, and drew Barb under his arm. She was just the right height to snuggle there. He sniffed her hair, the scent of her shampoo enchanting him, the most alluring perfume he'd ever experienced.

Emmett said, "Look at the hill tonight." They all peered up at the mountain looming over Northport's shoulder. "Remember last year, just about this same time, we watched them clear-cut? Now they're bulldozing it into view lots."

"It looks like a pine cone," said Ann. "All sliced up. Landscaping by Edward Scissorhands." She giggled shrilly and Dick cringed. In a lot of ways she was a silly twit of a woman.

"People really going to build up there?" said Emmett in a wondering voice. "You know what I heard those lots are going for? A hundred thousand, to start! Christ, the Andersons sold the whole mountain for about that."

Barb said, "But look what it's costing to grade and level, and put streets in and all. The Andersons didn't have that kind of money, to develop."

"No one's got that kind of money around here. Takes these Japanese—"

"Now, Dick, they're not Japanese. They're from Hong Kong," said Barb.

"What's the difference? Same thing, gooks taking over." Too late he saw the look in her eyes, the track her mind would follow. He plucked at her shoulder, but she'd turned to Ann and Emmett.

"Our Alicia, you know what she's doing? She and Dave are adopting a Vietnamese baby. Imagine, Dick and I grandparents to a Southeast Asian!"

Dick flushed, then trembled with a hot-cold shock. How could she blurt out this breach in family solidarity! How could she share this shame so blatantly, so ruthlessly! In the heavy silence follow ing her words, he heard the surf pounding a hundred yards away, and imagined that it mirrored his blood pressure. But he faced Emmett, laughed hollowly and said, "Yep. We're being invaded. My dad fought 'em in WWII, I was in Korea, and whaddaya know, my own daughter's bringing them in the front door."

"Dick!" exclaimed Barbara. "It's Alicia's decision, hers and Dave's. It's...it's going to be"

"Politically correct?" Dick's stomach knotted into a ball of acid. Through the window he peered into his own living room, golden, serene, empty. He longed to go back in, take an antacid, be alone with his thoughts and his TV remote. Would these people never leave?

Soon the Robinsons mumbled goodbyes and hurried away. Back in the house Dick sank into his lounger, flopping his feet up on the leg rest. Bitterly he listened to Barbara put the kitchen to rights. That's what mattered to her, getting the dishes done and the crumbs swept away and the counter cleared for the next meal. Little things not worth a hill of beans. She hadn't a clue, not a clue. The whole evening soured on him, that business about the lesbians, the way she let his stories down, and worst of all blurting out what Alicia was up to. And just a bit ago he'd thought he and Barb such soul-mates!

Later, after she'd padded down the hall to the bedroom, his tide of resentment ebbed. What did it matter? What the hell did anything matter? He gazed at his shag rug, now matted from traffic. That's what it all came down to: saving something worth less to pass on to someone who didn't want it. The Asians were going to get it all anyway.

Well, well. No doubt he was just tired—he'd missed his nap. To drown out the growing silence, he punched up the TV volume on his remote and channel-surfed. He stumbled onto a kick-boxing match between two small dark men of minority extraction, and settled into it. But gradually the roar of the crowd turned into the roar of the surf pounding on rocks a half block away.

The droning sound became quite soothing, almost enticing. Dick considered slipping his shoes on for a quick look at the water...then suddenly he was on the edge peering out at the wrinkled sea yellow with wake from a moon, now mysteriously full...such a broad sea...almost endless...nothing between him and Asia thousands of miles away...Surely he was safe enough...

Then the ocean yellowed even more, and the short regular waves became the loops of his shag rug...not lifeless now, but crawling, bleeding forth an army of ant-like creatures inexorably inching toward him, feeling up his legs, across his skin, covering his eyes with an insect-blindfold...

With a start, he awoke in his armchair, sweaty and trembling with fright. And stared at that hateful goddamned yellow shag rug. He thought for a second he was going to puke up his cherry pie on it.

Barb was right, time to get rid of it. Get something new, something flat in a nice beige. He leaped from his chair and stomped on his rug, flattening any loops still upright. He'd show them. He'd win this thing. He wasn't through yet.

SURVIVING THE SIXTIES

I'M A relative newcomer in Northport. But because this is the kind of town where no one cares who you've been or what you've done in a former life, I fit right in.

Blending with the locals as I do, I've slipped a bit, I know that. I've let my gray-brown tweed hair grow out, now wear it in a braid that unravels throughout my days of cabin-cleaning. Mitch, my current husband, owns and we operate Thayer's Sea Cliff vacation cabins.

I've also quit on make-up, now use only lip balm. Long fly away hairs stick on it while I race around changing the fourteen beds, scouring the ten toilets, washing at least some of the sixty seven windows of the rental units.

I wear the town uniform of sweatshirt and jeans, even though I am capable of some kind of style. I can twist my hair into a french braid, decorate it with fancy combs. And, from my teaching days, I still have collections of earrings, eye shadows, and perfumes. But I don't bother. Mitch says he doesn't care. We've been married seven years and maybe he hasn't even noticed my slippage. It's been that kind of marriage and it suits me. After all, not everyone wants, or can even survive extravagant displays, passionate fireworks. I maintain a cool rationality, despite the barrage of sex in the videos Mitch rents from the racks in the across 101 from the Suprette. (Yes, it has occurred to me that maybe that's why he rents them, and no, I don't care enough to ask.)

I do think, though, that my coolness bordering on apathy, and my preoccupation with a fantasy life that excludes him, has precipitated Mitch's doting affection for the dog. Sunny, his golden retriever, gives Mitch what he doesn't get from me: unquestioning devotion and companionship. That Mitch prefers the dog's company to mine makes no difference to me. None whatever.

Once in a while, though, something happens to wake me up, shake me up.

Take this ho-hum Presidents' holiday. I'm nodding into my half-life while mulling over resistant blanks in the crossword, listening to the weather channel warn of storms in the Cascades and Siskiyous. I don't care about storms. I love storms on the Coast, so wild but relaxing, too, because fewer people come then to mess up my clean cabins. So Mitch startles me when he sticks his head around the corner of the motel office and says, "Hey, Darlene, I just registered a guy from that high school you used to teach at. Think you'd know him?"

My heart races. "I dunno. What's his name?" No, it couldn't be Kurt, it couldn't be, the odds are—"

"Roger Dahl and his wife, Mae. You know 'em?"

My heart takes a tumble. "Oh, I remember Roger," I mutter, composing myself. "He taught industrial arts, welding, or some thing." I undergo an irrational flash of anger: how dare Roger, boring Roger Dahl check into my life when I haven't heard from Kurt all these years! But then my blood pressure gallops: he may have news of Kurt, maybe I can get some word out of him, some nourishing connection. I stand up, tuck in my shirt, smooth my hair. "Yes, I knew him," I say lightly. "So you're putting them in five? I'll run across and say hello when they get settled."

Then I moodily stare out the window to watch Mitch, the dog at his heels, trundle a load of firewood up to five's door. Yes, that's Roger Dahl answering Mitch's knock. He's grayer, and his features are less distinct than when I knew him.

But Lord, aren't we all having our rough edges sanded down? Besides, I didn't really know Roger—there were such divisions between people back then, between "academics" and shop classes, between the young and the old, between men and women (between me and Gary, my first husband). But I'm just going to explode if I don't get to mention Kurt's name again.

Also, and I'd hate like hell for anyone to know this, but not a day goes by that I'm not reminded of Kurt. Mostly it's in quick flashes, like I'll hear a song, or catch a glimpse of a wide sweep of brow or certain jaunty kind of walk, and I'm off, my blood racing. my heart pounding. My dreams, my dreams are full of these wild erotic encounters, in color. But I figure what you dream is out of your control, so I'm not accountable for that.

What I am accountable for, though, are these spun-out fantasies I construct during our slow off-seasons. When the motel's empty, like now, and I slouch in the office and work puzzles or play solitaire or listen to white noise on TV...yeah, then I'm accountable. Guilty, even.

At Riverview High School, Kurt Steiner had been hard not to notice. He was the dark brooding presence in the back of the room at faculty meetings, his aura that of the very dangerous seductive stranger.

Our first exchange, or opening salvo, had been at a meeting during which the principal asked why we all picked the same night to load the kids down with homework. He'd had complaints. I volunteered that at other high schools, each department had assigned days: English, Mondays and Wednesdays; history, Tuesdays and Thursdays, and so on. Teachers took turns, like we were always telling the kids to do.

Kurt erupted. "We've got to teach them responsibility," he shouted. "We've got to teach them problem solving, the ability to prioritize." He swiveled to glare at me. (Later I wondered how he knew I'd brush off compliments like flies, but would rise like a hatchery-bred salmon to the bait of a fight. I know,

I know, what presumption on my part, thinking he'd act up to engage me. One of my worst character flaws.)

I stayed after the meeting to explain the homework system. "If all departments abide by it, it works," I said. "And it's fair."

"Trouble is, life's not fair. The sooner the kids know that, the better," he snapped.

"But they're just kids," I wailed.

Kurt went on arguing, haranguing. Responsibility was his favorite word, he harped on it. At least that's what I told Evelyn, my girlfriend who rented the other half of our duplex, later that night when I recounted the scene. Gary, my husband, didn't want to hear about it. "Bunch of eggheads, none of them put together could earn an honest day's wage," he'd mutter. "Hogs swilling at the public trough." (His standard teacher insult.)

"Wait a minute," I'd say. "None plus none equals none. And eggheads and hogs, that's a mixed metaphor."

"Speak English, woman," he'd say, gathering up his tools to rush off for his nightly four or five hours of work. Days, he worked for the highway department. Nights, he was single-handedly putting together a three-bedroom modular out in the country. I'd started grumbling about it, not about the hours and hours he spent away, but that I'd have to live in it when he finished. I wanted to stay in town, where I could see other people's lights at night. Not Gary. He wanted to pioneer on his own acreage. We were at war over it, our words weapons. Like a spear, I'd thrown at him that it wasn't really a house, it was a kit, a thing that that came on a flatbed and all he had to do was put up trusses and match slots and tabs. Like a Legos game. But he'd brush that off, like everything I said. "Darlene, you put up fences when you talk," he accused, and roared off in the pickup.

But Evelyn listened. Evelyn didn't think I put up fences. She enjoyed hearing what I was up to. She complained that her own job at the telephone company was boring. "So, is he cute, this flirty, irascible guy? I think you've kinda got the hots for him," she said.

"Nah, he's like anybody. Well, yeah, he's sort of, oh, ar resting. But not really," I hedged, thinking of Kurt's wide forehead, his shiny hazel eyes with tiny flicks of yellow in their depths. Then I countered jokingly, "He's Mr. Family Man, Mr. Responsibility. I think there's a kid or two."

"Oh, kids," she sighed. "Kids ruin everything. You and Gary were right not to have any. Who needs kids?" Actually, it had been a tradeoff with me and Gary: if I gave up the family thing and worked, he said I could go back to library school when he paid off the property.

"Yeah, who needs kids," I echoed, thinking how much alike Evelyn and I were. The same age, twenty-seven, both of us were comfortable with and dependent upon the Pill. No scares, no surprises for us. And no children.

But she'd just gone through a messy divorce and was regrouping. Her term, regrouping. She claimed to be up and down about it, mostly down. But I envied her the freedom of her own apartment, the twin of mine next door, but so different.

I daydreamed about having my own place. I'd furnish it with bright cushions and Indian blankets in exotic designs. And baskets, candles, posters from the import store. I'd have racks of out rageous hats and paisley scarves, and big clunky jewelry. I'd have feather earrings and wrap-around skirts like sarongs and sexy sandals for which I'd paint my toenails. It was 1975 and I was caught up in the sixties madness. It had hit us late out there in Bend. We never suffered big city horrors like draft card burnings or "peace" marches or sit-ins in our schools; we were a decade behind with any new ideas—they sifted in like spores from the Valley or down from the Gorge—but when they hit us, or at least when they hit me, I was hammered.

"Gary out working on the modular tonight?" Evelyn asked. "I see his pickup's gone." She kept up with his progress—as a gauge, she said, as to how soon I'd be moving. She was going to miss me.

"Yeah, he's having trouble with the skylights. Still can't get them water-tight, and bad weather's coming on." I twisted down my mouth to show my disdain.

You poor kid. It's awful having to please someone else all the time. You should do your own thing, Darlene, that's what the kids say, and they're right. You only live once. Might as well live how and where you want. Tell me, should I hang a bead curtain between here and the kitchen? They're on sale down at Pier 21.

"Oh, yes, and get some incense, frangipani or jasmine or lemon," I barked, my voice hoarse with pot smoke. Evelyn had introduced me to the deliciously illicit pleasures of toking, "And some votive candles. Straw mats and batik. And a lava lamp.

She laughed. "Whoa, kiddo. You need your own place, I can see that. Oh, don't move out to the boonies! Show him who's boss!" She said that most women on their own were happier than when they had been married. She'd just read that in a Cosmo poll.

"Oh, Evie," I sighed, taking another drag and passing her the joint, you are so lucky, knowing who you are, being your own person. Gary, well, Gary doesn't stop to smell the roses, know what I mean?" I began considering a revolt against the move. It would be fun hanging out with Evelyn.

Where I did move was down to Kurt's doorway to hang out between classes. We argued. I said my favorites, Steinbeck and Twain, were better than his Hawthorne or Melville. I said my learning groups worked better than his worksheets and drills.

"Worksheets went out with buggy whips," I snorted.

"Buggy whips, yeah, that's what some of these kids need, an upper hand that'll smack them around, make them do the right thing," he groused.

"Maybe we should set up stocks out front, for gum-chewing, note-passing, whispering in class."

"Yeah, good idea," he said sourly.

Slowly our arguments took on a predictability, a jovial bantering. I'd draw myself up, square my shoulders in my gauzy Indian print blouse, flatten my stomach under my new denim skirt and pronounce, "Slavishly following the rules is not always an indication of progress. Do you ever try anything new? The kids might like something different."

"What they might like is beside the point. The point is, they do it, whatever. They learn to take responsibility."

He reacted suitably when I pointed out that he wore his responsibilities like a hair shirt. What he really wore was a new green tie that brought out the color of his eyes or maybe I was affecting him. I wanted badly to think it was my doing.

One afternoon we lounged in his doorway watching the football team practice on the field across from us. "Now, there's where the kids really learn responsibility, playing that game," I said, thinking that for once he'd agree.

But no. "Soccer is much better. Many fewer kids get hurt—"

"Many fewer? Many fewer?" I laughed. "What kind of an expression is that?"

"Well, how else would you say it?" We argued back and forth while kids milled around us, smirking, nudging each other. They'd all noticed my spiffy new wardrobe, my new boots, embroidered silk vest, watermelon pink angora sweater that shed a mess on my new black linen suit. They'd also noticed Kurt's new tweed jacket, his crisp pastel shirts. Some of the sharper ones had even spotted his new capped front tooth, and his slightly longer over-the-ears blow-dry haircut. I sure had.

I tried to act annoyed, disgusted. I wanted to glare into his green eyes, show my irritation. But I also wanted to preen and giggle, like the girls in my classes. I began wondering if I was too old to let my hair grow out and wear it parted down the middle like they did. Evelyn said, "Go for it! If it feels good, do it!" I was already trying to see without my glasses, was wondering what Gary would say if I got contacts.

I began waiting for Kurt, lurking around so I could watch him march down the hall, his long body lithe and lean. I noticed a new lift to his walk, a briskness—surely this was my doing, I was changing him, bringing out his best. I was as proud of him as if he were a golden egg I'd laid. I thought about telling Gary how much fun a proper argument was, as opposed to the kind we had, but he was too busy to listen.

However, Evelyn listened, she paid attention. She said she got a real hoot out of my duel with Kurt. She said listening to me was more fun than going to her singles group, or to a movie.

Kurt started staying after school so we could sit in his room and talk. While the janitor swept up around us, Kurt talked about his family, his worry over his son's slow development. The boy was two years old, and hadn't begun to talk.

"Is it so unusual for a two-year-old not to talk?" I asked.

"No, but he didn't walk, either, until he was twenty months. He's been slow all around. It scares us." His frown deepened. "My wife's taking him in for tests next week."

Kurt said he'd been slow, too, as a child. But his wife Saralyn was gifted, a successful artist. She ran a photography studio downtown, was much sought-after. "So, you see," he went on, "I have to be careful. Maybe there's resentment or envy or jealousy. Saralyn and I, we hassle each other a lot."

"Too bad, but I know what you mean. Gary and I fight, too."

"At our house, we're at each other all the time. I hope it isn't affecting Jason."

"When he learns to talk, you can ask him," I cracked, then wished I hadn't. I wanted to sheathe my tongue so he'd keep opening up. I took it as a compliment to me, a demonstration of the effect I had on him.

He did go on confiding his troubles. Another time he complained, "Saralyn and I came out ahead this month, then had the usual fight. I wanted snow tires for the Scout, but she needs this expensive new camera equipment."

"Oh, dear."

"But it's for the shop, it's got income potential."

"Of course. It's an investment," I soothed, but was deeply pleased at any clash between them. "It would be like me buying clothes when Gary needs a table saw." I was buying clothes, with Evelyn's help: at the time I was wearing a new cotton dress, bright Aqua, slightly gypsyish, folded into a million pleats. For coming and going, for effect, I pinned on a straw hat trimmed with a rose, and thought I looked smashing.

Kurt leaned back, lounged his long legs out into the aisle—we sat facing each other in a pair of student desks. "So, how's the new place coming? Gary done with the skylights?"

"Yes, it's cabinets now. He says it'll be ready before school's out."

Be nice out there, your own woods, your own creek. Everybody's dream."

"But not mine." I knew he was sounding me out—I did the same to him.

"I'd like to show you my place. I designed it myself." Then he barked, "Only thing, I've got the wrong woman in it."

This jolted me, the first open attack on his Saralyn. I read into it that he needed someone else, well, someone like me who understood him. Our line-up had undergone an adjustment. Now, Kurt and I were counterpoised against Saralyn and Gary. We were a team, had realigned ourselves in those long drawing-in autumn afternoons while the janitor smiled to himself, gliding around with his pushbroom, raising a cedar aroma from spilled pencil shavings. Against the intermittent roar of the practicing football squad, Kurt and I had begun to speak of our spouses as slightly contemptible impediments to our happiness. Later, when I described this de licious scene to Evelyn, she knew exactly what I meant, this switching of sides.

"You guys sound like a natural pair," she said. "Have you ever met this Saralyn?"

"No, but I will at the Christmas party. I wonder...could you help me with a knock-out outfit? You've got such a eye."

Evelyn talked about the wonderful new stuff down at the Emporium, just my kind of thing. She'd love to help me shop.

I geared up for that party like I was going to war, which I was, in a way. Gary took one look at me—tie-dye silk, fringed paisley shawl, velvet palazzo pants (bellbottoms gone mad with legs a yard wide), and my first (and last) platform shoes—and said, "I didn't know it was a costume party." He hated women in flowing trailing garments—they would use feminine wiles on him, take advantage. He would rather I wore jeans and boots all the time, as Evelyn did, despite her talk of shopping and her "good eye."

But I didn't care. I was wild to see Kurt at the party, and meet his wife.

The party was at the principal's house, and I pushed through those double doors, already searching for Saralyn. The gathering itself was mere backdrop to the drama of getting a look at the powerful wife, the woman who demanded and got vacations spent touring art galleries instead of backpacking in the Cascades, season tickets to the concert instead of cross-country skies, a housekeeper instead of a gardener. I honed in to find her, a smart bomb trained on target...

"So, come on," Evelyn said the next day, "how's this Saralyn stack up? She as sharp as you?"

"She's..." I drew a breath, "totally forgettable. A summer squash body, narrow on top, round on the bottom. Uptight frizzy perm. Sensible shoes. You see her kind everywhere, in Safeway sniffing cantaloupes, in Penney's buying white baggy underwear and cloth handbags, in the library returning Mitchener novels, read, and on time."

"I know what you mean! Next to her, you must have been a knockout." Then she asked, busy pouring more coffee, "Gary have a good time?"

"Who knows? Oh, you mean with that tie?" To my surprise, Evelyn had given Gary a Christmas present, a battery operated Rudolph the Red-Nosed Reindeer necktie. And to my further surprise, he'd loved it, had worn to the party. It had brought out a sense of humor I'd often accused him of lacking. "Yeah, he went around blinking his tie...but, Evelyn, let me tell you this. While I was listening to Saralyn play the piano—Kurt and a bunch of us were singing carols in the living room—I heard Gary out in the kitchen with the shop and PE guys, braying about how to cheat on your taxes. Yeah, I'm not kidding! In front everybody, how he's writing off the modular expenses as repairs on this rental. Then he went on about how he wouldn't mollycoddle welfare spongers, how he had to work his way up and so can they." I rolled my eyes and shrugged.

"You poor kid. Gary can talk pretty rough."

"But, then, Evelyn, the most romantic thing—Kurt followed me into the hall, right outside the downstairs john, he said he wished he had some mistletoe to hang over my head!"

"Aha! Now you're getting somewhere."

Still, where was I getting, I wondered, when school started again. Kurt and sat longer and longer after school in his room, talking, talking. At night, our two cars were the last to leave the lot. The kids joked openly about us, and the other teachers had long been giving Kurt and me knowing smirks, thinking they knew the score.

Yet the real score was zero. All we did was talk.

Yeah, but such talk! I'd like to get in there and cultivate those roses," Kurt whispered in my ear once when wore a floral top. Another time he sidled over and murmured, "I'm showing a movie this period. Come in and we can sit in the dark and make out."

Make out! Such a juvenile term, but weren't we acting like juveniles? Like junior high school brats? But ate it up, could barely wait through our 54-minute periods of class time to get out the door for more flirty talk.

Maybe what we did was innocuous, but my fantasies, oh, they were passionate, wild. played them over and over until they were threadbare. had Kurt follow me into the supply room, lock the door, and rip off my clothes. There in the musty dark smelling of newsprint, chalk, graph paper, there in the aisle between stacks of Moby Dick, Red Badge of Courage and Warriner's English Grammar and Composition, he would ravish me, such a choice word, ravish, an old-fashioned sort of violence, which also removed any onus from me. Or I'd have him follow me home, only not to the duplex but out into the woods where he'd force my car off the road and then chase me through the trees until, panting, weak, trembling, I'd stumble and he'd fall on top of me. (Again the violence, the dom ination, and again, I would be blameless.) Or I'd call in sick and during his prep period he would come over to the duplex, and pound on the door until I let him in, then he'd...but no, because here lay real violence: Gary would arrive unexpectedly and shoot us both.

All that spring while I shadow-danced with Kurt, Gary worked on the modular. Things came to a head when he finished it, in late May. "I'm not moving out there," I told him, a declaration I'd rehearsed earlier with Evelyn.

His mouth dropped open. "You're what?" "I'm not going. You go. Do what you want. I'm not moving."

He argued, he threatened, he pleaded. But no, I wasn't moving with him. Then silently, in a raging pout, he began sorting He argued through his things. He packed bare essentials. His clothes, tools, the camping gear, a card table, the deck furniture. more, he threatened—I'd be sorry, he'd show me then he took his special pets: his grandfather's beer stein collection, an antique musket, his sharp-shooting trophies. He was gone.

Alone, I paced. I played Booker T's "Green Onions" over and over—Gary hated Booker T. For dinner I had tutti frutti ice cream and red wine. I burned a hole in the wagon wheel coffee table with my incense, longed for some of Evelyn's good pot. When I went next door to see if she had any, and to tell her how tense and lonely I was, she laughed it off. "First reaction, kiddo," she said. "You gotta expect some adjustment, after being under Gary's thumb all these years."

Then Gary came back with the pickup, talked so nice, asked me so sweetly to come with him. But no, now it was a matter of principle, what would Evelyn say if I crumpled? So I told him to take what he wanted of the furniture because I was doing the place over with my own stuff. He said forget it, he didn't want the green plaid couch, the La-Z-Boy recliner, fuck it all, fuck all that shit, he shouted. He shouted—I was sure Evelyn was listening next door— he shouted that now I could do "my own thing" if I could figure out what the hell it was. I cried a bit, then went to find Evelyn, but her car was gone. But even when she was there, the next few days, she was distracted, busy, preoccupied.

Even worse, at school Kurt acted aloof, distant. As soon as I told him how it was with me and Gary, he became too involved with test papers or lesson plans to sit with me after class. He had to leave, he said, because the Scout needed repairs, or he and Saralyn were taking Jason to an new psychiatrist.

I got the message, yeah, I got it, all right. Safely tied to Gary, I was okay to flirt with. On my own, I was dangerous, as messy and uncontainable as an oil spill.

Just to make sure, I sashayed into his room one day after school. I needed to talk, I'd talk about rules or rights or responsibilities, or whatever rot—because I really did think it was rot.

He sat there like a sphinx, then pushed back from his desk and gazed into his lap at his hands, at his wedding-ringed finger. "Darlene, I've got responsibilities, to Saralyn and to Jason. Saralyn, well, she...she needs me. And little Jason, he's got problems, and after all, he didn't ask to be born. I've got...I've got all I can handle. I...I need my space."

Well, what had I expected, I scolded myself, driving back to my empty apartment. Nevertheless, I ached with my own stupid ity, my naiveté. I worried my situation around, fooled with it like it was a sore tooth. Had I ever hoped he'd leave Saralyn, for me? Did I even want that...responsibility? Now, of course, I denied it to myself. I couldn't have wanted that. But I missed him. I missed him bad. Not only did I pine for him, but I realized I'd grown to depend on him. Along with Evelyn, who was still acting weird, he'd become my best friend. Even worse, without him, I'd run out of fuel for my fantasy life. I'd even begun to miss Gary.

One day after school, I dolled up in my rhinestone cowboy shirt, western-cut jeans, and boots, daubed on some Arpege perfume—Gary had always liked it—and drove out to the modular with some of the stuff Gary had forgotten. But when I saw Evelyn's green Toyota parked next to the pickup, I flipped a U and spun out, back toward town. I should have known. All the signs had been there, but I'd been too damned stupid to see them.

Sure, I considered storming in, making a scene. I could have done it, Gary could have been shamed, brow-beaten. He'd always been straight-arrow...but I heard them laughing in there, they were laughing, having a good time. I suddenly realized Evelyn knew Gary better than I did, she'd made a study of him. She'd known he'd like that foolish Christmas tie—I never would have guessed that. She'd known he'd hate that ridiculous outfit I'd worn to the party. And all the hippie shit she'd turned me onto, the bangles, beads, candles—she'd known he'd hate all that, too.

A wave of rage for both, for all of them washed over me. I screeched to a stop and dumped Gary's stuff in the road: his country music records, his old army junk, the magazines that still came in the mail, Field & Stream, Shotgun News, his underwear that had been in the wash, and a pole lamp I'd always hated that had lights shaped like witches' hats. I considered driving over the pile, but just left it there. After all, none of this was really his fault. Gary had been the most injured party.

In September I transferred to another school. In November I quit and drifted to Madras, Baker City, Redmond; out of teaching and into temp work. I drifted to the coast, washed up here at Northport, where I thought I'd blend in, do my own thing. (Gary had been right: I never did figure out what it was, exactly.) Instead I met and married Mitch. Been washing windows and cleaning toilets ever since.

I watch number five cabin's door all afternoon, but the only sign of life is wisps of smoke curling from its chimney. The sky has changed from cobalt blue to dull pewter. Promise of a storm hangs heavily in the air, which now snaps with cold.

I have lit our own fire before the Dahls appear in the macadam courtyard. I watch them march cold-quick around wind-slanted shore pines, and disappear toward the ocean. Mitch comes to stand by me at the window. "Let's check on the sunset," he says. There could be a sliver of light out the bottom. And you could say hello to your friends."

After we bundle up, he whistles for the dog and we crunch over iron-cold rocks to gaze at the surf from the lip of the cliff. It is ebb tide, and the sea scratches lazily on pebbles it has hand-sorted. No one else is here, and I'm horribly upset, disappointed. But what will I say to these people, these strangers? Do I want to resurrect old painful times, in public? Don't memories, like milk, have expiration dates beyond which they curdle and sour? I am so tense I develop a dull ice cream headache.

It gets worse when I spot Roger and Mae picking their way up the trail from the beach. I mentally pull them forward, but turn shy at their approach.

"Beautiful place you have here," chirps Mae Dahl, a nondescript middle-aged woman in a puffy down coat.

Roger, yes, now I place Roger Dahl. He'd taught mechanical drawing (surely that's an oxymoron), not welding. He's a gray man trying to wear his scanty hair in a flat top. Again I feel a rush of anger for him: he knows Kurt, he knows things I badly want to hear, and stubbornly, although unconsciously, he will withhold them from me. But he says pleasantly, "It gets colder east of the Cascades, but it feels like twenty below here. Must be the humidity."

Mitch makes small talk about the weather, tells of our white Christmas a few years back. Then he says, disconcertingly, "Darlene used to teach at your school, at Riverview."

So, I smile and ask about a few of the teachers—as cover—then bring up Kurt. "How's the English staff holding up?" I say, then add cunningly, "Kurt Steiner, he still there?"

Roger looks blank for a second. "Well, I don't know, I guess so. Yeah, he's there somewhere. Comes and goes, does his job. Getting gray like all of us. Oh, Mae, isn't he the one having trouble with his kid? Wasn't there some run-in with the law a while back?"

Mae nods slowly. "Yes, I believe so. But the boy's okay now. You know how these kids are, they go through bad stages. I guess everybody does. Kurt and Sarajane—"

"Saralyn," I correct.

"Yes, Saralyn. Well, they've had a rough time, separated for a bit, but they're back together now. The last thing kids need is for the parents to split up."

Roger adds, "I didn't believe for a second that rumor that went around about Kurt...accidents do happen...people hurt themselves cleaning guns all the time"

Mae interrupts sternly, "Then let's not even repeat it, dear."

They continue with small talk, how to raise children, some nonsense, but I'm fixated on their remarks, hear them echo in my head. I visualize Kurt arguing with a twenty-something, the tiresome Jason. For some reason, I've got them in the garage, a fight over tools, over cross-country skies, over backpacking equipment. Then I see Kurt and Saralyn bickering endlessly, in the background a wall groaning under the burden of her arty photo graphs. I see Kurt trudging to class day after day, graying into anonymity, the lines from his bifocals throwing a shadow on his cheek. How I wish, although I know he has not, how I wish he has pined for me as I have him, how I desperately hope that he has suffered. These are not kind thoughts. I'm sure they show too clearly my flawed character, but I've paid my dues.

I regret that I hadn't sharpened up for the Dahls, put a rinse on my hair, worn makeup and my bulky knit sweater and my spandex stirrup pants. They could carry news of me back to Kurt, and I'd like them to report that I am holding my own.

But I have gotten some valuable tidbits from them. I am pleased that Kurt has had some trouble, pleased that he's stuck with his Saralyn. I'd be horribly upset if, after opening to me like a Japanese water flower, he'd broken loose with someone else. I want him always with Saralyn, the two of them yoked, uncomfortably out of step. I know that this is further evidence of my lack of character, but at least I'm honest about it.

The next morning, after Roger and Mae leave, I drag my vacuum around the dog, who doesn't offer to come with me, to number five. The promised storm has hit and wind and sheets of rain lash us. I'm in no hurry, there's no one checking in for the rest of this week. Then too, the Dahls have been neat and there's not much cleaning to do. So when I find, in the kindling box, an issue of my old hometown newspaper, I restoke the fire and settle in for a read. The front page shows that Bend is having the same old problems: scandals at city hall, fights for timber, water, grazing rights, the push for and against development. I read with a com fortable sense of familiarity.

But the society page jolts me. There, smiling up from a reception, fat and glossy, are Gary and Evelyn. I knew Gary had quit the highway department. He had made a bundle on the property. He'd turned developer, had cut down the trees, dammed the stream to make a lake for paddle boats, and had built a subdivision of 3,000 square foot "bungalows" for rich California retirees. His jowly face glows with a Kiwanis/Elks Club sheen.

However, Evelyn is the reason for the picture. She has just been elected to the school board, and has given a speech calling for more prayer in the schools, less drug education. I guess having children changes one's perspective.

When I finish reading, I roll a newspaper log and set it in the flames, immolating these familiar strangers. I plug in the vacuum and begin my cleaning, not even having to think—I've been over this room so many times.

Again I mull over what the Dahls said about Kurt—such a wealth of tidbits to play with, to work over. In a twinkling, I'm at it, I'm building new fantasies, dreaming, scheming away with the new factoids they've provided, which is the bone value those people, any people, have for me.

Let's see, I could be walking on the beach and from a distance I spot that lanky figure approaching me...no, too far away, too public. Better...I'm alone, in here cleaning cabins, a shadow darkens the room, a hand touches my shoulder, I turn and fall into those devilish green eyes with their golden highlights...I'm spinning into their depths, out of control...

NEWLYWEDS

INDIAN SUMMER on the coast, respite between summer wind and winter rain. Lucille was enjoying the morning in her yard, separating narcissus bulbs. Paper Whites, a buck apiece at Payless, so she also enjoyed the feeling of having got hold of a bargain. She thought smugly that she was one of those people who usually did; yeah, she got her money's worth.

Which was more than she could say for Robert. Then she reminded herself sharply that Robert was an artist while she was a mere technician whose job was to smooth her new husband's life into something pleasant. But the thought of him sleeping in there triggered a surprising rush of irritation on another account: he was keeping her from pruning the hydrangeas that grew under their bedroom window. She didn't want to disturb him, but how could a grown man sleep in like that? It smacked of self-indulgence, of a sapping juvenile selfishness. She stopped short of spineless, but her father wouldn't have. She imagined him jeering, "Layabout sluggard. Sleep your life away. Shall we wake you up to die?"

But Robert wasn't like her father, thank god, which was why she'd married him. Not that she'd had that many offers. At her age, with her history, she'd been lucky to get Robert. So let him sleep away the mornings, at least until he got a job. Not easy on the coast. Few openings for CPAS, Robert's profession, because half the business done was by way of barter, eliminating paper trails; and tax season was several months off.

Besides, she was enjoying herself. She stripped off her garden gloves and caressed a handful of rich dark earth, soil that had been sandy and sterile when she and Ed, her first husband, had bought the house. Mulching and composting—she knew what to do in the garden. Her cat Scout did her part, too, bivouacking here on a regular basis. Maybe that was why the bulbs had done so well, these elongated ovals, hard, pointed with purpose, mysterious as crystals. Lucille pushed them firmly into new settings, working steadily to the end of the bed. Then with a final smoothing pat, she paused and inhaled the loamy fragrance. Earth perfume. Her grandmother's cellar had smelled like this, rich with dark hidden treasures, underscored with a hint of danger for the uninitiated...

Just then she heard the toilet flush, followed a few minutes later by the whir of the coffee grinder. Robert was up. She stood, unkinked her back, and went to tend to him with an uneasy excitement, as if she had a beautiful but temperamental animal in a cage, a glossy Florida panther, or an iridescent green and gold Amazonian parrot with clipped wings. She loved this feeling of possessing an exotic treasure, but it was also wearing her out.

She often found herself reviewing a list of possible catastrophes, testing which would most likely strike and ruin her new happiness. Robert would get tired of her and go back to his mother's in Eugene. He'd begin to sulk, as Ed had done. He'd withdraw, disappear, like Curtis, her last live-in. Or she'd get fat, or develop cancer. The house would fall down or burn up. The earth would buckle, open and swallow her.

She had to admit, though, that in some ways, Ed and Curtis had been easier than Robert. They, and most of the men she'd known, had been locked into their male identities in such a blind way that they'd been restful to be with. But Robert was gentle, too gentle, too in-tune with the new sensitivity. She couldn't relax. And there was something about him, an ineffectiveness, something bordering on the prissy...but no! She erased the frown she felt gather around her eyes after a good look at the shaggy hydrangeas by the back door, and replaced it with what she hoped was an accepting smile.

Robert was shuffling around the kitchen in his blue and white terry robe, barefooted, hair tousled. He looked vulnerable, and tame the way she liked him. Ah, yes, but sometimes she yearned for a flinty, virile, passionate barbarian, capable of uncom promising fits of love. What did she want! She didn't know. But how could she wish to change anything about him? He was perfect as he was.

Robert poked his head into the service porch where she was scrubbing her earthy hands. The house was so quiet," he said (sheepishly, she thought). "I didn't know how late it was."

Lucille came into the kitchen, laid her cheek against his back and hugged him as he fussed with the toaster. "I didn't want to wake you, so I worked out front. You need anything? Canadian bacon, cream cheese, or that marmalade in the stone jar you like? There's a good pink grapefruit, sweet and juicy, I saved for you."

He yawned, began relating some complicated dream which interested her only until she realized she wasn't in it. If she had been telling it, she would have added him in, even if it were a lie. Yes, sadly, this demonstrated the difference in their attachment. Then, in spite of herself, she began surveying kitchen damage. Tuffs of black cat hair, tongue tracks in the butter: Simon, Robert's cat, had been allowed on the counter again. And Robert had used one of her good silver forks to mash garlic and brewer's yeast into Simon's cat food. There was going to be trouble over this cat...but Lord! here she was, letting a cat call the shots in her new marriage. The important thing was that Robert was here in her kitchen, her Robert whom she adored.

"It's a beautiful day," she said when he finished the tiresome dream story. "We could pack up a picnic, or walk on the beach. Or we could stick around here, work in the yard."

He stretched. "I've got to wax the T Bird. This sea air, sure fire rust. Oh, don't forget my mother and Angela are stopping for supper on their way to my sister's in Newberry."

Lucille stretched her lips into a smile. "I know, dear. Your mother and Angela, yes." Angela was his twelve-year-old daughter who lived with her mother, one of Robert's exes, in Eugene.

Robert gazed off. "Let's see, a broiled fish, I think. Fresh fruit, a bit of brie for dessert."

Robert was a splendid cook, an artist. ragouts with sweetbreads and mushrooms on wild rice. Tender He created exotic crisp stir-fries with bright vegetables. Casseroles with three kinds of meat...oh, he was extravagant! But Lucille's concern about the food bills, not to mention the twelve pounds she'd put on in four months, went out the window whenever she heard him singing in the kitchen.

He went on rather dreamily, "A nice halibut, green salad, broccoli." Lucille knew he was balancing flavors, contrasting tex tures, designing plates of food. Slivers of red pepper, shine of black olives, sprigs of parsley...he had an eye. Except why could he not see, with this fine eye, how her silver differed from his stainless!

"Fresh stuff's expensive, Luce, especially halibut, but I want us to eat right."

Lucille melted into a warm dark puddle of love. He wanted to take care of her. She longed to burrow into him, but gently so as not to alarm, so as not to reveal her raw nerves, her need, her ragged insecurity.

"Oh, hon," she signed.

Misreading her, he added quickly, "I know you're carrying the load for both of us, and you're not making much at the Chamber of Commerce, but I'll get on my feet soon, you'll see." He flooded her with a misty warm unfocussed gaze, and she realized he wasn't wearing his contacts. Without them, his vision was as cloudy as if he'd smeared Vaseline over his eyeballs. But Lucille gazed back at him, willing him clarity.

"I know, hon," she murmured. She reached for his hand. "Let's wax the car together. I want to do whatever you want to do." She felt idiotically close to tears.

However, after he whistled out with polishing cloths and expensive preserving preparations, she fussed in the kitchen, gathering up coffee grounds from the sink. If only he'd lift them out in the paper filter! Then she plunged greasy dishes, her good Blue Willow china she used only for company, into hot soapy water. She heard him back the T Bird around and exchange greetings with the neighbors. He was so friendly, he already knew more of them than she did. She smiled and swished water over a frying pan, but panicked in a gap of silence from outside. Her hands dripping, she rushed to the window, but, oh, he was still there, bent in rapt attention to inspect a blemish on the car's angular haunch. He loved that car. She liked it, too, but not the way he did.

Later, though, out in the yard, she became jealous of it. The caressing way he applied wax, the way he lavished attention. But then she noticed again the shaggy hydrangeas, full of brittle heads as big as basketballs. Also, the skeletal remains of fuchsias still swung from hooks in the sun porch. They needed cutting back and packing in straw for hibernation under the house. And in that high corner of the yard...Lucille paused in mid-wipe, visualizing an area of rocks interplanted with Irish moss...

"Lucille, you're leaving streak marks," said Robert at her elbow. "Step back and get some perspective, can't you see them? It's important to work this stuff into the paint, it's a space-age mix of polymers and carnauba wax, has to be applied right."

She felt a flicker of resentment which then flared when she noticed his cat Simon lying in the primroses, smashing them flat. The cat defiantly stared back, and she suppressed an urge to turn the hose on him. The poor cat. She was ashamed. She owed this cat, she ought to love it.

Because, in a way, cats had brought her and Robert together in the first place.

It had been an agonizingly slow shift that day at the Chamber booth, and Lucille was dozing on her hand, gazing out at the rain. Then into the parking lot slid a classic 1957 Thunderbird, and she sat up straight. Those distinctive lines, cross between a race car and a phone booth; the color, opalescent blue; the port-hole windows; baby moon hubcaps.

She watched a man climb out of it. Tall and thin, with just the right amount of gray in his curly brown hair, he headed toward her door. She grabbed a stack of Arts & Crafts Faire fliers to fold and stamp, just as she would have reached for a beach cover-up had she been wearing a bathing suit.

"Hello," she chirped brightly, her voice a careful mix of business and cheer. "What can I do for you?" she asked, then blushed. Good-looking men put her off.

But he was relaxed, easy, folded himself into the chair opposite her desk. "You look like a local," he said. "Tell me, what's to do around here."

"You mean where does the bus stop for Disneyland?" Her standard quip. Then she added, "What does a local look like?"

He laughed, revealing perfect teeth. She thought orthodontia, tennis and skiing lessons, white collar jobs, wives. (Yes, she found later, he'd had them all.) "No, no bus to Disneyland. I want the essence of Northport. And a local, well, a local looks wholesome, sensible, natural." Then he turned to scan a relief map by the door, labeled with a green arrow pointing at Northport that read YOU ARE HERE. "What I want is wholesome, natural, too. Tell me," he leaned forward, "Where do you spend time when you're not working?"

"At home doing yard work," she snapped. Then to soften it, There are tide pools a mile or so south. Go to Huckleberry Wayside and follow the path—"

"No, not that. No signs saying keep off the grass, watch for sneaker waves. I want the real unfiltered thing."

After a second or so, Lucille said, "Okay, Lava Rock." She flipped over an orange flier and began drawing a map. "Here's the path, starts at Seaview Terrace, it's called 1908 Trail for the year it first appeared on county maps. It zigzags along the headland and goes down to the beach here. Then about here, Salal creek becomes a waterfall," she placed an *X*, "then pools below in a misty little bowl fringed with ferns and orchids."

"Lovely."

Lovely? Lovely! The word struck her like a blow. would have said "awesome," or "bitchin';" Ed "cool," or "super," but Ed had been awhile back, and no great shakes with words anyhow. Curtis Lovely would have rankled them both, but this man across from her looked sincere, so she went on with Lava Rock's real attraction.

"The tide pools are good here, not all picked over. But the real thing is there's a sea grotto with an octopus. We call it 'Otto's Grotto' for this fellow. A big one, must weight fifty pounds. He likes crackers."

"Wonderful." He folded the orange map into his pocket. "I'm Robert deNiro." He held out a hand. It seemed smallish in her grip, and she noticed fine curly hairs creeping from under his cuff. Curtis had had stiff black hairs on the backs of his fingers, like fur patches.

"Sure you are, Robert. And I'm Jane Seymour."

He chuckled, and after a bit of leave-taking, ambled out to his T Bird. Just as well. She was on the verge of saying something stupid like "Have a nice day," or "I like your car." She already regretted telling him about Otto. Maybe he'd do something mean like feed it a cigarette. Curtis had done that once. Quite a fight they'd had over it, too.

No one else came in so Lucille had plenty of time to review every word she'd said. Had she simpered? Been rude? She worked herself into a bit of depression, then kicked herself for being vulnerable. That crack about looking like a "local"...she checked herself over in the bathroom mirror, applied new coats of lipstick, blush, mascara. She went at her hair, plastered it down, fluffed it up. She narrowed her eyes, but under them, dark shadowy areas remained, the skin folded into tiny diamonds. Well, well. She'd have to go on being who she was.

Back at her desk she ran through a list of her weaknesses, her false starts, her quirks, misadventures. No wonder Curtis had left, packed up and pulled out for Portland. Just like this Robert, well, not to Portland, to Eugene, according to the guest register. But somewhere. Away from here. Away from her.

Love is a sickness; marriage the cure, Curtis used to say, conveniently forgetting that he'd picked it up from her. She'd picked it up from Ed, who'd read it in graffiti down at the Drift-In. What the hell. Anyone who's been married knows it's true.

Her shift wound down. She locked and left. Typical February on the coast, cold and wet. Fluorescent lights from the Suprette wept into puddles in the parking lot. Time of afternoon when odd jobbers appeared for beer, bait, and ice. threading through rows of beat-up pickups equipped with gun racks and dogs, the kind piloted by Roy Orbison look-alikes; through ranks of Toyotas and Datsuns painted cartoon colors; between tiers of twenty-year-old, four-door former luxury cars stuffed with kids, cans, and Kleenex. Here were the real locals, Dan'l Boones caught in a time warp.

"Scuse me, ma'am," mumbled a guy trying to get by. He wore a baseball cap backward over a fuzzy ponytail, and toted a suit-case of Bud. "Good boy, Jinx," he cooed to his black Lab dancing welcome, toenails clicking, in his pickup's bed. "Good boy, Jinx."

Well, so he probably shared a sleeping bag with his dog, big deal. BFD, big fuckin' deal, Curtis would snap. These guys, the real locals, a nice bunch, Lucille thought. Nicer than Ed and Curtis put together, both of whom had been handy with criticism, belittling remarks, accusations. Good riddance. Feeling lighter, Lucille jauntily swung her string bag.

But not for long.

There by the road, blown against a hedge, a bit of orange. Her carefully drawn map...but no. She sighed in relief. Just some one's mimeographed garage sale notice. Why should she care, anyway? Whether he went down to see Otto or back to Eugene, mox nix to her. But why had she told him about Lava Rock? He might cart off buckets of agates or tear up sea palms the way tourists did. She wouldn't let a strange animal into her house to claw the furniture or make a mess on the rug. Why then let him into her treasured places?

No, she wouldn't let him in here, she thought coming into the peace and order of her own house. She perked up, she always did, surveying freshly vacuumed oriental carpets and sofa cushions plumped—no longer squashed under a ghost impression of Curtis's body—magazines fanned out just so and misted ferns full of curled new growth like party ticklers, and leggy Christmas poinsettias still in bloom. This was how she liked her home, everything hung up, put away, cared for.

Scout, her calico, appeared to rub her ankles and lead her into the kitchen. Lucille admired the order there, as well. Dishes done, counters uncluttered, dusted mini-blinds cocked to let in slanting slices of view, mainly of camellias in scarlet bloom. The scent of lentil soup filled the air. The quiet. Muted tick of the clock. Faint wash of surf a half block away. Soothing murmur of rain. Heart of the storm, here. Why would she let anyone into this peace?

She fed the cat, then made ready for a fire. Newspaper bow knots under a teepee of kindling, a few paper logs rolled from Curtis's *Shotgun News*. Curtis had pored over its cheap newsprint, lusting for a Colt Gold Cup or a Walther squeeze cocker or an S&W model 629 like Dirty Harry's. She'd given Curtis the subscription for his birthday; then when he left, it kept coming and she burned it up with a ferocious joy.

Soon the rain turned to mist. Lucille grabbed the log tote and went out for real wood. One side of the garage was lined with firewood that was cut, split and stacked so tightly it had almost reformed into the original logs. Curtis had been good with wood.

Ready to lug a load back in, she suddenly saw the blue T Bird glide up the street from the west. It idled to a stop and Robert leaned out to yell, "Why, it's Jane, isn't it?"

She straightened and frowned. She was supposed to joke back, "You, Tarzan!" But then she remembered her Jane Seymour joke and relaxed into a lopsided smile. "Mr. deNiro, did you enjoy the trail in this rain? My name's really Lucille, Lucille Flint."

The trail was lovely, Lucille. I saw cormorants, ospreys, even a wimbrey." He went on about agates, shells, green and purple urchins. And Otto who had swirled slowly in his pool, as if it had been set on cold-water, gentle-action cycle.

While he talked, Lucille noticed his nice eyes, so blue. And dimples, yes, dimples. In consternation, she dropped her gaze and startled herself with her own reflection in the baby moon hubcap. She looked like an squash in her yellow outfit, she wondered why he wasn't laughing, or if he was.

"...coming back with crackers," he was saying. "The next minus tide."

But Lucille began inching toward the house making excuses. She was busy, had a fire to attend to. She had a cat. Anything to escape the horrible misshapen vegetable she'd become.

"Oh, you have a cat. Me, too. I like cats." He smiled again, then the Thunderbird glided away. Lucille gazed at its back, hoping for something off-putting, a sticker reading EAT SPOTTED OWL, or SPECIAL PEOPLE: SPECIAL RIGHTS, but saw only the perfect chrome donut housing the spare. He wouldn't ruin his baby with stickers, she thought staggering in with the wood. He was one of those guys fixated on his car, an extension of his penis or something. She'd read about that in a MS article.

But those nice blue eyes! Those golden curly hairs on his wrist! Just when she'd gotten her life so tidily sterile, was so insulated and safe. She stamped on the entry mat, threw open the door, and dumped the wood onto the hearth. Scout flattened orange ears and rounded her back in surprised disapproval. Lucille cooed apologies. "Good Kitty, good Kitty, my last good friend," she soothed.

Everyone has to have something to hold onto, to believe in. Curtis used to say, "I believe I'll have another beer," and Lucille would laugh and scurry off to refill his styrofoam beer sleeve. For herself, she'd just believe in her cat. It was her family, all she had left.

A week or so later, Lucille was puttering in the yard when the T Bird slowed to a stop by the rhododendrons. Her heart raced. Robert climbed out holding up a box of crackers for Otto.

"Hope he likes salted tops," he said. The lady at the Chamber booth told me you were off today, but wouldn't say anything else. I think she suspected I was up to no good."

Lucille smiled, imagining Eunice's reaction to a man like this asking for her, Lucille. To cover her agitation she then babbled garden talk, and took him on a tour of the yard. She fantasized tak ing him around town, showing him off in the Suprette, in Melody's Gift Boutique. Maybe they'd run into Curtis contritely returning to her, thinking she'd waited for him, would be available, receptive, unoccupied. She'd show him. Possessively she'd hold Robert's elbow while calling out so sweetly, "Hello, stranger. This is Robert, my new friend..."

She abandoned her gardening to go with him to feed Otto, then explored tide pools that she'd looked into a million times before. They progressed to dinner at the Quarter Deck, most chichi place in town. It specialized in California cuisine, and was decor ated with redwood beams, plants, and old copper utensils. Sipping a G&T in a cozy booth, Lucille smiled thinking of Curtis coming in, seeing her here. He'd scorned the Quarter Deck, said it was pretentious, but that was because he'd never been able to afford the prices on its hand-calligraphed menu. Poor Curtis. He hadn't done well on the coast, had never found work in his field of technical illustrator. He'd eked out a pittance in maintenance at the Pueblo, a big motel north of town.

"Something amusing?" asked Robert.

Lucille said quickly, "I was thinking I'd take Scout home a piece of this fish, but I'm going to eat it all myself."

He talked of his cat, Simon, said on his next trip over he'd bring catnip for Scout. Lucille had been about to offer him some from her garden; instead, she effused her gratitude with wide eyes.

He did come back with catnip, and 4-inch starts from a sale at K-Mart, tomatoes, cucumbers, bell peppers. Lucille hadn't the heart to tell him how poorly these did in the coast cold, but took them with thanks. She listened with joy when he said he was going to spend time in the area, to see if he could escape his allergies. He talked about cooking and eating healthfully, about air pollution, about cats being better than dogs. He said little about his mother or Angela. Sometimes Lucille forgot that he had a family.

Rather quicker than he should, he was staying overnight. Lucille knew that early risers were spotting his T Bird in the drive, frosted with morning dew. It was the equivalent of tacking a notice on the Suprette bulletin board. The gossip, the winks, nudges. There she goes again, another one..." But this didn't happen, as far as she knew. The locals, the real locals, liked him, were friendlier than they'd been to Curtis, or even to herself. But Curtis had been hard to like, and she was stand-offish.

He helped around the house. He explained, again, how to program her VCR. It had been Ed's—he had liked to tape boxing matches, then played them over and over. Robert talked about *feng shui*, then rearranged her furniture into a grouping for company despite her telling him she didn't know four people to have in.

"We will soon," he said and she swooned at the we, added it to growing list of hints that they had a shared future. He sharp ened knives; he moved in some of his favorite cooking utensils; hung spice rack, a matte-finish oak ladder affair. He encouraged her to dump antique spices.

"What's an antique spice?" she asked.

"Anything that predates the Crusades," he said prying the oval off the top of fuzzy can of fennel. She laughed, partly in relief because sometimes he seemed too earnest, almost humorless.

(But she didn't laugh later remembering his need to upgrade her kitchen, to reorganize her, when he created an oil slick in front of the stove frying chili rellenos, or splattered the window over the sink with whipping cream, or dribbled cantaloupe seeds down the side of the counter. Then she thought, what the hell! But that was later, months later.)

In the evenings they made love on the oriental carpet by the fire, Lucille feeling bare, brave, sensuously up-to-date and loose,

Scout watching quizzically at a safe distance from the thrashing legs. Mornings, padding around in slipper socks—which he'd moved in with other personal necessities such as his robe, allergy medicines, contact lens solution—he cooked breakfast: broiled tomatoes and eggs on rounds of corned beef. He served up loving platefuls on tray to her in bed.

One rainy day they watched an entire Charlie Chaplin Film Festival on TV: *The Kid*, *The Gold Rush*, *City Lights*, *Modern Times*, *The Great Dictator*, *Monsieur Verdoux*, and *Limelight*. Never got dressed, lolled around on pillows and blankets, a wonderful day. Lucille remembered it as the height of indolent love.

They married in June. The night before, Lucille suffered terrifying dreams. Ships sinking. Houses burning. Bones breaking. Radioactivity erupting. Worst of all, him calling, his voice hoarse with regret, "Lucille, I've been thinking, this isn't going to work..." In a terrorized sweat she got up to unplug the phone. Then plugged it back in. If he changed his mind, she had to know, the sooner the better. But he didn't and they wed, on schedule.

Then began the clean-up. Lucille put on an old sweatshirt and a pair of Ed's army pants to wash windows, scour the kitchen, wax floors, haul ashes, vacuum sand and pine needles out of the carpet. Scout, back raised, tail fluffed, hissing and spitting, watched the noisy activity and Robert's enormous tuxedo cat who was installed with the last of Robert's things. "She'll just have to adjust," Lucille told Robert. Everyone had to adjust. Life is a process of adjust ment: Lucille had also said that to Curtis. He'd resented it, said she was preachy.

The Thunderbird gleamed in the October sun, blue paint shining deep and rich. Lucille drew a sigh and gathered up polish cloths while Robert lovingly buffed the chrome. He used a special chamois for this, not to be mixed in with cloths employed in the washing operation. Suddenly Simon leaped from the squashed primroses to step delicately along the hood, leaving muddy prints.

"Oh, get off!" Lucille cried, flapping a cloth. The cat held his ground, staring malevolently.

"Hey, easy, easy," said Robert. "He thinks the hood's warm, see, he'll get up there and stretch out. He's at least fourteen years old, my good buddy." He'd told her several times how he'd met Simon. It was his last year of college. Everyone except Robert had gone home for Christmas, he was alone in the dorm. Then the cat strolled in. Out of gratitude Robert had fixed it a frozen turkey dinner, had loved it ever since. Lucille was bored with the story, had cat stories of her own to tell.

"But look what he's doing," she exclaimed. "You wouldn't like it if Scout got up there."

"In human terms, Simon's ninety-nine years old. Scout is just a kid. Tell you what, I'll give you a hand with those hydrangeas. I know you want to prune them back."

But when he appeared with the shears, she wasn't happy. He didn't prune things right, he didn't stop to check for new growth, but blindly lopped away, sacrificing tender pale green shoots into the mounting brittle pile of refuse.

Soon though he made his excuses. "I'd help you finish, hon, but I gotta run up to the Suprette. And, uh, Luce, I'm short, mind if I dip into your purse?"

"Of course not. Take what you need." Mind! Rather than mind, she experienced a rush of power at supporting him, a heady sense of control. Their money situation, although stressful, suited her exactly, bringing him down, her up. At the same time, she felt anxious...he spent money like a teenager in the mall...what the hell ailed him! But, no, can't think that, she stifled it. He was wonderful, she loved him so much, she was so lucky to have him.

Once she'd asked him, "Why me? Why'd you pick me?"

"I told you up at the Chamber office, I was looking for someone sensible, someone who'd be fair." His face closed like a fist. "I've had it with manipulators. Like Alice. Or Maureen." Maureen had been his first wife, the mother of Angela.

"How does Maureen manipulate?" Lucille ached with jealousy over his past, wanted badly to hear rotten things about his other women.

"Maureen uses Angela to get to me, you've seen Angela, poor kid. All that weight, her bad skin."

"Yes, but she's only twelve. Pre-adolescent girls—"

"It's not that simple. Maureen feeds the kid junk, fast food, chocolate-covered marshmallow cereals, frozen crap."

Lucille had met Angela only once, at the wedding. She'd been a blimp of a girl, packed wretchedly into a puffy pink dress accentuating the weight. Her limp tan hair hung like a ragged curtain. The only color in her sallow skin had come from a network of pimples between her eyebrows. Deep in the girl's sullen eyes, Lucille had caught a glint of desperation. The kid needed help; that it was probably going to have to come from Robert was something Lucille didn't like to think about.

"Listen, you get Angela over here in this sea air," Lucille said, alarming herself, "and we'll feed her right."

Robert threw an arm across her shoulders. There, you see? That's why I picked you, Luce. You're a good person."

Lucille savored the compliment, but later thought it a bit flat. What did "good" mean? Was he so limited in vocabulary, his perception so shallow, that all he could come up with was "good"?

In the beginning, she'd thought the merest crumbs from his table would nourish her, but now she wanted more. She wanted meat, potatoes, vegetable medley, arugula salad, cranberry sorbet. And she worried that he wasn't up to it, he couldn't provide.

Robert's mother and Angela arrived that afternoon. Lucille put Angela to setting the table, and the girl sparked a bit with the chore. At the wedding she'd been like a stone—but who wouldn't turn to stone watching one's father marry a stranger? Now, though, she talked.

"My mom's got blue dishes, too," she said. "But hers got circles, not pictures. Don gave them to her, he's her new boy friend.

I like Don better than that other guy. He was a dweeb." Angela smiled, and Lucille caught a glimpse of Robert in the girl.

That's nice." Lucille was torn between her part in the dinner damage control and eavesdropping on Robert and his mother in the living room. The woman presented a purpleness. She favored grapish-toned dresses, and her frizzy hair resembled a cloud of grayish pink cotton candy. Robert was her only son, born late in her life. He had three much older sisters who, like the mother, doted on him. They didn't need toys if they had baby Robert to play with," Mrs. deNiro said once. Right now Lucille overheard the plummy voice, "Did I tell you I ran into Linda in Nordstrom's..." Linda? Who was Linda? Lucille considered, fleetingly, pumping Angela for information.

"What else is there besides this gooshy fish?" Angela asked at her elbow. "I hate fish."

"...looking tired, Robert. Are you taking care of yourself? Getting enough rest, dear? An old house like this, well, don't burden yourself with chores. It is her house."

Robert laughed bitterly. "I'm not working, Ma. Rest is all I do. Luce's carrying the whole load."

"Yes, but it was her idea you come here where there are no jobs in your field, dear."

Lucille turned to Angela and said brightly, "Besides fish, there's rice pilaf, broccoli, and salad. Your dad made the dressing. Special, for you."

Angela wrinkled her nose. "Yuk. He puts stinky white stuff in it. Smells like dirty socks."

"If you'd rather, you can have Thousand Island."

"...not her idea at all, Ma. You knew I wanted to get out of Eugene. And I'll find something."

"...with your talents, Robert, you're wasting your time."

Angela said, "My mom, she's got hair longer than yours, it's down to here. She says she's going to give me a perm, not a perm, a body wave. Is that what you got?" She blew an enormous pink bubble with her gum; then when it popped, she gathered shreds of it from her face. She wore a lime green sweatshirt of nubby stretch material run to balls. The top was embossed with a Disney *Little Mermaid* design. All wrong, Lucille thought. This girl was an autumn, not a spring or summer. Dark gold, forest green, russet brown. Those were her colors. Lucille itched to get at her, make changes.

"...but I told her you'd married again, a woman in business on the coast. It's almost true, isn't it? You could have married a business woman, Robert. Isabelle Stevens was quite gone on you a while back. You could have married her."

Lucille turned to Angela. "No, my hair's naturally curly," but Angela was under the table grabbing at Simon. Lucille's own cat Scout always disappeared when there was company, and Lucille admitted she'd like to do the same thing. 'Here, let's let the cat out, Angela. You want to see my flowers in the backyard?"

"Yeah, I guess. We don't got a garden, but our condo's got a balcony and I fly my windsock there. You guys don't got a neat windsock like mine."

"....marrying an older woman like you've done, Robert..."

"Ma, Luce's only a few years older than me..."

Older than I, Lucille wanted to snap, banging out behind Angela and the cat into the yard. Poor Robert! None of this was really his fault. "See, Angela, these are dahlias, here're the last of the poppies, the geraniums—"

"Cool. What're these green things?" "Bells of Ireland. Would you like to cut some?"

I suppose. I'll take 'em to my mom." After a second of silence, the girl went on, "Lucille, can I ask you something?"

"Yeah, shoot."

"What are you to me, exactly? I mean, how're we related? You're not my mom, well, course not. Not my grandma," an em barrassed giggle, "but...are we anything to each other? See what I mean?"

"Sure, I see. Well, I'd be your..." her stomach gave a sour lurch, your step-mother. I'm your step-mother." She hated the sound of it. "Listen, let's just be friends, okay? Forget that other stuff."

"Cool."

Cool: Angela's verbal hiccough. Nevertheless, Lucille rattled on about her garden, all the while thinking, the only flower out here is me, a bloomin' idiot.

"Look, Lucille, what's that?" Angela pointed, then walked toward a grassy stretch studded with conifers bordering the yard.

Lucille followed her. "It's mushroom season, Angela. See the red one with the warty top? *Fly amanita*, poisonous. Those white specks are strychnine, so don't mess with it. Wash your hands if you touch it. But these purple ones are woodland russula, edible. You can tell with a spore print. We'll do one in the house."

Angela rubbed the top of the purple mushroom gently. "Same color as my grandma's dress. Can I show her?" She felt the gills on the underside, knelt to sniff. Could it be that she had an instinct for gardening? Lucille's spirits lifted a bit.

"Sure. Snap it off carefully. Mushrooms grow from under ground fungus, and trees feed on them. You can't have a forest without fungus."

"Cool."

"And you, too. You need nutrients as well." But she'd gone too far, and Angela turned away.

On opening the back door, Lucille heard Mrs. deNiro's voice trail off...was the word *annulment* hanging in the air? or was it her imagination? Robert was scurrying around the kitchen, tending to his dinner. Mrs. deNiro watched, queen-like in her regal get-up, from the dining room doorway. Lucille's ears rang, her nerves pulsed. Then Angela said, "Look, Grandma, Lucille's mushroom's the same color as your dress."

Mrs. deNiro shrank back. "Get that nasty thing away from me! And wash your hands, you don't know what's been around it, slugs, dogs, rabid creatures in this desolation!"

Angela's face fell. "I thought it was neat." Roughly now, she turned the mushroom in her hands, bruising the purple into brown.

Lucille said quickly, "Never mind. Come, Angela. Let's make a spore print in the service porch. Then we'll pick those flowers for your mom."

"Don't bother. They'll be dead before we get them home," snapped Mrs. deNiro.

Lucille's eyes met Robert's over the girl's head. He looked miserable, mouthed at her, "I'm sorry."

In the service porch Lucille flattened a dark brown sack, to show the yellow spores. She set the mushroom on it, gill side down, and covered it with a fruit jar, explaining the process to Angela. All the while she pondered the alarming number of females running loose in Robert's life. She imagined deNiro women in her dining room clustered around the Queen, whispering in her ear, giggling, drawing together in a cabal. And the three sisters, two divorced, one widowed; the former wives; this daughter. Now Linda, Isabelle. Who were they? She'd heard Robert say he'd wanted to get out of Eugene...had she been merely an escape hatch to a man accustomed to using women as escape hatches?

At the table over dinner, Lucille smoldered with resentment. She should have stuck it out with Curtis. At least she'd known where she stood with Curtis, and he never went near the kitchen. But then again his personal habits had driven her nuts. Dagger sharp crescents of yellow toenail clippings in the rug. Toilet seat always up, unless he'd used it to prop his feet on for a dusting: then it was covered with his foot powder. The scattered bits of tooth-flossings sprayed on the mirror like cement. No, that had been no good. But at least then she hadn't been double-teamed; her adversary had been just Curtis, not a raft of unknown women.

She refilled her wineglass, leaned back to watch the Queen chatter news at Robert about people she didn't know. The woman also pleaded with Angela to eat. "Just this much, honey, then I'll buy you a soda in Newberry." But Angela whined, squirmed, sulked, ate only the croutons off her salad, and a breadstick smeared with butter.

Lucille turned to study Robert. He was squeezing lemon on his fish, frowning. To be fair, he was not enjoying himself, but that wasn't Lucille's fault. She hadn't foisted these women on him. She drank off her wine, refilled her glass. Why had she let this man and his complications into her life?

It had been so simple. She began rehashing her days alone with the cat, painting their memory in a wine-glazed wash of existential colors. She remembered one day coming home from the Chamber office in tears—a cranky man had harassed her about everything in town—when Scout had run out to greet her with unconditional love. Lucille had been so grateful, so delighted with the cat's sinuous dance to can opener music, she'd fed her the whole tin.

Scout, where was Scout? Lucille hadn't seen her all day. Abruptly she scraped back her chair, preparing to rush into the kitchen, but she caught a corner of her placemat and tumbled her entire dinner to the floor. Splat. Her plate upturned a messy heap of food, splattering all over the Bokhara rug. broccoli, her salad, her rice, the buttered breadstick, her wine. At least it been white, she thought wildly.

"For god's sake, Lucille," said Robert in the shocked silence.

She stumbled from the room, slammed out the door. Madly, she strode up the street the twilight. The evening had turned chilly, but she was on fire, full of electricity and rage. She knew the signs: she and Robert were going to have fight, their first. It was overdue, and it going be good one. She understood that he was not the cause, but he was going to be the reason. This would not surprise him. He must have seen coming.

He appeared at the door behind her and yelled something. She ignored him, flew up the street with no idea where she was going. She was love with this moment of allowing her feelings free rein. She felt dangerous, firecracker just put to light. Blow up time. And she knew why she'd not blown before: if she'd let him see the person she really was, he could not possibly love her. But right now, the corner 101 and Cape View Road, she did not care.

Gradually, though, she ran out of steam and began to falter. She waited for gap traffic, then trotted across the highway. She trudged up road that wound like vine up the hill. Puffing, sweating, frightened...what was she doing, acting like a wild woman? Wasn't she playing right into the Queen's hand? Yes. Giving her ace play against her...

Finally she paused in vacant lot and looked out over town. She could see her own house from here, tranquil and seemingly deserted, like piece in board game.

As Lucille watched, the Queen and her attendants appeared. She saw the Buick back out, nose toward the highway, then swing north toward Robert's sister's house. Bitterly Lucille imagined the gossip this episode would generate. And it was no one's fault but her own, this humiliation.

Exhausted, all she wanted to do now was go home. Oh, she'd been mindless, she'd had her freedom and she'd squandered it. Like one of those chickens on the freeway after the poultry truck turned over. They'd wandered around, out of their cages for the first time in their lives and all they'd known how to do was go back in the cage. Freedom was beyond them. Freedom had been be yond Lucille; she was a factory chicken, couldn't live without a cage, without a man, was afraid to try.

In the meantime, what to do? What would happen to her and Robert? Surely this wouldn't be the end, surely they would make up? But under her panic, Lucille felt a layer of relief grow, an easing of pain, a calm relaxation. As when fever breaks and the road to recovery stretches ahead. She welcomed health, she welcomed the eroding of her passion for Robert, the crumbling of her worship. He was just a man, such as men are. Now she could take up her real personality, but was this good or bad? Did other couples go through this experience? Surely they must, and they must manage some adjustment. After all, no one stayed a newly wed forever.

Lucille sighed and looked around. Her adrenaline had run its course, and she was cold. She stumbled back down the hill, and in front of her own house saw that Robert had left the light on. She noticed, happily, that his mother had parked badly and had run over the Paper Whites on her way out the drive. This couldn't hurt the bulbs, but Lucille would point it out to him.

Ammunition.

She crept around to the back, no point dragging pine needles in on the rug. As she passed the bedroom window, she heard the TV tuned to the news. Robert had gone to bed. Lucille glanced at her newly pruned hydrangeas; at least the day hadn't been a total waste. Then she saw Simon and Scout squaring off in the bushes. Before she could flap at Simon, the tuxedo cat bolted. In hot pursuit, Scout took off, letting go with a kind of yowl Lucille hadn't known her capable of.

But Lucille's exhilaration evaporated in the service porch. Robert's clutter was everywhere. Boxes, bags, kitchen gear, tools she doubted he knew how to use. She stopped to inspect the progress of Angela's russula. A yellow star of spoors had begun to appear on the brown sack. When complete, Lucille would mail it to her. The girl could be an ally, or at least a piquant new ingredient in their family stew.

Robert had made only a faint-hearted attempt at cleaning the rug. This pleased Lucille and she gathered up shampoo, rags, and sponges and set to work to do it right. She was on her knees over the soiled area when Robert appeared, again in his robe.

"Luce " he said. Then, "Wait! That's my carwash sponge!"

She looked up and snapped, "For chrissake! If you don't want to see me use it, go back to bed."

He let his shoulders sag, and turned toward the bedroom.

Lucille worked on the rug feeling in some ways better than she had for months. The relationship had entered a familiar phase, one that involved a bit of testing.

WAR STORY

JIM LARSON let the front section of the newspaper slide from his fingers into a heap at his feet. He leaned back in his recliner and sighed, forcing himself to relax against a feeling of claustrophobia, of stagnation. A glance down at the headlines—drive-by shootings, a child killed in a hit-and-run, an eighty-year-old woman raped—made him shudder. The world out there was coming apart.

He was appalled. Not at the news: he was used to that. But at his reaction to it. He'd never thought himself a fan of entropy; nevertheless, he was smitten with the raw power, passion, the violence that seethed everywhere in cities and towns, everywhere but here in this backwater burg on the Oregon Coast.

He gazed through the sliding glass doors to his deck overlooking the Pacific Ocean. When a new feeling of suffocation choked him, he launched himself up and out.

Leaning his elbows on the deck railing, he took a couple of deep breaths, trying to get some air in his anxiety. He made himself breathe it, the green aroma of fungus, of dry-rotted sawdust. The smell of nothing going on except the slow disintegration induced by nature. He told himself he ought to be glad for such peace, if this was peace, but he was not. A prisoner, he was a prisoner, cut off from the passion and excitement that gripped the rest of the world. And he'd done it to himself, this marooning.

He forced himself to focus on the ocean, a flat sheet of aluminum from this lofty distance, seemingly so smooth that not even a crinkle disturbed its surface. And the sky, an unrelenting arch of gray—as if a lid had been clamped down to hold him in. He ached to get out. He ached to...well, to expound with the guys in the lunchroom, analyzing current events, Supreme Court decisions, trends, fads, the eddy and flow of campus life.

The guys in the lunchroom used to listen to him, they'd paid attention. "Jim, what do you think of Judge Rehnquist's comments about women going to military academies?" someone would ask. Or "How about finding signs of life in rocks from Mars?" And he'd think of something profound or witty to say, and guys would quote him all over the department. He felt a bit of a smile creep over his face, imagining his remarks admired and repeated.

What he did hear, though, were sounds of laughter. Jim turned to watch his wife and daughter work in the rhododendrons bordering the drive. Or rather Terry, his new wife, worked while Brenda, his daughter and their guest, followed her around. They could pass for sisters, same long blond hair flowing from under straw hats, same trim figures in tee shirts and jeans, same stance and energy. They could even be twins. They were exactly the same age.

Jim watched Terry pick through dead blossoms on the shrubs. The rhoddies had given up early this year. Had they given up? Was it early? He tried to remember last spring, the first one that he and Terry had been full-time residents here, but he couldn't bring up any details. Tell the truth, the last few years were a blur. First there had been the scandal that, due to old resentments, jealous ies, departmental politics, had washed over the school like a tsunami. To escape it, before it brought him down, he'd taken early retirement. Then he'd been too busy relocating, too full of the romance of his new marriage, the glow of writing his book.

Well, well. He rubbed his hands together, tried to make himself feel brisk, efficient. Get a grip, he told himself. All this anxiety...it was because he wasn't writing. Here he was, a natural writer with the passion and talent—yes, he had talent, he was sure of it—to get his knowledge, his grasp of the broad patterns sweeping contemporary American life down on paper. But he'd found his words and ideas bottled up in him like gas. Wasn't his fault, though, the lack of progress. Lately he'd been distracted by his daughter's visit; however, this was Brenda's last day. Tomorrow she'd go home...and carry back tales to her mother Claire, Jim's ex-wife.

He prickled with apprehension. But he wondered why. Surely he didn't care what Brenda told Claire, who bore him no ill will. She'd forgiven him for leaving her to marry his student, Terry. What did bother him was the suspicion that Clair was laughing at him. "Silly old goat," he could hear her saying.

Was he a silly old goat, marrying a woman so young? After having evaded so many, how had Terry got to him? He frowned, trying to remember.

Jim hadn't even noticed Terry sitting with his daughter in the second row of Intro to Soc until mid-term when he'd passed back blue book exams. In her loopy handwriting, she'd written a facile essay describing patrilineal and matrilineal descent lines. It had been the easiest of the choices Jim had allowed, and he hadn't been impressed. Just another big-haired blond with acrylic nails, in a bulky knit cotton sweater over skin-tight acid-washed jeans.

Every year his classes were full of such girls. For one thing, he was rumored to be an easy A. Then too, for the last ten years or so (since his true passion for teaching had died), he'd developed a sparring banter with the sexy ones that seemed to be a hit. He'd had more than one girl come onto him. They'd sit in the front row with their legs apart, or they'd brush their boobs against him as they leaned over his desk cooing questions or murmuring comments.

But then, blue book in his outstretched hand, he'd fallen into Terry's gray-green eyes flicked with gold; he'd been struck by the soul he'd glimpsed in those wonderful eyes so relentlessly fringed with lashes. He'd gone on to admire her smooth oval face, like a pearl set in the gold masses of her hair. His fingers longed to touch the smooth skin under her ears, to feel the curve of her cupid's bow mouth. He thought he could smell her perfume, a light flowery scent like lilacs.

He began studying her, covertly at first. Her reflection in the glass case holding his artifacts. Her rapt attention to his lectures, so flattering that even he, jaded as he was, got interested in his subject. Then he ogled openly, staring as she crossed to the pencil sharpener, or stood to wiggle into her jacket.

He started playing to her, his appreciative audience of one. She laughed at his jokes, the stale ad-libs he'd penciled in the margin of his notes a decade earlier. She laughed in all the right places, not rudely as some of them did when he turned his back to write on the board, but with genuine appreciation for his sense of humor. She had a wonderful tinkly laugh. Reminded him of the bell on a candy store door, a sweet promise of goodies. He was half surprised no bees, no butterflies, no bits of glitter wafted in her wake, so sweet did she seem to him across the room.

Then one day he'd fallen into step behind her in the hall. She was wearing spandex bicycling shorts and he drew back a bit to admire her ass, a perfect little upside down Valentine. When she flipped back the mass of her hair to laugh into the face of her girlfriend, whom Jim abruptly recognized as his daughter, Brenda, he was torn between delight and chagrin.

Just then Brenda had swiveled and caught him gawking. "Dad," she said, "you look like you just discovered an intact Dead Sea Scroll. This is Terry McKinna. She's coming out to the house for the barbecue." To Terry, "My dad does great chicken and ribs. Be sure and bring your swimsuit. Pool's too cold for them this early, but not for us." A sardonic chuckle.

Jim had stood there with a silly grin, thinking of the wispy little suit this kind of a girl would wear.

Jim wandered in from the deck, shooed Terry's cat from his chair and swatted at floating cat hairs. The whole place was haired, either with Terry's long blond strands or with black puffs of fuzz from this animal that seemed to be able to aim and shoot fur balls at him, as a porcupine is said to do with quills. He sank into his recliner, still warm and rocking from the cat, and reached for his yellow pad and a pencil. But instead of writing, he drew another deep defeated sigh and punched on the TV with the remote.

He channel-surfed over a man talking of the environment in dire tones, a game show all applause and laughter, a panel discussion on AIDS, commercials for stomach medicines and cleaning agents, movies of varying vintages, and an interview with an author of a best seller on serial killers. The thought of a best seller energized him into jabbing off the set and leaping up to pace around, cursing loudly enough to rattle the cat into bolting.

"Jim?" called Terry, now downstairs. "Who are you talking to?" Then more softly to Brenda, "Your dad, he's uptight, you know?"

Jim heard Brenda rumble a rude stagy laugh and say, "Tell me about it. What's buggin' him?"

"It's the book, I think. Just don't bring it up, okay?"

So when they entered, sun-warmed and smelling of greenery, he felt condescension ooze from their flow of gardening talk. He pouted while they got lunch on the table, an eggplant casserole leftover from the night before. Jim had disliked it then and he wanted them to feel his displeasure at seeing it again.

As if to thwart his fit of pique, they persisted in a sunny discussion of nasturtium beds, rhododendrons, the carpet of wild strawberries Terry had encouraged instead of grass. Then Terry said, "I turned the compost pile, Jim. You should see. It's really cooking now, full of worms, big fat ones."

Brenda clattered her fork onto her plate. Talk about a lunch topic. I'd rather discuss writer's block. Oops, sorry, Dad."

Silence hung in the air like a bad smell. Terry and Brenda both glanced at Jim, assessing the damage, but Jim just went on chewing. He pointedly removed a long blond hair from his food, then got up for a steak knife to dissect peel from a gray-brown slice of eggplant. He surgically trimmed it as if it were a carcinogen.

Terry said, "Sorry about that, love. I should have remembered you don't like moussaka. We'll have pork chops for dinner, okay?"

"We don't have any," he said peevishly.

"I know. Brenda and I'll stop in the market on our way home, Oh, I forgot to tell you, we thought we'd run up to the outlet mall since this is her last day. Give you a chance to work in peace."

"The outlet mall? Again? You were just there," he said.

"No, not since before Christmas. clearance. Brenda wants to go, well, I do, too." They're having a spring clearance. Brenda wants to go, well, I do, too."

"Yeah, Dad, I'm shopping for a birthday present for Mom. She's been looking for an apricot colored top."

Brenda went on describing the shade as Terry bustled around clearing the table. Jim leaned back and watched her. The nipped in little Valentine ass had spread a bit. Now it resembled a pair of pancakes run together in a pan too small, but she was still a looker. She still turned heads down at the Suprette, enough to give Jim an occasional attack of jealousy.

But not over the young ones, no, not them. Not since she'd told him the basis for his...selection, for want of a better word.

Yeah, she was a looker, not as sharp as she'd been at that barbecue. The memory of her then still made him sweat.

At Jim and Claire's little faculty party, Terry had pulsed like an extra heat source. True to his expectations, she'd worn a spec tacular swimsuit, a french-cut hot-pink nylon number that had caused a discernible hush to fall over Jim's buddies when she draped her long limbs on a lounge near the pool. Jim carefully busied himself basting ribs with his homemade sauce, while Terry basted herself with some preparation, in the process flex-

ing into provocative positions. Through the smoke, he thought
he could smell her lotion, a scent oozing pure sex.

When she stretched languidly, he collapsed into a chair and
gawked. Then she stood up like a ballerina, no pushing up
sideways as Claire had to do. She straightened her suit, tugging
at the little triangle of material that covered her bottom and
daintily entered the water. Jim knew all the guys, middle-aged
academics like himself, had noticed how her nipples dimpled
through her top, how the backs of her legs had retained the
faint imprint of the lounge webbing.

The Golden Girl. His Golden Girl. He was as proud of her
as if she were his creation, and at the same time angry at her
for bring such an unsettling presence into his life.

He was still staring moodily into the crowd of his guests
when Claire appeared at his side. She was into the "fat" end of
her wardrobe, blamed it on menopause (but after he left she
lost forty pounds), and was wearing a red and green flowered
Mother Hubbard thing he particularly disliked (she called it
her "gypsy look). It had large floppy sleeves and billowed out
yards of material from a square-cut yoke.

"Can't believe it, can you?" she said.

"What?"

That we were once that young. I never thought we were going
to get old." She laughed wryly to show what a good sport she
was about it, and Jim glared at her retreating back.

The nerve, her including him in her rush toward dottering
old age He watched as she flapped over to talk to another fat
white broad who also wouldn't dare put on a swimsuit. He
frowned, wondered why Claire didn't do something about a
black mole on her neck, so visible now that she chopped her
hair off painfully short. Just then a breeze raised the hem of
her baggy dress and revealed ripply white thighs. She didn't
shave her legs above her knees. Claire had that Irish coloring
of raven black hair with white skin, and Jim had once found it
attractive. But now he was dizzy with distaste, and he savagely
basted ribs, wielding the brush as if it were a sword.

Then his pulse raced when Terry crossed the lawn to place her precious little bottom in a chair next to his.

"Professor Larson," she purred, "did you happen to catch the National Geographic special about Ashanti and Machu Picchu, about how they could have come into contact?"

He looked down into her flower face, admiring the golden fuzz above her upper lip, her perfectly aligned teeth, the dimple in her little chin. She'd been one of those girls who'd gone to summer camp and rode horseback, who'd always had a date for the prom. "Why, no, I didn't see that program," he lied and leaned forward to smile into the soul in her eyes.

Just then one of his teaching buddies passed behind her chair and smirked at Jim over her head in an oily way. Jim didn't care. Let them joke all they wanted.

The next day at school, he still didn't care. Nothing bothered him, the nudges, the jabs, the knowing looks. Not even the misshapen potato with a growth like a penis some smart-ass crammed in his mailbox. What the hell. He'd gotten lucky. That was all there was to it.

Once he even asked Terry about it. At the time it was Tuesday, Jim's half-day—they were sprawled on a waterbed in the Starlight Motel off the old truck route. He asked her, "Why me? You coulda had anybody. I'm old enough to be your father." To make sure, he raised his head to glance at the gray plumage of his crotch. He felt like a kid, like she'd taken twenty years off him.

Terry propped herself up on a round smooth elbow and traced a gold-painted nail across the lines in his forehead. She laughed, that golden laugh. "Jim, this is weird. You're not going to believe this, but I've had the same dream over and over. I'm flipping through the pages of a photo album and I know on the last page is a picture of the man I'm supposed to marry. I get to the last page, and it's you, it's you. Well, it's a little like a picture of my dad, he died before I was born, but it's really you."

Jim had lain there, shocked. He suddenly realized all he

wanted to do was run home and tell Claire this crazy story about this crazy girl. Claire loved hearing about other people's dreams. But he couldn't do that anymore. The marriage had unraveled. And Claire, lulled by almost three decades of his fidelity, hadn't even realized it yet.

From the deck, Jim watched Terry back the Volvo around. He heard the girls (he thought of them as girls) giggle together, such an irritating sound, like nails on the chalkboard. They were happy, he supposed, to escape his dark They'd remained best friends through the break-up, Brenda announcing her support for Terry. Brenda was tolerant, able to understand how one's inner child expressed longings the adult ignored. The affair, she said, had been Jim's destiny; he was wrong to worry about it.

"You have to center yourself in your own existence," she'd said. You can't go messing with your karma. Besides, Mom just doesn't understand. She never even listens to Bill Moyers, or anyone else who'd help her get the big picture."

Jim had stared at her blankly. He'd noticed that she never had a steady boyfriend. Wasn't it because she'd seen up close the perfidy of men? Hadn't she decided not to get caught in the same trap as her mother? More fuel for his unease.

The car crunched down the gravel toward 101. Now, with the house to himself, he planned to work diligently, to make up for the wasted morning. But before he knew it, he was reaching for the remote, telling himself that he might as well shoot the whole day, get it over with.

But what the hell...he had to get up to remove a post-it note stuck to the TV tube. "I love you" in Terry's childish scrawl, encased in a heart. A horrid wash of emotions shook him. He was somehow pleased, but also exasperated that she'd known he'd turn on the set; and he suffocated again with a feeling of entrapment, he wadded up the bit of paper and stuffed it under his chair.

He surfed onto a riot scene in some Islamic city, Kabul, he thought. Like giant crows, women shrouded in black skittered away from a crowd of men brandishing sticks, the images jerky and uneven, as if filmed from the back of a truck.

So ugly. Not like his riots in the sixties which had been clean, holy things, dedicated to investing people with freedom, not taking it away. He remembered himself and Claire, never his passionate lover—they'd reserved real heat for their causes—but his best friend in those days, backpacking baby Brenda as they marched for civil rights in Berkeley. Claire had worn her long black hair parted down the middle, swinging like a curtain around her face. Beads, fringes, bell bottoms, a vest made from a faded American flag she'd worn them, too, like a costume for a party. It had been a party, deadly serious, but a party all the same. They'd smoked a little pot, everyone did, so what? He sneered a bit, thinking of Terry's attitude toward grass. So pure she was, so goddamned pure. Jim longed for a little grass right now. Maybe that was what he needed.

He got up to pace the room, mulling it over. What the hell did he need? He picked up Terry's half-finished crossword—she never did get it all—and tried to fill in her blanks. Giving up— he couldn't finish it, either—he tossed the paper aside. Claire would have finished it. Claire was smart, all right; she'd had answers for everything—tax issues, the economy, government regulations versus private property rights. She'd even managed to understand liters, kilometers, pounds and pence during their trip to the British Isles, which, he told himself, he shouldn't have to trouble with. Up till now, he'd managed to surround himself with the kind of woman who dealt with those details.

But there'd been that other side to Claire, that pain-in-the-ass know-it-all side. He could almost hear her now braying about something distasteful, unacceptable: his constipation...her hot flashes...or care of the clitoris, fer chrissake! He'd found Claire's "liberation" repugnant, didn't miss that, no sir. But she was one sharp cookie, she could write a book, maybe she should write his book. The thought made him sweat again, tremble with incipient failure.

Late in the afternoon Terry and Brenda giggled in, loaded down with plastic bags. Terry showed him new jeans and tees exactly like her other jeans and tees. Jim smiled and nodded, but wondered if no one sold anything but casual wear anymore. He shoved his yellow pad under his chair after noticing that he'd doodled over and over *The Great Escape*, the movie he'd wasted his afternoon on. He loved this movie, had already seen it twenty seven times because he'd used it in a unit with the unfortunate title of "American Pluck." Unfortunate because his sophomores couldn't resist rhyming "pluck" with their favorite word, and because half the main characters weren't American at all. No matter. Watching Steve McQueen always raised his spirits, and Jim now felt better than he had all day.

True to her word, Terry had gotten pork chops for supper. She fixed them in a microwave cooking bag that was supposed to produce a sort of gravy (but didn't, Jim pointed out so peevishly that he made himself set the table, to atone).

"Dad," Brenda wailed, chopping up a salad, "you're in my way. Just go back in the living room with the TV."

Happily deserting the kitchen, he turned on TNT, still at its Steve McQueen festival. But Terry objected.

"On Brenda's last day?" she yelled over some playful music from *The Reivers*. It was the scene where McQueen lets the kid drive the car, one of Jim's favorite. "Can't we just have some peace and quiet? Or something good? I could run back to the Suprette and rent *Thelma and Louise*. Everybody's seen that but us."

"Yeah, Brad Pitt's in *Thelma and Louise*," said Brenda. "Or we could get *The Bridges of Madison County*. I totally loved the book."

Jim vetoed them all. Through dinner they debated on a board game. Brenda liked Scruples, but they needed partners for that. Terry favored Yatzee, but Jim said crisply, "If I wanted to add up columns of figures, I'd balance the checkbook."

After eating, they dragged chairs out to sit on the deck. Jim opened a bottle of brandy and drank from a tea-stained cup.

Along with all their good dishes, Claire had gotten the snifters they'd bought in Waterford, Ireland. Jim was the only one who cared; the girls stuck to drinking herbal teas or wine coolers (*soda pop*, Jim called them).

Terry and Brenda worried about the unseasonable heat, said it was due to global warming. Jim disparaged this concept. Thing is," he said, "global warming's got its up side. Getting hotter one place means someplace else'll grow new crops. I'm planting pole beans and tomatoes next year, if this keeps up."

He found himself telling stories of what a picky eater Brenda had been as a child. When she'd discovered where meat came from, she'd announced tearfully that she was going to eat only wieners. She'd thought football players had chickens stuffed in their suits for padding, that peacocks laid eggplants.

Terry did not find his stories interesting; soon she was fidgeting, yawning. She said she was going to bed. She needed more sleep than Jim did, went to bed early, got up late. So Jim found himself uncomfortably alone with his daughter. When had he last talked to her without the filtering presence of his wife? He felt tongue-tied, marooned in the warm dark with a stranger.

A breeze stirred the alder trees down toward the point. Through them he saw tiny white lights flicker, the lights festooning Thayer's rental cabins. He sat up straight.

"You remember that trip we took back east, and you collected lightning bugs in a jar?" he asked her profile. He realized she was avoiding him, too.

She grimaced. "And I went around shaking it to make them light up, like flashlights. Then they all died. Why did you let me do that?"

"They were just bugs." When Brenda went on frowning, he added, "It was a different time then. Our ideas, our values change." He felt a small lift. Could it be true? "By the way, how's your mother? Is she really okay?" He didn't wish Claire any harm, but writing out that check every month…

"Oh, doing great. She passed her real estate exam, works part-time in an office downtown. The bookstore was okay, but this's a real career. Got a new hairdo, kept all the weight off." Brenda paused, then said slowly, "Dad, I don't know if I should tell you, but Mom's got a serious boyfriend."

An unexpected shock prickled hair on the backs of his hands. "You don't say," he managed to mutter. "Anybody I know?"

"As a matter of fact, it's Phil Meechum."

Jim sat upright in a rush of fright and anger. "What? Phil? Where the hell's his wife?"

"Left him for a real power player who wears jungle print ties and toodles around in a Beemer."

"My god! What's the world coming to!" He leaped up to pace the deck. Then he made himself sit down: no point in tipping his hand to Brenda, who'd tell Claire. So in the growing dark he babbled away on neutral topics, while his mind boiled with Phil Meechum, the teaching buddy who'd taken Jim's place as department head. Phil, an idiot, who read only the sports section, who ranted and raved about some goddamned Blazer's game, who put the coffee pot back on its burner, empty.

Jim tortured himself with images of the two of them, Phil and Claire, cozy in his, his book-lined study, a cheery fire warming them. Ah, no, because he'd given up the house to keep his pension, and he'd taken away his books. Too warm for a fire anyway.

Then he imagined Claire reading Phil some tidbit out of the paper, looking up over her half-glasses with that smirk he'd detested. He'd hated having Claire read him the paper, as if he couldn't read for himself. In fact, she'd treated him as if he were a child, her child.

After their divorce Jim thought he'd dwell less on Claire, not more. He was worn out with her, dragging her around like a broken leg. At the same time, he wanted her back, so he could pick a fight. No good fighting with Terry: first she cried, then she pouted. For days.

Mercifully, Brenda soon turned in. Jim sat there, staring out into the dark. Life is like a Russian novel, he thought. Something you checked out of the library to read on the beach. After a hundred pages or so, if you get that far, you recognize the characters despite their plural, multi-syllabic names, but the plot's grown tedious and you're not enjoying the story at all. However, you have to finish the damn thing before it's due back, and when's that? You have no way of knowing since the date's stamped in blurry ink you can't read. Jim played with his analogy, wished for someone to tell it to. Claire. She'd loved Russian novels. But she'd one-up him, ruin his sense of achievement.

Jim studied the lights around Thayer's cabins, now swimming in a bit of breeze. Something niggled at him about Thayer's... oh, yeah, they had that golden retriever puppy Terry'd wanted so badly. But Christ, he didn't want a dog. He'd had dogs. Been there done that. Something else about Thayer's...yeah, Darlene Thayer, a juicy piece, that. One he could get into if he wanted to because she oozed restlessness, boredom. No wonder. Mitch, her husband, was about as interesting as his woodstove. But why would he put the make on Darlene? Been there, done that, too.

Sex hadn't even started for Jim until Terry. Well, before that there had been a formal sort of screwing. But real full-body sex had eluded him, and now he knew that it was over. However, he had had it, for that short period. And he'd had a passion for his causes, although he now couldn't remember exactly what they'd been.

The air had grown chilly, and he got up to carry in chairs. In the cold living room he longed for his sweater, but didn't want to go in the bedroom for it and wake Terry. He curled up under the couch blanket and punched on the TV against the silence. Soon there would be plenty of that.

He was relieved TNT was still at its festival, now showing an early McQueen, The War Lover. Feeling war-like but used up at the same time, Jim settled down. Tomorrow he'd soldier on, he'd find something to keep himself from sliding into the dark, from guttering out like a candle. But he knew it was over, it was finished, and he didn't even know what it was.

BIRDS OF THE COAST

I'M OUT for my walk. Down Sea View Terrace, across Salal Drive to the field with the path mowed in it, out to the headland by Thayer's Cabins. Darlene and Mitch's dog, that nice retriever, has taken to barking at me. Poor thing, she misses her puppies, the last of 'em just given away. Then beyond Ally's place—which is quiet now that her daughter's gone—I hook onto Trail 1908 and follow it to the beach. About an hour out and back, three miles give or take. I use this time to sort myself out.

For example, what to have for dinner. Spaghetti or chili or meat loaf—I left a pound of ground turkey thawing out on the counter. Charlie—he's my husband—Charlie's on a restricted diet and can't eat beef or pork anymore so I've learned to cook with turkey, even beans and tofu, although Charlie hates tofu so it's a bit perverse of me to inflict it on him.

Or I puzzle over transplanting the orange rhododendron out of its cold windy northeast corner of the yard, or let it acclimate where it is (or die). Or if it's worth a trip into Newberry for Safeway's three for a dollar cantaloupes; but they're probably the size of hardballs, and as juicy—It's hard to get good produce here on the coast—so I usually decide not to go.

I mull around Tony, too. He's our only child, grown and gone now, but still teetering on the edge of this so-called global economy. I don't know if it's that, or some lack in him that causes him not to take hold, but he doesn't (at least in my opinion).

He's over in Eugene, bouncing around from job to job. He's sold sneakers in a sportswear shop, weirdly colored and constructed sneakers. I don't care what you call them, trainers, runners, hikers, walkers—they're all sneakers to me, which I suppose tells you more about me than Tony. And he's been a greeter in a Wal*Mart, pushing a cart and a smile at you by that fishtank near the entrance. Currently he's doing telephone solicitation, trying to sell memberships to a health club. The kind that'll fold in the night, and leave him holding the barbell, so to speak.

Charlie doesn't even want to hear about Tony anymore. Just to mention Tony gets Charlie so steamed the veins in his forehead throb. He turns red and rants about lack of foresight, wasted oppor tunities, stupid decisions, etc. So I don't bring up Tony. Why give Charlie a heart attack? Anyway Charlie's so deaf these days I have to yell to make myself heard over ESPN or C-Span blaring away. That's another reason I'm out here: to get away from the TV.

Well, I enjoy it, too, rambling around. On Ocean View Drive, this street here, Northport's best residential area, I keep track of who's painting their siding what color. Last year it was all marine blue-gray; this year it's buttercup yellow which I don't like as well, but who asked me, right? And I check out who's got company or who's out of town. Who's letting blackberry canes come up in their planters, whose lawn needs mowing. Mostly nobody's. These folks all have gardeners who mow, weed-eat, and prune efficiently and impersonally, mindless as giant insects under their safety goggles.

This street used to be a ribbon of gravel winding between shore pines and brambles. Right here where these people have built a spendy gazebo, I used to pick blackberries. Still plenty of berries around, but I miss the ones I got here. Somehow they were juicier, sweeter, maybe due to mist off the sea; or the longer time it took 'em to get ripe. Middle of September they were perfect, right after the end of Charlie's vacation and Tony went back to school (or did they just seem sweeter because I had the house to myself again?). And there where they've paved the whole yard for RV parking, I remember a carpet of mushroom that always sprang up after the first real rains of November. I used to stuff the Thanksgiving bird with 'em—that was back when Charlie could eat stuffing and giblets and turkey skin and gravy. And beyond that cement block wall there's a path that Charlie and Tony used to climb down for a bit of fishing off the rocks. They used to catch perch, bass, salmon.

Now the rocks are off-limits, and the berry brambles and trees have been cleared for these big houses, vacation "cabins," that stand empty most of the time. Still, this is a nice walk. I can see the ocean beyond sideyards not walled off, gray-green rollers churning onto basalt rocks. Smell it, too, salty and fishy and pungent. And hear the roar and hiss of caterwauling water, and maybe a gull scream or an oystercatcher pipe. At the end of this road there's that trail leading down to the beach; that's where I'm headed.

Well, that's all true: I do need time and space to worry and sort myself out, and I do like to see what's going on. But the real reason I'm hoofing it around town is that Charlie's wearing me out. He retired last year so he's home all the time now. Before that he left the house at seven and came back at six. Kept those hours for thirty-two years working as a sheriff patrolling 101 and a handful of other highways with numbers, and he got his fill of the bleak side of life. Blood and gasoline and broken glass, belligerent drunks and arrogant bigwigs, or kids so young and dumb they make you hurt just to look at 'em. So he's earned his rest and should get to do what he wants. And what he wants is to stay in the house; I go into a room and Charlie's there listening to a congressional hearing on C-Span or a PGA tournament on ESPN. Or fiddling with something, making a mess, leaving pieces of stuff scattered around; or he's rooting through the desk or the file for a misplaced scrap of paper or a receipt, or directions that came with his battery-powered screwdriver the VCR Don't get me wrong, I'm devoted to Charlie. But... he's there all the time.

I once took a quilting class with a woman, Marcy from Las

Vegas, whose husband had just retired. He waited for her in their car out front. If she was late finishing her project, or we spent a few minutes talking after class, he came in looking for her. "You about through?" he'd ask. "How much longer?"

Now Charlie's not that clingy; he's just...there. Eighteen hours out of twenty-four, he surrounds himself with TV noise. Me, I like the place quiet; I find my own silences comforting. I like my solitude. I know that sounds antisocial, as if the rest of the world isn't good enough for me, isn't up to my elevated standards, my lofty requirements.

But it's just the other way around: I'm not up to the world. Being with people fatigues me; just one encounter eats at the marrow of my energy. After an interaction, I replay the whole ex change in my head, turning it this way and that way; I rerun the conversation, evaluate the wins and losses. And parties, well, I hate parties; takes me a whole week to digest a party. Ha! me at a party....Might as well be a spotted owl at a loggers' convention. So, to be honest, it's self-preservation that leads me to spend time alone.

Which makes it crazy that I ever took up with Lark.

I first met her at the bench where the trail drops down to the beach. I was sitting there contemplating a bit of the bay when she plopped down next to me. "Isn't this nice, the view, the air?" she said. "Who needs fancy exercise equipment when you can walk these trails? By the way, what're those birds on the rocks down there?"

I told her they were turnstones, experts at precision formation flying, like an airborne school of fish, or the Blue Angels.

"And those snaky ones riding so low in the water?"

Cormorants, I said, and pointed to one on the rocks drying its wings, holding them out like it was posing for a portrait.

The woman introduced herself: Lark Springhill (a smug smile at the poetry of her name), in Northport for the summer. She was "storing up psychic energy" for another year as an administrator in a Portland junior college. Without mentioning my need for psychic energy, I introduced myself: Myrna Secord, Northport resident for more than forty years.

"Wow! she exclaimed. "A long-timer...you've seen some. changes around town, oh, boy, I'd love to hear your stories!" And I admit I puffed up, feeling so worthwhile and unique. Like a ten foot sturgeon, or a California condor.

As if it were something we'd agreed to, which later I wondered about—my courage, or cowardliness, or audacity; or her courage, or cowardliness, or audacity—we got up and started down the trail together. She asked about plants as we walked along. I rattled off everything I knew about sea pinks, viola duncas, purple asters, scarlet pimpernels—how they're called "poor man's weatherglass because they close up in bad weather.

She told me she was new in the area—a fact I found so obvious I wanted to snap "No shit, Sherlock!" the rude way Tony would have done—and that she'd seen me walking around town. She too liked to walk. She wondered if we could make a thing of it, walking together down the path to the beach so she could "pick my brains about stuff," also one of Tony's expressions. In fact, I think, now, I took her on, then, as a positive way to relate to a kid like Tony, gum-snapping, smart-alecky.

Yeah, I ate it up at first, this attention, so flattering from an attractive girl younger than Tony, but with a lot more sense. I began waiting for her at the bench, looking down the trail for a tall lithe figure in a rather dashing straw hat and heather-green outfit. She seemed interested in what I had to say and I lectured like a professor on Indian shell middens, pillow basalt, wave-cut terraces. If I didn't know, I made it up, to impress her. "People used to dip smelt here, used to bring up wheelbarrows full of 'em. Smelt don't run anymore, not like that. It's overfishing. And El Niño out there heating up the Kuroshio Current."

Kuroshio Current. Listen to me. I think I heard that term somewhere...so it wasn't really a lie. Just a little fancy stitching on the plain cloth of truth. Charlie would have said it was bullshit.

Twenty-four thousand gray whales this year, that's up from

nineteen thousand last year. And they don't go all the way to Alaska, just hang around off shore because of an unusual bloom of plankton. It's this global warming." Well, it sounded good, and I enjoyed her looking up to me with those wide green eyes. She was impressed with me. I was impressed with me. I was a California condor soaring aloft on updrafts of her esteem.

She began walking with me into town and asking about the people living along Ocean View Drive. I told her as much as I knew, and then some—still so full of myself I was. I pointed out the house, that one there with the wooden butterflies, where a woman older than me lives with a guy young enough to be her son; not her husband either. Least they use two different names writing checks around town. In that pink two-story with round windows next door, there's a woman who drives an almost new Mercedes, but has the gall to redeem food stamps up at the Suprette.

And in that one, the pale blue one with diagonal siding, there's a man who sneaks up to the recycling bins by the Suprette with his whiskey bottles at night because he's ashamed to own up to them in daylight. This same fellow, I added, goes into rut in the spring and starts hanging out in the Drift-Inn. Every evening he marches by in new corduroy pants so stiff they swish. Those new pants and a natty new flannel shirt: his courting outfit. His rut lasts a couple of weeks; then he goes back to old flannel shirts and silent washed-out jeans and knitted caps. He's always on foot. Rumor has it he's gotten too many DUIIs to drive anymore. Rumor also has it he's the black sheep son of some Portland nabob who pays him to stay outta sight.

In short, I told her the village gossip. The question is, why? Me, so secretive that I don't even like people seeing what I've got in my cart up at the Suprette.... Why did I go out on a limb like that? I don't know, except I just lost control with her listening so intently, so earnestly. I sang like a canary, then dragged myself home, exhausted.

Then it got worse.

One day we walked by my house, which is not on Ocean View Drive but one block east in a section the locals call Old Town. I live in that pale green one that needs paint and a new roof. Charlie says he'll get around to it, the maintenance, as soon as he sorts himself out. Besides, our warped and mossy old roof doesn't leak—why fix it if it ain't broke? that's what Charlie says. Anyway, we blend in with the neighbors—they're all a little seedy, which keeps our taxes down.

Walking by with Lark, though, I noticed our shabby yard, warped porch, peeling paint, and I made some comments in a sarcastic tone that surprised me. Then I went on about the TV noise, the mess in the living room, and before I knew it I was telling her some Charlie stories, and at the same time telling myself to shut up.

But when I did get hold of myself and quit in the middle of my tale, she'd pick up the thread, wouldn't let it drop. "He really went out at two in the morning to bullhorn at some people sleeping in the park parking lot? How rotten!"

"But it's day-use only; staying overnight's illegal," I said, defending the very situation I'd just the breath before condemned. "If you let 'em stay, the word'll get around and every night the parking lot'll be full of freeloaders."

"Motels around here are expensive. What if they couldn't afford a place to stay?"

"They were driving a fancy new rig, one of these sport utility things. If they could afford that, they could afford a room. Least that's what Charlie says."

"Ridiculous!" she snapped. "That doesn't mean they have ready cash."

"Still, the law's the law," I said feeling cornered and... exhausted. "Look," I said, hoping to distract her, "see how many scoters today...sometimes people think they're puffins, but you have to go up to Yaquina, or down to Heceta to see puffins."

Another time I let slip that Charlie and Tony don't see eye to eye, and told her about one of their run-ins—all the while telling myself to shut up, to no avail. I was out of control.

She said, "You mean Charlie wouldn't even loan your own son some camping gear?"

"Yeah, but last time he borrowed our stuff, he brought it back dirty. Took me a whole afternoon with Brillo pads and pipe cleaners to clean up the Coleman stove. There was a dent in the cooler, and a tear in the tent. Besides, Charlie was mad at Tony because Tony forgot his birthday."

"But Tony's just a kid," she said. "So he's thirty-two. Every child matures at his own rate. After all, what is it to 'grow up'? 1 was lucky. My mom absolutely knew how to raise kids, she let me and my brother set our own limits, our own goals. And it really paid off. If I ever had any kids, I'd know exactly what to do, I'd just copy my mom. She's so totally aware, so totally jazzed on positive vibes." Then she rattled on about how her mother once out-foxed her into buying some outfit by pretending to object, the old Tom Sawyer bit. At the time we were walking down the trail to the beach, and I listened to her loud voice while watching a line of brown pelicans skim just above the surf, like a ribbon unfurling. I wanted to call her attention to it, but couldn't interrupt because she was really into it, the story about her mother.

Then it occurred to me that I could keep her attention off me and my poor family by getting her to talk about her own. Now she was the condor, and I was a sparrow flopping in her slipstream.

Two or three weeks into our walking partnership, I'd spot her loping toward the bench and my stomach would churn and my shoulders would ache with the burden of carrying her presence down the trail with me. Why didn't I tell her I'd rather walk alone? Because I'm a coward, and because I dissemble with people I don't like; in fact, with people I don't like I'm extravagantly courteous to keep them off-balance, to keep them from discovering my true feelings, which, I seem to believe, would give them some kind of power over me.

So when she'd ask, with a smirk, least I saw it as a smirk, what I was up to, hoping for incriminating details, I'd throw her off by asking about her mother or her brother or her ex-husband or her boyfriend or her job in Portland. Although listening to her bored me, especially about the job. She worked impossible miracles, despite incredible odds, with a raft of nincompoops. But keeping her talking gave me less chance to expose myself.

I'd begun to have bad dreams. One that really upset me went like this: I'd been given a small fawn to raise, a sweet but useless creature I had to carry around in a basket on my head. Three or four times a day it demanded that I stop what I was doing and feed it. People gathered about me in an admiring circle to coo oh how sweet, how cute. But it was in my way, I couldn't get anything done with this damned fawn. And I had much to do, I never knew in my dream what it was, but wasn't getting at it.

Out on the trail, Lark changed tacks. She finished chewing up the people she worked with, so zeroed in on the town and how badly it was run. "You really ought to enforce strict zoning codes," she said. "Look at that, letting modulars in with these custom houses! Everybody loses value when that's allowed to happen. My mother's been on so many committees working on zoning problems, she is so good at working up restrictions."

"But there's a law about discriminating against modulars," I said weakly, sweat trickling down my sides.

"That doesn't matter, if you're clever you can get around any law. And all these overhead wires...why don't they bury utilities, why don't they run conduit down these streets! They have in other towns on the coast, progressive towns. These wires just look awful, it's like living in a spider web."

Limping along, gasping for breath—I was so tired I had to look where she was pointing because I don't see telephone poles and wires anymore. They've become a part of my landscape, like the clearcut above town. "Well, the expense—" I started to say.

"Expense! But it would add so much value to get rid of those wires! Look at that pole there, right in front of those people's view. How many wires on it? I count seventeen...now, can't you just imagine how it would be without that mess up there?"

That night I dreamed I was at a funeral but didn't know whose. I went around asking who died, but the people gathered by the grave ignored me. I panicked and started scrambling here and there and got tangled up ropes the pall bearers had slung under the casket. was going down into the pit with this pine box, but couldn't make sound wrapped in ropes which had turned into a sticky silky cocoon, as if been trussed up by a giant spider. I woke up scared to death...what way to go; plus, suddenly realized it had been Charlie's funeral. Then I heard ESPN down in the living room—he was watching an NFL preseason special and I was so relieved I didn't even mind the blaring TV.

Lark had to go to Portland one day and it was like being let out of a cage, walking by myself. felt lawless and free. When a man on Ocean View Drive said, "Where's your friend? You're all alone today," felt bad sayin' yeah, poor me, I was by myself, deserted. felt guilty, too. A betrayer of trust, mean as magpie. I resolved to be better, more tolerant, a real friend to Lark.

But she came back with two sets of wrist weights. She said we were wasting time just walking when we could get seriously fit, we could develop upper body strength and raise our metabolisms by adding only a few extra pounds. We couldn't just walk, though. Not that simple. We had to bring our arms together in front so our elbows touched; then out sideways as high as our shoulders; finally straight out to the back—all of which bothered my bursitis quite a lot but she said I'd get used to these routines, and they were the best thing for joint problems, which were caused by faulty nutrition. I'd practiced bad food combinations that had resulted in an explosion of free radicals assaulting my joints. Or was it electrolytes...anyway, these aches were all my own fault.

She was critical of my performance. "No, not like that, see? You're not raising your arms high enough. Look at our shadows.... See me? how I'm doing it? Now look at you. So it hurts a little. No pain, no gain. Wait, that's not right, either," she scolded. "Okay, that bothers you, do this." She alternated arms, flinging them straight up, but when I tried to do that, I heard cartilage crack my elbows and shoulders. She couldn't hear it; she was like Charlie, slightly deaf, the result, she said, of too many rock concerts when she was teen. She'd begun to remind me of Charlie in other ways. It was like listening to Charlie rant about Tony when she went at the city, its lack of planning, design, foresight.

One day I was too depressed to go walking so I didn't show. She came to my house, knocked, and asked up at the bench. Charlie (while I hid in the hall) if I was okay. I listened to them talk, mutter, mutter, a staccato of a chuckle. I heard him tell her I was just taking a day off. I was a good old gal, he said, but sometimes I tried to do too much and canning twenty quarts of peaches had got me. He was lying for me! He was covering up for me, protecting me, and I felt such a rush of gratitude, of amazement because I hadn't said anything about how she was bothering me.

Then I got a look at my face in the cloudy old hall mirror, and saw that my irises were black, my face pale and drawn. I was tuckered out even without canning any peaches.

After she left 1 crept into the living room. "Well, what didja think of her?" I asked.

He glanced up from a tennis match on the television. "Oh, she's okay. Like a lot of these kids, she's got more answers than there are questions. She left you this."

It was a video and Charlie punched off ESPN to play it for me. It showed how to power walk. Heel, toe, head up, pump the arms, heel, toe, breathe, breathe...wore me out just watching it. It was like swimming, only on dry land. "What on earth!" I exclaimed.

Charlie took off his reading glasses, rubbed his nose, then said, "What's this power walking got to do with you?"

"Lord knows."

"Listen, Myrna, I understand that you're out there blowin' off steam, me bein' underfoot all the time after you've had the house to yourself—"

"Oh, Charlie, it's not that."

"Sure it is, and I don't blame you, but I just 'bout got a handle on it, this feeling I've been put out to pasture. I'll get busy soon, quit brooding around. Thought I'd start by painting the kitchen."

"Yeah, but I'm the one who paints the kitchen. You just go on with your tennis match, dear. Besides, I'm out ramblin' around town because I enjoy it, keeping up on the neighborhood."

"Then do it, the hell with power walking."

Charlie was wearing the pill-covered gray-beige cardigan with a cowl collar he'd bought in Butte in 1975, the year we'd visited his sister. His hair's getting gray and fuzzy and kinda sparse, and he looked a bit like a rock, all kinda rounded with wear. My rock. Maybe a little hard and stubborn, maybe even a little mossy, but solid and dependable. Clear-eyed and dear. "Yeah, the hell with power walking," I echoed, feeling suddenly pretty good. And safe.

It's September now, a month I like quite a lot. Many of our visitors go home, in September. Lark has gone home. She left me the wrist weights and video, thank-yous she said, for the company. What she really left me, though, is a new appreciation for my set-up here in Northport. And for Charlie.

I feel...normal. And relieved. My nightmares have returned to the usual. I dream, for example, that Charlie opens a jar of my blackberry jam and it didn't jell, it pours out goopy syrup on his toast; or that I'm marooned on the end of somebody's couch at a Tupperwear party. Meaningless mundane catastrophes that fade as soon as I wake up.

Today the sea is rough, and there's the feel of a storm in the air. Clouds sit so heavy and low I can't see a chevron of geese overhead, but I can hear them honking their way south. The mountain wears the storm like a puffy gray collar. From where I am on the bench, the clear-cut seems to have disappeared; only thing sticking out of the weather up there is the big yarding tree that survived the saw by being harnessed with the cables that dragged out its fellows—a Judas goat of a tree.

I am perverse enough to like bad weather—wind, sheets of rain beating against our old mossy roof. Maybe it's the drop in pressure that elates me.

Charlie's in a good mood, too, these days. He's working on a project. He's using his battery-operated screwdriver to build a shelf for his videos, mostly sports blooper films. Then he says he's going to do some maintenance around the place. I told him there's no hurry, to relax, enjoy his retirement.

There's good news from Tony, too. He's progressing, at least I think it's progress. He has moved to Bend. Bend's a couple of hours farther away than Eugene, out of striking range, so to speak. Charlie pulled some strings and got him a good job in a sheet metal shop. Charlie always told Tony to think sheet metal; heating and air conditioning are the waves of the future.

I'm going to fix Charlie a real meat loaf for supper, although it's part tofu. With enough garlic, onions and catsup, he won't notice. I'll tell you it's a relief to go in the store and not have to look around for Lark. No more tiptoeing, slinking down one aisle and up another, no more dodging the straw hat, the heather-green outfit. I'm free as a bird.

Yet I miss her, too. I find myself saving up crumbs of gossip to tell her next year when she comes back—she said she'd be back. Which is okay by me. I can handle it.

FOUR CHRISTMASES

I. BEGINNINGS

As a holiday, Christmas isn't what it's cracked up to be, Sonya decides. So much hassle before...before what? She can't end her thought with any bright reward, anything with enough energy to get her going.

Finished hacking up the onions, she wipes her eyes, brushes back her hair, turns the cutting board and sets about dicing the rough slices. All she wants is go back to bed, and to sleep through the night. But she's very tired today, every day lately. Her advancing pregnancy has broken her sleep (*Macbeth has broken sleep*, she thinks grimly), this new baby tap-dancing on her bladder so that she has to struggle awake and out of bed to pee every hour on the hour.

Moreover, this intense nocturnal activity ominously signals the arrival of another one with its days and nights mixed up. It had taken months to get Danny sleeping nights, months of staggering around with Danny on her shoulder, on her arm, on her hip; of balancing Danny and a bottle, Danny and a book, Danny and a mixing bowl, a bundle of laundry, Danny and the crossword puzzle. And Frank always in the background grousing about how he had to get some sleep, he had to get up at 7:00 and go to work, while she could go back to bed. Sonya still resents this. Steadily, keeping pace with her spreading girth, Sonya's resentment of Frank has grown. It closes her throat, tightens in her chest like a knot. She would like to talk to someone about it before it swallows her up, but can't think who. Her mother? No, the woman is unapproachable, not to be trusted with this heavy bitterness.

Scraping the onions into a skillet of melting margarine, she thinks, *I should be wrapping presents*. She has bought Frank a power screwdriver, and he has for her a portable mixer (she will wrap them both), but instead she eases herself down at the kitchen table. She pushes aside dirty breakfast dishes, Frank's half-finished crusted oatmeal, Danny's congealed egg and dark banana slices. The smell nauseates her, so she lights a cigarette. But it nauseates her as well, so she grinds it out in Frank's oatmeal. She peers down over her watermelon belly, considers her swollen ankles as if they are not related to her. She is wearing mules, the only footwear she can get on her puffy feet.

But Danny has noticed her disappearance, and begins nattering on the other side of the counter. Knowing that he's winding up to fuss, she calls quickly, "Here, Danny, I'm here." He crawls around the partition and Sonya regards him impatiently. He is fifteen months old, but has not yet begun to walk. His clinging dependence exasperates her. Her mother is right (although Sonya would not admit this to her): she is going to have a tough time managing another baby when this one is so slow developing.

"Come to Mama," she says, and he creeps forward like a giant bug and tries to climb her leg. Babbling to be hoisted up to her lap, he emits an odor, and she knows it's the bubble of gas before his bowel movement. The baby's face reddens as he begins to strain.

"Okay, kiddo, let's go sit on the duck. Come on, Danny—you gotta do this. It's for Mama, hon."

But when she straps him onto the potty seat perched on the toilet, he begins to whimper. At first she talks reassuringly, coos at him; but when he wails, she scolds, then she argues. The child is fair, thin skinned like herself, and he fusses until his face

is blotchy red before she gives up. Immediately off the potty
chair, though, he delivers a diaper full of hard little marbles,
like deer droppings.

He has been constipated, and Sonya admits to herself that
this forced potty training is the reason.

He is also teething: no wonder he fusses, thinks Sonya as she
changes him, then pats aloe vera into red areas around his nose.
His nose has run for six months solid, and Sonya is thinking
allergies. She has just spoken to Frank about having tests done.
She cringes, remembering his reaction. "For Christ's sake!" he'd
roared. "We haven't got the money! We haven't got Danny paid
for yet. God knows how we'll pay for this new one."

"Come on, Danny," she pleads. "Give Mama a break and take
a nap. I've got so much to do." But when she leaves him in the
crib, he shrieks. She considers letting him cry it out—that's
what Frank says to do—but she knows from experience he'll
go on until he's hysterical, until he's convulsed with sobs and
drenched in mucous.

Smelling onions burning in the kitchen, Sonya gathers up the
baby like a sack of laundry and hefts him over the crib bars. "All
right, all right, you win," she grumbles. "Let's have some peace,
willya?" Waddling heavily back to the kitchen with the baby on
her hip, she feels the flimsy trailer creak on its cinder blocks.
She plops the baby on the floor at her feet. The playpen is so far
from being an option it makes him scream even louder—that
they've used it to fence off the Christmas tree.

He settles into dragging pots and pans out of the lower
cabinets while she stuffs the turkey. It's a big bird, twenty-five
pounds. Frank said why cook a small one when a big one is no
more trouble. But now Sonya realizes dinner will be late. Actually, she has no idea when the bird will be done— it's her second
turkey. Last year she cooked the first one until it dissolved in
the pan. She steps around Danny as she lugs the heavy roaster
to the oven, but sighs in relief that at least some of the dinner
preparations have begun.

A sensible plan, Frank's parents coming here for dinner, then

Frank will bring her mother over for Christmas day. Holiday weather in Northport is apt to be too cold and wet for dragging babies around. Moreover, travel logistics have become horribly complicated. Frank has no patience for loading down the truck with high chair, potty chair, diapers, diaper pail, extra clothes, porta-crib, bedding, baby food, and bottles—although Sonya is determined to wean Danny from that hassle, at least, by the time this new one arrives.

Again Sonya settles her dinosaur bulk at the uncleared table for a cigarette break. But it's as if her pressure on the seat cushion activates Danny's bowels, and he now, with his job finished, crawls to her with a full load in his diaper.

This time she's angry. "Why can't you learn!" she shouts and roughly hauls him off. Even seeing the duck makes him scream, but she straps him on it anyway. This is her mother's toilet training instruction, this association exercise. Her mother claims to have trained Sonya herself by the age of one year. "It's possible if you do it right, if you let them know who's boss," her mother says firmly. But Sonya knows she's not as good at being boss as her mother, and that she will have two babies in diapers at once. This prospect induces a shallow panic that tightens just below her throat.

Danny screams himself blotchy again before she relents. It has become a battle of wills, and she knows it, but is committed to this struggle. When she can stand it no longer, she changes him and hauls him back to the kitchen. She puts him on the floor with his pans, and starts to gather up dirty dishes so she can use the table to wrap presents.

Oh, she is tired! She sits, lights her interrupted cigarette. However, this one nauseates her, too. Her heart thuds sickeningly, her palms sweat, and bitter metallic water wells up under her tongue. To counter the attack, she stumbles over to the couch and curls into a fetal position, the only way she can rest now.

In settling herself, she discovers a pocketful of change in the cushions, a quarter, two dimes, a nickel, some pennies. Money for the vacation jar. A weekend away, oh, to die for...but where to go? In silence broken only by the whir of the heater and the drone of rain outside, Sonya muses blurringly... the mountains, the Mackenzie River, Portland, Bend, anywhere away from, well, not away from Danny, of course, nor from Frank. Just away...away.

She dozes, but bolts awake when she hears Frank's pick-up crunch down the gravel lane leading to their single-wide. She flushes with alarm—she's achieved nothing, no packages wrapped, no dishes washed. There's a hint of turkey in the air, but it's hours from being done. Fleetingly she wishes the Court-house, where Frank clerks during the week, was open a full day on Christmas Eve. Nights and weekends he tends his father's gas station, Bosco's Chevron, on 101; between he takes classes in law enforcement at the JC.

Sonya is suddenly struck by the ominous quiet in the trailer. Then she hears the door to the pickup slam, and Frank's hollow footsteps sound on the soggy deck outside it's been raining ten days straight. What is Danny up to? She pushes off the couch and waddles around the kitchen counter. "Danny...oh, no!" she wails.

Danny has gotten into the cupboard under the sink. He has shaken cans of cleanser into puddles of dish detergent and has fingerpainted a sticky mess all over the floor. "Oh, no," cries Sonya again, fighting back tears. But Danny smiles at her from the cat's dish, which has been kept inside because of the rain. He has cat food around his mouth, and has also mixed some into his chemical mess.

"What in hell is going on!" explodes Frank, glaring at them from the door. He has that look around his mouth that tells Sonya he's been drinking. This makes her wary. In their eighteen months of marriage, she has learned not to take him on after a certain point.

"He got in that cupboard under there," she says more crisply, more in-control than she feels. "I told you to put safety catches on those doors. Well, don't just stand there, come here and help me with him." She lowers herself into the mess, the Hindenburg settling to its moorings.

He picks up the baby, who immediately begins to cry. "Can't you at least watch him? That's all you have to do," he says.

"Oh, yeah, all I have to do. All I have to do." The tears rise again; again she stifles them.

"Jesus, look at you," Frank mumbles with distaste. Sonya realizes she's still in her nightgown, over which she's thrown one of his old flannel shirts. But more gently he adds, "Hey, I'm sorry, hon. You feel okay? It smells good in here, like turkey's cooking, but it's awful hot. Let's get some air, clear out the cigarette smoke."

Sonya says from the floor, "I'm okay, but this is not so much fun, you know."

It used to be fun, being with Frank. When Sonya worked split shifts at the phone company (the only job she'd ever had—it lasted four months), Frank would pick her up for lunch and they would talk for hours. Then with a six-pack after work, they'd park out on the jetty and talk and laugh and, yes, make out (back under cover of deep trees on the fringe of the lot) like the passionate teenagers they were. They listened to Stan Kenton, Billy Eckstine, and Fats Domino on the truck radio, and made wild optimistic plans. Frank was going to build his own house. It was to be a low-slung modern marvel with natural wood cabinets, showpiece walls of pink granite hauled in from the Cascades, and a heart-shaped indoor/ outdoor swimming pool. Sonya was going to go to college, to be the architect of this marvel.

Yeah, it had been fun, once. She'd been a queen then, dispensing favors. Now she is a brood sow, a stone around Frank's neck—not that he said that, well, only that once, but he'd been drunk, and afterward had apologized abjectly. But she never forgot it.

Still holding the baby who is whining in a steady drone, Frank squats, shifts Danny's weight so he can throw an arm around her. "No, this isn't much fun. But it'll get better, you wait and see. Let me help, what can I do?"

Sonya makes swipes in the mess with a sponge. Panting with the effort, she gasps, "You can carry this watermelon around awhile. See how you like it." Then she adds softly, because she's so afraid, and so vulnerable: what would she do if he took off? "I'm sorry, too, I'm really sorry. You can change his clothes. Put on his blue crawlers with the plaid shirt your mother gave him." She's wild to get him involved with Danny. She fears Frank has not bonded with the baby. He'd wanted a boy, all right, but a dark, curly-haired a tough handsome bright-eyed bambino like he had been, not this pale whiny clinging vine. She wonders if she herself has accepted the baby. It's another secret, a nightmare.

The baby continues to fuss, leans toward Sonya with his arms out. When Frank rebalances him and heads toward the bedroom, Danny cries in earnest, puddling Frank's shoulder with drool. "Come on, kiddo," Frank says. "Let's get ready for Grandma. You wanna look nice for her, don't you?"

Sonya can tell when Frank has set him down by the increase in crying. Frank shushes him, yells to her over the noise, "Where's the shirt?"

"Third drawer," she yells back.

More shushing, drawers opening, closing. More crying—she pictures Danny blotchy-red, drooling, standing at the crib bars. Later he'll rock himself to sleep, banging his head against the wood, scooting the crib around their room. She sighs, sponges more goo from the cracked linoleum floor into one of the pots Danny dragged out. The turkey really smells now. But she should be further along with dinner preparations, and wonders vaguely about a jell-O salad.

Frank yells, "Why is he crying?"

"How should I know," she answers.

Frank comes to the doorway holding out a small shirt. "Is this the one?" he asks.

"No. It's the blue plaid."

"Then you come here and do this."

She climbs to her feet and lumbers to the bedroom. Just as she'd imagined, Danny stands there sobbing, waiting for clean clothes, balancing on the crib bars. Again Frank asks, "Why is he crying?"

"I don't know."

Frank's face darkens, he compresses his lips. "I'll by God give him something to cry about!" He rushes the baby and delivers a stinging slap on his bare rump.

"Oh, no!" Sonya sobs and grabs at Frank.

He pushes her away and whacks at the baby. Now Danny is hysterical, shuddering with sobs. Red handprints light up his white backside.

"Stop this!" she screams.

Frank is shaken, backs off, rubs his hands over his face. Sonya wraps Danny in a blanket and carries him to the rocking chair. This poor helpless baby, this tender thing. Tears roll down her cheeks. She vows to do a better job, make it up to him. She cradles him, molding him around the lump of the unborn baby which is kicking her on all sides, as if claiming an urgent new priority, as if it were twins. Her grandmother had been a twin...but, no, the doctor would have surely known by now. She croons to Danny in a voice thick with tears and guilt. After a bit his ragged crying settles to long shuddering sobs and his eyes glaze over.

Frank comes to stand by her. "I need a drink. You want one?"

"No." She retracts from his touch.

"Listen," he hisses, "I can have a drink in my own house on Christmas Eve if I want one. You make me feel like a criminal!"

"I'm not the one making you feel bad."

"Sonya, this kid is like having a wild animal in the house that we can't cage, or send to obedience school. I want you to talk to my mother tonight. Ask her...ask her..."

"Ask her what!"

"Ask her why he cries..." he trails off. "God, I don't know, ask her why he isn't walking yet."

But Sonya knows why he isn't walking. Her poor baby is

overloaded with his father's resentment, his mother's fatigue and guilt, and his German grandmother's toilet training. No baby could walk with all that.

Sonya also realizes through a film of fright that she is unsuited for the job she has taken on. She sags under the enormity of it, under a sense of her own sheer inadequacy, and the irreversible damage she has done. Her existence is a prison term, in solitary. But no, she tells herself with a mental shake, no, she's overreacting. She's just horribly tired, what with Christmas and all.

Soon Danny heaves a long sigh, then his breathing settles into deep regularity. He's asleep. Sonya struggles to get up, but finally has to hand the baby off to Frank. He lays him in the crib, and they tiptoe out.

2. PROJECTS

"All right, girls," Sonya announces crisply, "it's time to clear up because I want to set the table." She carefully wipes her hands on her Christmas apron. It is printed with trees upon which sequins are glued, to simulate ornaments. It was last year's Christmas gift from the twins, and she wears it to please them.

Angie and Vera, named for their grandmothers, murmur a bit, then gather up their materials. They are putting the finishing touches on Christmas angels folded from old Reader's Digests, surprises for their namesakes. Just then the dining room door from the garage opens and their older brother comes to stand by the table. He fingers a pair of scissors, touches Vera's angel. It has been spray-painted gold, and has red wings cut from construction paper.

"Ma," squeals Vera, her dark eyes snapping, "tell Danny to leave my stuff alone."

Sonya looks over from the candied sweet potatoes she's dotting with marshmallows. "Don't be silly, Vera," she says. "He's not going to bother your decoration." But she's not sure: strange things do happen to the girls' toys—pieces to games go missing, bike tires become flat, skate keys disappear, tiny slits are cut in doll clothes. Of course these could all be accidents.

Sonya turns to Danny and smiles. "How's the secret project coming, hon?" It's hush-hush, his Christmas surprise for her, but Frank has let slip that it's a bird feeder. It isn't going well, and Frank has complained bitterly about Danny's awkwardness, his carelessness, his lack of interest. Sonya will be glad when it is finished: something in the garage—the sawdust or the spray paint—irritates Danny's allergies and he has been wheezing and coughing at night. Actually, she will be relieved when Christmas itself is finished and they can go back to their ordinary lives. For all of them, ordinary life is school. The kids share a sixth grade class (Danny has been held back a year), Frank is studying for the bar exam, and she is taking bookkeeping classes at a trade school downtown. "So, you about to finish?" she asks again, still smiling.

But Danny says sourly, clicking the scissors, "I would if Dad would get off my back. He's always pissed."

"Don't use that word, Danny. What's the matter?"

"He says I left his saw out to rust, and I didn't."

Angie bears off her angel, identical to Vera's except it is sprayed a glittering silver. She throws over her shoulder, "Well, he can't blame us. We never go near his tools." With the twins, it's always "us" or "we." It's always a team.

Sonya, sensing a quarrel, interposes quickly, "Now, now, that's enough. I need you girls to get out the good placemats, and Danny, you run to the store for a few things. Milk, whipping cream, sweet pickles, cranberry sauce...but, let's see. Maybe you should all go—"

"Yeah, and I know why, too," smirks Angie. "You want us to keep an eye on Danny's sticky fingers, make sure he doesn't steal anything again."

Danny's pale face reddens and he sputters, "Shut up, goody two-shoes. Ma, make her shut up."

"Mother," says Vera primly, "has Danny had his Ritalin?"

Sonya's face burns with resentment. These little devils know exactly how to get to Danny. They nip open little holes in his self esteem and bleed him dry, and Sonya cannot stop them. As a result, she rushes to protect Danny, and says furiously, "You know he doesn't take that anymore. Of course you're not going along to keep an eye on Danny. It's to help carry things."

The shoplifting experiment, after all, had been an isolated incident. She had dragged Danny down to return the snorkel set and apologize to the manager. Moreover, Frank had talked to Danny. Very harshly, true; but between them the point had been hammered home.

They still don't want to go, but she bribes them with dimes for ice cream (Frank would object, this close to dinner). Then she watches them walk down the driveway, Danny shambling along, his shaggy blond head bobbing like a chicken's with his "tough guy" gait. Poor Danny—he is not tough, and this act underlines his frailty. In contrast, the girls are self-assured, as smooth as a pair of black olives. Sonya suffers a pang of jealousy: they never need her if they have each other. Getting into them, between them, would be like inserting a knife between blocks of the Great Pyramid at Giza—there's simply no space.

She sighs with relief. So handy living close to stores after the isolation of the trailer in the woods, although this tract house in a Newberry development has as much texture as white bread. She hurries to light a forbidden cigarette, the real reason she wanted them all out of the house. Flipping the stove hood onto high, she smokes greedily. She'd love to quit, but can't with finals so close. Danny smokes, too: she has track of the packs he snags from her cartons in the service porch. This doesn't worry her as much as the gin and scotch he siphons from Frank's bottles, which he then waters back to original levels. But all boys experiment, don't they?

To reassure herself, Sonya glances around the room, savoring the solidity, the prosperity they'd hit on. They'd had a bit of help from Frank's father who'd died and left them a little money. But mainly their own efforts have achieved the solid oak table with matching chairs on the bright oval rug, the spinet in the corner (the girls practice faithfully), the desk stacked with Frank's texts, and her own accounting books. Just looking at her books raises Sonya's spirits. She loves the sanctity of numbers, the thrill when credit and debit columns balance. It's something to really depend on, something sure with no fuzzy gray areas, no guessing as with people. With kids.

Yes, they are actually finally getting somewhere after a disastrous beginning—three babies within a year and a half. No one's fault but her own. She'd never caught on to the tricks of the slimy diaphragm. Thank goodness that mess is over; now she's safe with tubes tied securely. So what can go wrong? If only Danny ...if only Danny holds together...for Sonya knows there is something not solid within the boy, something that she either caused, or donated to in his genetic make-up. She is uneasy, wary.

She stubs out her cigarette quickly when Frank's station wagon swings into the driveway. He comes in, frowns, then says, "You've been smoking again."

"And you've been drinking," she retorts.

"So what? You know there's always booze at the office party." Then he adds, "Have you seen the mess in the garage?"

"No. What mess?"

"He's got glue all over, and the top is off the tube so it's all dried up. He's left my paint brushes to dry, too. He never takes care of anything. And he's used my good chisel to pry something and there's a nick in it."

"Well, this project was your idea. Why do you get him into something that's over his head?"

"Because every man needs to know how to use tools, and he's got to learn. Where is he?"

"He's gone to the store with the girls." Quickly, hoping to divert him, she says, "Your mother called, wanted to know your shirt size. Maybe she'll get you that Pendleton you liked down at the Emporium." Their own presents to each other are still likely to be dull, based on need rather than pizzazz. This year

under their great fat Christmas tree, she has for him a Black &
Decker 1.5 hp router; he has for her a food processor to chop
up the onions, peppers, and tomatoes for the spicy Italian sauces
he loves. The girls are getting Magic Make-up Mirrors; Danny
a Heath Kit walkie talkie set. This was over Sonya's objection.
"But he'll have to put it together," she had said. "You know he
hates that." Moreover, he has no friends; who will he talk to
on it? "Well, here come the girls now," she says, "but I don't
see Danny."

They watch the twins march up the driveway, heads up, shoulders back, victorious soldiers in the army of what's Right and
Proper. They burst into the kitchen, plop groceries down, and
rush to Frank. "Daddy! You gotta see our Christmas angels,
come look at our angels!"

As they tug Frank off, Sonya hears him say, "You girls are the
only Christmas angels I'll ever need to see. How's my sweet
hearts?" Sonya feels for Frank a thin sliver of contempt to let
these little snips lead him around. He has no judgment.

She calls after them, "Where's Danny?" Sotto voce, "Should
we tell her?" Then louder, "He's coming, Ma. He'll be right here.
We told him not to, but he doesn't listen to us."

"What? What?"

Just then Danny comes in with an armload of flowers, winter
roses. He sniffs the air. "You been smokin', Ma?"

Besides her cigarette smoke, the air is now heavy with the
turkey cooking. But Sonya smells only the roses and the fresh
green scent of bruised stems. "Danny, oh, Danny, you didn't
pick those from Mrs. Jorgenson's hedge, did you?" They'd just
had a run-in with her over Danny untying her dog. Danny had
explained to Frank, "Dad, I can't stand seeing that poor puppy
on a three-foot rope, day in, day out."

Frank had said, "I know, Dan, but it's her dog. You've got no
right interfering with her private property."

"She doesn't deserve a dog."

More sternly, "Dan, did you hear what I said? Stay out of her
yard! How she treats her dog is no concern of ours."

"It is too!" he'd thundered back. Frank had gone on arguing with him, with Sonya wringing her hands. She hated them to argue. Why couldn't Danny just leave well enough alone!

Now here he is with the woman's flowers! "Why, Danny? Why?" Sonya moans. "You know you can't go in her yard and pick her flowers."

He thrusts the blooms at her, the ends roughly sawed with a pocket knife. They're for you, Ma. She won't miss them. You don't have any flowers and she has too many. She never picks them."

"But Danny, we don't have any right to her private property. What's hers is hers, not ours."

"She can't own things like flowers, or dogs. They just happen to be under her control, but she doesn't own them. Take these roses, they grow right next to the street. It's like saying she owns the street, or birds that fly through her yard. Or my Frisbee. Re member when it landed in her stupid old petunias and she wouldn't let me get it?"

Oh, yes. And Sonya remembers that someone soaps Mrs. Jorgenson's windows on Halloween, someone orders her pizzas from Little Caesar's, and someone steals her outside Christmas lights with disheartening regularity. But it could be anybody because all the kids hate Mrs. Jorgenson. Even the girls hate her, and Sonya doesn't like her much, either.

Frank appears in the doorway between the girls, an arm around each. "What's going on?" he asks carefully.

"Danny picked some flowers, big federal deal," Sonya snaps, going for a vase. Better to take the bull by the horns.

"Whose flowers?"

"Don't ask. You already know whose."

Frank starts forward. "Danny, how many times have I told you—"

"Not now, Frank," Sonya interposes.

He turns on her. "Don't get between me and my son, Sonya. You always undermine my authority. That's a big part of the problem. Now, we're going to get something straight, for once."

Then, "Danny," he's bending into Danny's face, "you don't touch anyone else's belongings." He grabs Danny's shirt, shakes him. "You don't touch anyone else's things."

Danny squirms away. "I didn't touch her things, Dad. A thing is dead, a lump of concrete. A flower's alive—"

"No, Dan," shaking him harder, "a thing is her stuff, any of her stuff." His face is now white. "You leave her stuff alone. Alone. You hear me?"

"Frank!" Just then the phone rings. "Get the phone, Frank."

But Angie has scampered off. She calls from the hall, "Dad, it's Mrs. Jorgenson." She draws the name out, imbuing a dire tone.

Frank strides off, and Sonya hisses, "Go to your room, Danny." He slinks out, but there's a bit of a strut, too. He's defeated but defiant, and Sonya's heart turns over. She's angry with him, and afraid she wants to yell at him, "Why do you have to take him on! You know you can't win, not yet, anyway." The girls have watched the whole scene cold-eyed. It amazes Sonya that they are not more sympathetic. Is there no childhood bond between her children at all? Are they complete strangers?

From the hall phone Sonya overhears Frank's side of the conversation, phrases like "it'll never happen again," "certainly make this up to you," "yes, winter roses are special," "I understand your anger," and "always a difficult age, yes." When he's finished, he lays the receiver down gently enough, but then stomps off toward Danny's room. There's more yelling and some scuffling. In the kitchen Sonya wishes for a cigarette, longs to interfere, considers creating a diversion: she could burn herself, drop something, send the girls off to get Frank. But finally, after a spate of deafening silence, Danny's doc slams, and Frank reappears. Now his face is flushed an angry beet red, and his mouth is a clenched line. "Well?" asks Sonya.

"He's not getting any dinner, and he's grounded for a month."

"Oh, no!" she cries. "It's Christmas Eve, your mother's coming. This is too much." She flings a towel into the sink. "Where's your Christmas spirit? Don't you have a heart at all?"

"Listen, he's got to learn! He's not sitting at this table, and that's all! Now, stay out of this." She averts her eyes while he pours himself a large scotch from the watered bottle.

The tense evening frays everyone's nerves except Mrs. Bosco's. Since her husband's death, she has become lost in her own fuzzy world. Sonya thinks that is not a bad place to be, considering the poisonous atmosphere around her table. She is white cold angry with Frank for this scene, is convinced he picks on Danny to get to her. However, the rest of them play-act the jolly family-at-dinner with Danny's chair conspicuously empty. Frank tells his mother Danny isn't feeling well, and the old woman accepts this blankly.

"Why don't you tell her the truth," Sonya hisses as she passes him potatoes over the vase of stolen roses she has used as a centerpiece to pique him. He merely glares, then goes on prating neutral nonsense, more white noise than real conversation. Sonya's ears swivel like a satellite dish when Danny's door opens and he pads to the bathroom, then back again. He has begun to cough, and she knows he'll have an asthma attack tonight. The girls chatter, more background noise.

The meal gotten through, they gather around the tree for gift exchange. Sonya has wrapped for Mrs. Bosco an electric blanket she's complained of the cold lately. But the old woman stares stupidly when she shakes the electric cord loose from the fleece. Frank explains advantages blithely, but Sonya knows the woman is too old to incorporate new gadgets into her lifestyle. They'll get this back, unused. The folded angel from Angie gets more response, as does a collage of family shots that Frank has mounted in a frame.

The last few years the woman's gifts to them have come from the dismantling of her own household. This time it's a rich antique ivory damask tablecloth with matching napkins, for a rectangular table. Sonya's is round. Frank does get the Pendleton shirt, a red plaid. Sonya thinks he'll be quite handsome in it with his dark good looks. His curly hair shows only a bit of gray at the temples, and Sonya realizes, through her filter of anger, that women find him attractive. The girls unwrap fuzzy pink parkas, and Danny's present is set aside for later. But Sonya guesses it's another car or airplane model to glue together. She sees Frank's hand in this: he is determined to get Danny interested in his own boyhood hobby. Danny hates models.

At the end of the evening, Frank guides his mother's two-tone Rambler out of the driveway as carefully as a sailor would a jet on an aircraft carrier. Sonya sees a day coming when the old woman quits driving and gives them the car, too. After the girls go to bed, Frank works on the rest of his scotch. When he's sucked the bottle dry, he stretches out, begins to snore open-mouthed on the sofa. Sonya stares at him, wondering how he can sleep with her targeting him with hostility. Then she glances at her accounting books on the desk, and feels an urgent need to get to her studies. Someday she'll land a job, and get the hell out of here, take Danny with her. She'll show Frank. He'll be sorry he acted such a jerk.

She nurses her fantasies until Frank has reached coma-like depths. Then she tiptoes out to the kitchen and puts together dinner for Danny. She has heard his tight cough, and has caught a hint of his incense. He burns it to cover the smell of his cigarette smoke.

She selects tidbits carefully for his plate—a slice of white turkey breast surgically trimmed of fat, a scoop of mashed potatoes dabbed with butter—Danny hates gravy—a spoon of peas, a roll smeared with honey. She adds a slice of pecan pie, her favorite, and picks off large pecans from the rest of the pie to stick on his piece. Earlier Frank had chided her about this pie, said it was no wonder she was getting fat. In Danny's milk she swirls chocolate syrup, the only way he'll drink it. He's always been a picky eater.

She lines a tray with one of her new/old damask napkins, and slips down the hall, one criminal abetting another. Danny's room is fogged with exotic smoke. Sprawled in his bed, which is rumpled into a sort of nest, he looks very young and fragile, a sickly chick struggling to survive. His blond hair is thin and straggly, his brows and lashes invisible in his pale face. His eyes are bloodshot—either that or he's been crying (which he would never admit). He is roughly snapping into pieces a plastic model of a bi-plane. "Phew," she whispers, "let's get some air in here. You're going to make yourself sick."

"Who cares?" he mumbles blackly. He looks up from the rubbish he's made of his model to stare at a poster of the ocean featuring shafts of sunlight slanting through blue-green water. A school of brilliant orange fish undulates around giant feathery plumes of seaweed swaying in an invisible current.

This poster is one of the few things in the room Danny values. He'd expressed an interest in deep sea diving and Sonya had pleaded with Frank for scuba lessons, for Christmas. But Frank had grumbled, "The way that kid's accident prone, he'll go out there and drown. Besides, those scuba shops get you hooked, then they stick it to you for this or that. It's an expensive racket, and I'm not paying. Why can't he make stuff like other kids? That's what I had to do, and all by myself, too. My old man was too busy making a living to mollycoddle me."

"How about some dinner, Danny," Sonya says. "Aren't you hungry, hon?"

He barks, "I hate him. Why'd you marry him?"

"Now, now," she soothes. "You'll get over this, and he will, too." Sonya doesn't believe this herself, but feels she must play the part of go-between. "Thing is, Danny, you've got to leave Mrs. Jorgenson's stuff alone."

"I do leave her stuff alone. She's a witch, anyway."

"I mean leave her dog, her flowers, and her Christmas lights—"

He moans, "Ah, come on, Ma. Not you, too!"

"Okay, sorry, dear. Here, eat some dinner. See this nice damask napkin? It's Grandma's present. She gave us a whole set. There's something out there for you, too."

"Big deal." However, he sits up straighter and begins to pick at his food.

"Atta boy," croons Sonya, as if addressing a sick puppy. "I'll come back for the dishes in a bit."

Returning down the hall, she sees a crack of light under the girls' door. Sonya peeks in, but they're both asleep, cradling their new parkas. Such an aggressive pink, Sonya thinks, then wonders if it will match their new recital dresses. She softly opens the closet door, pulls on the light and searches through their clothes. She steps on a sack, hears the tinkle of glass breaking. What could this be? The girls are compulsively neat, not likely to leave things lying around. She opens the bag...it is full of tiny white outdoor Christmas lights—like the ones Mrs. Jorgenson is missing...aha! Sonya is momentarily stunned, then immensely, horribly pleased. Why, these little devils! She grimaces. Wait till she tells Frank what his "angels" have been up to! It is the most delightful event of the evening.

But the next morning when she'd told him about her discovery, he merely chuckled and said mildly, "Those little scamps!" He was drawn and pale; pouring coffee, his hand shook.

Sonya demanded roughly, "Well, aren't you going to have a fit? Aren't you going to run around and yell and grab their clothes and shake them and ground them for a month? You would if it was Danny."

"Yeah, but Danny always gets caught. He sets himself up. The girls are, well, smooth. Winners. Besides, nobody likes Mrs. Jorgenson. She deserves what she gets."

"If that's not a lawyer talking! That's cynical! You are so unfair, I don't believe you! What kind of value system do you operate with? Those girls drag you around like you've got a ring in your nose—your little darlings!"

Sonya was enraged, nonplused. She never again confided much to him about the children. But then too, after Christmas, with relief, they all went back to pursuing their own projects, too busy to bother with the hassle they'd made of their family life. It was like stuffing something nasty—a used diaper, or crab butter—down deep in the trash so you wouldn't come into contact with it again when you emptied the can.

Mrs. Jorgenson's dog went missing after the holidays—it chewed through the rope, disappeared, and Danny celebrated its freedom.

The bird feeder Danny gave Sonya was mounted on a pole in the yard—the trees had been clear cut when the development went in—but no bird ever went near it. Sonya told Danny it was because they kept cats.

That summer Sonya put the unbuilt Heath Kit walkie-talkies in a garage sale, and meant to use the money to buy Danny an aquarium. But in September she got too busy with classes and forgot about it. She would have sold his present from Grandma Bosco, too—it was an expensive radio controlled model of a B-52, the military airplane they were using to carpet-bomb Vietnam. But Danny had fiddled with it, had lost too many parts, and it was worthless. As a boy Frank had always wanted such a thing, so Sonya took an evil delight telling him she'd dumped it.

3. JOBS

"So what time is Danny getting here?" Frank is wandering around the kitchen. It is not a question, but a complaint, a criticism. "We're not that far from Coos Bay, only a hundred miles or so. Easy drive in two hours."

"Frank," says Sonya crisply, "are you going to stand around and get in my way, or are you going to let me finish with this turkey?" When he moves aside, she works efficiently on the bird.

Efficiency is her mode these days. She has her life firmly under her control. She has quit smoking, does a Jane Fonda tape every morning before going to work, and watches her weight on a scale like the one the doctor uses. The reason for this iron discipline: when they moved back to Northport a few years ago, she opened her own accounting firm, which succeeded beyond her dreams. Frank was City Attorney until his heart attack last year; now he works part-time from an office in the house. Sonya refers to it, behind his back, with an arch smile, as his "puttering around."

Besides this role reversal—she whisking away in her Mercedes for the office every morning, he sclocking around the house in his slippers—they have changed in more subtle ways. Her step is firm and brisk in her sensible but stylish shoes; she walks with her shoulders back, her head high and steady enough to balance a dictionary. She wears her hair, now showing artful touches of gray, in a deceptively simple style. Its upkeep dictates a standing appointment with her hairdresser every Friday at three—a sought after time that shows her clout in the community.

Sonya has worked on herself as if she were an extra job. She has schooled herself to be the kind of woman who can run a meeting. She knows Robert's Rules of Order, and how to make her voice and opinions heard in a roomful of people. She even talks of a run at the mayor's office—she has served on City Council twice and there has never been a woman mayor in Northport before.

Frank, in contrast, has let himself become shaggy, soft, and threadbare. He deals with tradesmen and repair people in conciliatory tones. He clips coupons and drives all the way to Newberry to redeem them. Now he does Christmas, the shopping, wrap ping, the cards—he jots chatty notes to their relatives in distant cities. This pleases Sonya; she enjoys thinking of him fighting crowds, fussing with ribbons, and waiting in line at the post office. Christmas has become bearable, with Frank running in circles instead of her.

Some things, however, don't change: she still tackles the turkey, and he tackles Danny. "So, where is he?" Frank asks again in a plaintive tone.

"Now, Frank," Sonya replies lightly, "you know Danny. He gets sidetracked."

Danny works as a "salvage consultant" in the harbor at Coos

Bay. He scuba-dives to clean boat bottoms, retrieve lost gear, and repair docks and boat slips. Now that the twins have been launched—they received Master's degrees in music from a college near San Francisco, and are in Germany on scholarships (their first Christmas away from home; Frank misses them dreadfully)—it was deemed possible to buy Danny a boat of his own. Danny said that was all he needed for total happiness, and Sonya badly wanted him to have it. To think of Danny as happy would lift a great weight from her psyche.

Frank continues to fidget, and Sonya murmurs, "Easy, dear. You know what the doctor said about nerves and high blood pressure." Her tone is consoling, condescending, calculated to soothe him, as one would a temperamental child. There is much buried anger in this, which Sonya has used to fuel her career. "Besides, what's your hurry? All the two of you do is argue."

"Sonya, you don't understand the bond between a man and his son. Besides, I need him here to watch the game with me."

"Danny hates football."

"No, he doesn't. It's UCLA and Georgia Tech, and he'll love it."

She chuckles wryly. "Why would he love that?"

"UCLA is rated #1 in offense, Georgia Tech #1 in defense, the best of both coming together. Plus the Heisman Trophy winner and the runner-up...oh, never mind...believe me, Danny will love it."

Sonya is not convinced but says "Of course, dear. Now go sit down. He'll be here soon." Frank returns to his pre-game warm ups and she to her turkey.

Alone, she contemplates her kitchen. It's an oak, copper, tile state-of-the-art creation overlooking the Pacific Ocean, and it fills her with a warm glow of satisfaction. She loves this house; this is her house. It contains none of Frank's nonsense, no imported rock walls, no greenhouse with grow-lights for winter tomatoes, no indoor/outdoor pool that neither of them would get in. She is married to this house with its cathedral ceilings and gray-stained beams and soothing open feeling of space more than she is to Frank. This is the way it goes, she thinks: women of a certain age are like cats. It is place they bond to, not people. Especially people who aren't going to last very long. Frank has perceived this change in her; he has also perceived his own tentative existence. For he allows her to interrupt him, to contradict; he puts up with her correcting him in public, in meetings: it is easier than a fight. He is no longer up to a fight. Sonya wishes her mother could see this power shift—the woman had thought Frank overbearing and pompous—but she's been gone several years now. All their parents are gone. Sonya and Frank are the senior generation, and Sonya is secretly surprised that their wisdom does not match this status.

But now with Danny coming, the house is not enough to lighten Sonya. She feels heavy with ominous foreshadowing, as if waiting for the third act in a Shakespearean tragedy (she just finished *Macbeth* in an enrichment course at the extension JC). She knows from experience that Danny will arrive wide-eyed, artificially breezy, accompanied by a large louty dog, to loose into this house of cats. He will carry in boxes of inappropriate gifts, part of it food. He follows a specialized diet, like a faddish child. He'll bring unsalted rice cakes, raw nuts, wheat germ, unsulphured dried apricots—as if what Sonya serves is unwholesome. Their conversation will be remorselessly impersonal before settling in on the critical evaluations that pinpoint their own shortcomings. Who will start the ball rolling? Sonya compresses her lips, determined it will not be herself. But the truth of it is that as soon as Danny arrives, she takes up again that old failed life.

She feels her stomach tighten. Not that Danny is demanding, oh, no. It is a self-inflicted guilt cycle. For she is the one who dredges up miscues, defeats, mistakes: the time she left him alone in his carseat while she ran into the bank; the Superman costume she sewed for him that drew jeers from his classmates; the tennis lessons she forced him into, then watched him jerk and twist around on the court like a grasshopper in a hot skillet—just because she had school-girl crush on the instructor.

Does Danny remember these tortures? Sonya hopes not. She stares out the window of her dream kitchen, searching the ocean for answers. She draws deep breaths, focuses the cross hairs of her attention on a lone cormorant in the surf. This she learned in Tai Chi, also offered at the extension JC.

It is now halftime in the game, and Frank wanders out to the kitchen. "So, where is he?" he demands. Turkey aroma fills the air; soon it will be done.

But Sonya replies mildly, "Frank, you know what they say about a watched pot..."

Just then a truck scarred with patches of primer and rust clatters up the driveway. It coughs and jerks a few times before dying. Danny uncoils from the cluttered cab. He is taller than Frank, but very thin. He clucks encouragement to his dog-of-the month, a Lab/shepherd mix that he lets make a quick circuit of the yard. It pees copiously on Frank's rhododendrons. Danny yells for it when it takes off after a cat.

Watching from the door, Frank mumbles, "Would you look at that! Where's the sandals?" Danny wears his blond hair below his shoulders, and a Levi jacket over a purple tee shirt tie-dyed to resemble a sunburst. His pants are frayed bell bottoms.

"Now, be nice, Frank." Sonya steps out to deliver the ritual hug. "Right on time, dear," she says brightly. "I just now took the turkey out of the oven. Here, let us help you unload. Oh, you're so thin, Danny. Are you eating right?" She releases him, shocked with the feel of his hard body, the sharp ribs through his shirt.

But he hears this as criticism. "Of course I eat right, Ma. Probably better than you do." He smiles aggressively.

Frank says, "Geez, what kept you? Game's half over." This draws Danny's attention away from Sonya, and she is relieved. "Dad, I told you it'd be afternoon. You don't listen to me. What game?"

Frank recites a summary of key plays while they drag in Danny's gear. Besides the usual chaos of food items, there are unwieldy packages for under the tree which this year is a scotch pine in a planter, Sonya's effort to be "green." While her men distribute these prizes, she escapes to the kitchen. She is ashamed of this cowardice; at the same time she rejoices in having something to do. She also rejoices there's wine with dinner—Frank is allowed one glass which smoothes him out remarkably. (It smoothes her out, too, but this is not something she wants to admit, or wants them to notice: a chink in her armor.)

They float through the meal on neutral topics: growth along Highway 101, the weather, the availability and cost of energy. Suddenly they splash into dangerous waters—President Carter's inflation problems. "If he'd just let business take care of business," Frank begins.

Danny sits up (he's been slouched over his food). "At least Carter has had some business experience, Dad. Ford, Nixon, Eisenhower, and this new clown Reagan, none of them has any business background."

Frank glowers. "Carter knows only peanuts—"

Sonya jumps in. "Have more turkey, Frank. The doctor said white meat—"

"Nah. I'm going to watch the rest of the game." He scrapes back his chair. Then to Danny, "Come on, it's third quarter."

Danny gives him a hard mutinous look. "I don't want to watch the game, Dad. I need to work on my truck. It needs a tune-up bad, you heard it out there in the driveway. I don't have any place to work on it at home." This startles Sonya; she thinks of this house, which he barely lived in, as his home. "Let me have the keys to the garage, Dad."

Frank frowns. "You sure you know what you're doing out there?"

"Oh, okay, Dad, I see where you're comin' from. Okay, man, just forget it." Danny bangs his chair under the table. He begins to cough. Sonya turns to glare at Frank.

"Dan, wait a minute. Here." Frank throws him the keys, and stomps back to the TV, his shoulders sagging. He is defeated, but victorious, too. He has Danny in a no-win situation.

Danny drags on work coveralls, they read MIKE'S JIFFY-LUBE on the pocket, and disappears into the garage. Sonya retreats to the kitchen to put together a package of leftovers for when he goes home. She is in an uproar. Of course she hadn't wished for them to get into a fight, God forbid one of those fist fights like before Danny left permanently for Coos Bay...but a bit of a dust-up...no, not that; a mature discussion would at least inject some real meaning into this paralyzing atmosphere. She's angry at them both, they are still stubbornly unmanageable at Christmas when she wants...well, she doesn't know what she wants, but she is sure that this is not it.

She slashes away at the turkey, then gathers up scraps for the dog. She opens the door into the garage, almost stumbling over the pooch puddled on the step like an oil spill. The open door lets in Danny's blaring radio. He's listening to the Beatles, Three Dog Night, and Donovan—music that Sonya likes, too. Frank yells from the den. Tell him to turn that down, willya?"

She begins to relay the message, then realizes that she is playing the role of go-between again. So she returns to her left overs, torn between ignoring the whole thing, or yelling back to Frank to do it himself, or going out quickly to keep Frank out of the garage. Oh, yes, she thinks clattering a knife into the sink, this is exactly where they left off last time! She's sure she hates both of them.

They come together again for gift exchange when the game is over and chores are done. Since Frank does the Christmas shopping, he gives himself Sonya—a plastic recliner wrapped in plastic, with built-in "magic fingers" massage and heating unit. When he plops in it and smiles, she thinks wickedly that all it lacks is the ability to play Dean Martin warbling 'That's Amore" when he farts into the cushions. Frank gives her a food dehydrator, a thing she has no use for whatsoever. She plans to return it for a word processor.

She and Frank are no longer united in their efforts for Danny. Sonya presents a certificate from a Coos Bay pet shop for a saltwater aquarium, the settling of an old score. In criticism of this (Frank sees an aquarium as burdensome and useless as a Grandfather clock, or a giant rubber plant), Frank has bought him a floor jack. Danny trundles it around—it rolls like a grocery cart stuck on a lettuce leaf—then kicks it a few times with his desert boots.

The twins (everyone has been careful about mentioning them, not wanting to draw a parallel between them and Danny, between success and failure), the twins have sent presents from Germany. Sonya gets a set of nesting dolls, Danny a foot-tall beer stein (he doesn't drink, has just completed AA's twelve-step program), and Frank the splashiest gift of all, a Black Forest cuckoo clock.

"By the way," says Danny gazing at it, "did you ever know it was Vera who overwound your eight-day clock and broke it? You blamed me. And it was Angie who burned BOSCO into the dining room table with a wood-burning iron. She stole Mrs. Jorgenson's rake, too, not me."

From his chair, Frank remarks mildly, "You don't say. Well, you did your share."

"Remember that picnic when the crows ate the top off the cake and you thought it was me?"

"We sure picked on you, didn't we?" says Frank sarcastically.

Sonya says quickly, "I do remember that crazy cat we had that shimmied up the pole to the bird feeder and stretched out its flat top for his sun baths. Remember that, Danny?"

But Danny isn't sidetracked. "Remember the Easter egg hunt in the yard when you said I stole all the eggs and it was the gulls?" He gets up, paces around the floor jack. "Dad, it's just that you program a loser by the things you say and do. This guy in my EST group was explaining how it works."

Sonya says firmly, "I think we ought to finish our presents. Here, Frank, this is for you, from Danny." It is an enormous clump wrapped in the Sunday comics, secured with duct tape. Frank uses his pocket knife on it and exposes a collection of pale green glass balls about the size of cantaloupes, attached to a corded net.

"Excellent!" pronounces Sonya. "You know what they are, Frank?" She knows, from a beachcombing class. "Dad, these are Japanese fishing floats. They wash up in the bay after a storm. And this net is old. New ones are nylon. I thought you could hang it in your office, a wall decoration."

Frank leans forward, a bemused look on his face. "Yes, this is nice, Dan." He rubs his chin reflectively.

It's Sonya's turn. She unwraps a heavy basketball-sized package that turns out to be a rock. "Wow, Danny! An Indian grinding stone. This is a real artifact."

"I found it in the bay, too. It's prehistoric, from when Indians summered on the Coast to harvest shellfish. There used to be hundreds of Indians, by the size of the shell middens. Before the Whites pushed them out to starve."

Frank leans forward. "Now, wait a minute. I don't want any lectures about how rotten we were to the Indians. It's survival of the fittest, is all."

"Oh, sure. I'd like to see you survive out there."

"Well, I don't have to. I'm in here because I used my head, not my back. Not like you're doing."

Danny draws a wheezy breath, getting set to fire back, but Sonya jumps up and yells, "Fer chrissake, I want this stopped now!" (Her assertiveness training group would be proud of her). When they both gape, she goes in a commanding tone, "Now, it's dessert time. Who wants whipped cream on their pie?"

Despite knowing none of them wants the damned thing, she rushes out to slice up the pecan pie. Then she watches Danny pick the nuts off his piece. "They make my mouth hurt," he says.

"For God's sake, why didn't you tell me? For years I've been loading you down with extra pecans."

"I did tell you. You don't listen to me."

Frank has turned on the TV for game analysis, and she stonily watches the meaningless discussion thinking of years of wasted pecans. She feels tense and worn out, wishes it were already tomorrow so Danny would go home and they could return to their routines. Christmas is the pits.

Later that evening Danny did go home. He threw the floor jack in his truck and peeled out for Coos Bay, despite his earlier plan to stay overnight. It was because Frank got on him about his hair. He said Danny looked like a girl from the back, and talked to him in a high wheedling voice. Then he went on about how Danny could save a lot of time blow-drying, creme rinsing, and styling by getting it cut short. Finally Danny barked that he'd taken enough crap for one day and burned rubber on the driveway making his getaway. Frank remarked sarcastically that at least the tune-up had been a success. When he first got here, that piece of shit couldn't get out of its own way," was how he put it.

Sonya scolded him. "Why do you rag him so much about his hair?"

"What do you care?" He answered mildly, "All I did was point out how much time he could save by wearing it short. That's what you tell me, that you keep your hair short to save time. Remember when you used to wear it long, to please me? But you said it was too much hassle."

He gave her a wide-eyed guileless look and whistled out to the garage for more firewood. Then he burst back in, furious. "Have you seen that mess out there?" he yelled.

"What mess?"

"All my tools in the wrong place, a coffee can full of oil, dirty rags stuffed here and there. A fire hazard, that's what he left me!"

"Oh, for heaven's sake. Calm down. That doesn't sound like a fire hazard to me. You make such a big deal out of the garage. Like it was a temple or something holy."

"If he'd done that in your kitchen, you'd have a fit!"

"Now, Frank, you're going to make yourself sick," she soothed while he glared at her. "Why don't you relax in your chair. See if the news is on. I'll get the firewood, if it's going to upset you."

But later, alone in the kitchen, she admitted to herself that she would have had a fit if Danny had run amok out here. However, she'd not admit this to Frank. The fact was, she didn't admit much to him anymore. The less he knew, the better. Knowledge was ammunition, and she wanted him unarmed.

If Danny had run amok in her kitchen, as he had in Frank's garage (because he really had), wouldn't there be an element of revenge in it? Wasn't he trying to pay back the misery of earlier Christmases, that awful one before the twins were born, those muddled messes when they were growing up. All of them growing up together? Oh, she'd made so many mistakes raising him! She'd been a horrible mother, she had no maternal instinct at all. It had been criminal for her to have babies, especially three so close together.

She hunched her shoulders up tighter around her ears—she had been so tense all night. This marriage, it was a poor thing she and Frank had created from their union. But at least they'd stayed together, had avoided the epidemic of divorce that had cut down so many of their friends. Surely that was good, much better for the children, wasn't it? Sonya wasn't sure. But, as her process-oriented psychology group had pointed out, she'd done her best, hadn't she? Hadn't she?

She wasn't even sure about that, but it was Christmas, a time that always unhinged her. She'd feel better in a week or two. Tax season always raised her spirits.

4. FAMILY LEGEND

Christmas again! It seems to roll around five or six times a year now. But Sonya doesn't care anymore, for she has given up celebrating the holidays. She has decided Christmas is an archaic, even barbaric ritual, geared to helping stores clear stock before inventory. It is a pawn in the deadly consumer society-global economy game, and she will not play it.

Of course this radical abdication is easier now that it's only she and Danny to get together. For Frank has been gone almost a year; he'd had a heart attack and passed away in his beloved chair just as the Bills were squaring off against the Cowboys in the Super Bowl. He had loved the Dallas Cowboys, relished the comeback of "America's team." When they'd stomped the Bills, it must have burst his poor heart wide open. At least this is how Sonya had pieced it together when she'd come in from shopping and found him. Or maybe it had been the perky little Dallas cheerleaders in their blue and silver outfits. Frank had once taped a movie about them, played it over and over again while she was at work. But whatever it was, Frank had hated being ill, and to think of him freed from his ailing heart tempered Sonya's grief.

The twins don't come at Christmas. They know better, having experienced winter in Northport, and sensibly confine their visits to summer. Besides, it's a long way from Boston where they are specialists in music therapy for emotionally disturbed children. Then too, Christmas is their busiest season. Seems that if you're going to have a spell, you'll have it at Christmas.

Both girls have married well enough to send nice gifts, although Sonya tells them not to. For Sonya, there's usually an extravagant assortment of cheeses, dried fruits and jams from Harry and David's; for Danny, sweaters of silk and cotton blends, or nubby natural-weave shirts from shops like Banana Republic, L.L. Bean, or Land's End. Frank used to get gift certificates from Abercrombie and Fitch, or Brookstone. He'd loved those Brook stone catalogs, would pore over them for hours before ordering exotic gadgets like self-coiling downspouts, automatic coin rollers, or solar-powered driveway markers.

Oh, poor dear dead Frank! Suddenly Sonya finds herself engulfed in a wave of grief, loneliness, and, yes, relief, and feels a hot rush of tears coming on. She collapses on her cot—she's moved a light bed into the dining room so she can close off the bedroom wing of the house and tries to frame this mix of emotions into a haiku. As she reaches for her journal, though, she realizes her mood is too massive to compress into seventeen syllables. So she falls into loopy longhand prose, such a pouring forth of feeling that she doesn't hear Danny's pickup in the driveway.

Suddenly he is there and she is startled by his rapping on the glass of the sliding door, looking in at her. It gives her quite a start, too, just like when that hobo wandered into the kitchen when she was making a sandwich. After that, she'd had to re-think her philosophy about locks being anti-egalitarian.

"Danny, hon!" she gasps, opening the door. The dog rushes in past her to lick up crumbs of food in the cats' dishes. She frowns at it, then says, "I didn't hear you."

Along with the ritual hug, he gives her a quick looking-over. "You okay, Ma? What's going on?" Sonya sees herself through his eyes—her wild shaggy hair, the baggy sweats, the Birken-stocks over Frank's ragwool socks. She has let herself go, re-laxed into retirement. Last spring she sold the accounting firm and now spends her time "brooding around." That's how Frank would have put it. But she prefers what her encounter group says: she has gotten her priorities straight and has given herself permission to become the person she really is. Yes, much nicer, and closer to the truth. "I'm okay. How about you?" His eyes flatten when she pulls away to look at him.

He's wearing a misshapen wool sweater covered with pills from hard usage. Sonya recognizes it from the package the twins sent last year—it was an expensive Irish cable knit, and she longs to lecture him on the proper care for woolens. (But she has been to enough workshops to understand his need to ruin it.)

(Just as she has also understood her own veiled message to the girls when she offered them her office wardrobe—three-piece suits stored in their plastic bags from the cleaners. For Sonja is tall and thin, while they are the real Bosco women, short and stocky. As babies, they'd been so beguiling with their round black eyes fringed with long thick lashes. However, Sonya has realized, with a pang, that they will not age as well as she and Danny, that their complexions will turn muddy, and at a certain age, they will sprout mustaches.)

"Did you have a good trip, Danny? What's wrong?" she asks, for his mouth smiles, but Frank's frown puckers his forehead.

She goes on, "What is it, Dan? Something wrong with the boat?" She thinks it must be the boat, the boat she had made possible, since he has no wife or child. Yes, it is her fault, his unhappiness, his grim situation. It's like the aquarium she saddled him with, that he carts around from lodging to lodging.

"Nothing's wrong." He sniffs the air. "Am I too early?"

"Early?" she squawks, her voice filmed with panic. "No, of course not. I've got a bean casserole ready to pop in the oven." A turkey is no longer required: Sonya has gone vegetarian with a vengeance. "No fuss, no muss," she adds wildly, suddenly aware of the desert of time stretching before them. What will she do to fill it up? There's no football to watch, no turkey to cook, no packages to wrap and unwrap, no tree to put up or take down. She and Danny are going to have to relate, they are going to have to get along. And they no longer have Frank to blame for their failures. It is daunting.

They unload his cargo, and Danny talks of the economic slump in Coos Bay. The days of big salmon runs are over, everyone has a boat for sale, no wonder he can't sell his. "Clinton's just got to talk to fishermen, too, at the Timber Summit," he says firmly.

"Thing is, Danny, fishing's an extractive industry. You can't take and take and take. If we would all just quit eating the poor things—"

"Ma, that's too simplistic. Anyway this crisis in fishing is something I didn't create, but I'm paying for. It's just not fair."

Well, that's life, she thinks but murmurs, "Best we can do is what the bumper sticker says—Think globally, act locally'."

His frown deepens. "Live like a bumper sticker. Yeah, that'll fix everything."

Sonya is irked, but she thinks of a diversion. She says they must walk on the beach, to a new house being built just above surf line. "Five bedrooms, three baths for one old lady. Talk about over-consumption..." She leads him down a path through salal, salmonberries, and shore pines to a sandy stretch behind the house. Her head is ringing with nonsense—Frank would have said bullshit—and she blathers about costs of construction, use of space, septic approval. But her body pulses with Danny's presence beside her, the gravitational pull of one planet to another. He still affects her. He is still dangerous to her.

"So, see what I mean?" They stand before an ugly new edifice with a mansard roof. Three garages, this woman needs three garages!"

When he turns round puzzled eyes on her, she fragments further, and begins to spew geologic facts—her latest extension course.

"See, this land can't sustain such pressure from development. The septic tank will have to have leach lines out to here...we're living on a sea terrace carved out of basalt; igneous and sedimentary rocks are all we have here. Makes me laugh, your dad wanted granite walls in his dream house. Granite! It would have had to come all the way from the Wallowas!" She does laugh a bit hysterically, and goes on about intrusions along sill lines, breccia embedded in clast, and twisted coils of basalt pillows. Danny lets her spin, watches her as if she's a wound-up top.

Then they come upon a tide line dotted with velella, tiny jellyfish washed up because of an unusual west wind. She cradles one in her hand and announces like a professor, 'They're called 'wind sailors' because they don't have motors, only sails and rudders. They're at the mercy of the wind and tide, of forces beyond their control." Like all of us, she adds mentally.

"Jesus Christ, Ma!"

She looks up wildly, almost expecting a sneaker wave. "What? What?"

"I come all the way up here and you lecture me about some shit! I shoulda stayed at home. You don't pay attention!"

"Danny, what is it?" She turns to him. His face is white, clenched, and she sees Frank in him.

"Diane's pregnant. She's gonna have a kid and she says it's mine!"

She stutters, "Why, why...that's...uh...that's..." while trying to think who is Diane. (And she is aware of relief, of an unholy glee she herself is not the cause of Danny's bad mood; nor is it her contribution to his life in Coos Bay, the boat.)

"Wonderful, Ma?" His voice drips sarcasm. "No, it's not wonderful. I don't want a kid, I haven't got time for a kid. Or money. She doesn't want a kid, either, but she won't...she won't do what I tell her about it."

Slowly they retrace their steps, the dog bounding ahead of them. Sonya notes their footprints in the sand, the two of them and the dog, as if they were the only creatures left in the world. She is aware of a deepening depression, but pushes it firmly aside. "Well, Danny," she says, "if every baby born was planned for, I don't think we'd have a global population problem." Her words clatter coldly, like stones down a well, and she immediately wishes them unsaid.

"Oh, great! That helps a whole lot."

She goes on with it, clutching at straws, "It's true. wouldn't be here if my mother had had a choice."

"Me, either. Yeah, Ma, I can count, I know I was about five months premature."

Even now, in this age of casual, no-fault pregnancies, Sonya is stung. She feels like crying, and when he lays his arm across her shoulders in a rough embrace, she flinches. Danny notices this, and drops his arm. "I'm sorry, Ma," he croaks. "It's just that I'm so trapped. You don't know. You couldn't know."

"Oh, but I do know, Danny. Just the same, at your age—"

"Okay, okay," he says roughly. So I'm thirty-seven, and at my age, you had a nineteen-year-old and two seventeen-year-olds. That doesn't make me want to marry her. God! I only met her a couple of times. She was supposed to know better! It's not fair! Aren't people supposed to agree to have a baby?"

Sonya turns away from this disconcerting childishness—as if agreement caused babies. Instead, she fastens on his earlier comment. "Oh, yeah, Danny, believe me, I know trapped feelings. Your dad and I— "

He interrupts, says in a rush, "Yes, yes, that's exactly what I've discovered, how it must have been for Dad. The old man, he was some kind of guy, you know? To hang in there, steady as a rock." His voice rises, cracks with emotion. "He was trapped, too, but he maintained, he was so honorable, so strong, and he's gone and I can't tell him."

For a second, she flushes with anger, sees again baby Danny clinging to the crib bars, Frank's handprints reddening on his rump. However, she murmurs, "Yes, he was all of that."

He goes on in a blubbery tone, "He tried so hard to teach me about tools, how to fix things, and I couldn't learn. I'm not very mechanical, Ma, but he wanted me to know so much."

In spite of herself, Sonya conjures up that last lethal fight over some greasy misplaced tool—when, from the house, Frank rifled to Danny in the street a sleeping bag and kicked him out for good. But she says softly, "Oh my, yes, he was a mechanic, all right."

"A genius. That birdhouse, those models. Dad could always fix anything. What a guy he was!"

"Of course, dear, yes," Sonya murmurs. She wants to go on with this veneration of Frank, but she's a bit miffed. What about her part in it? She begins to tell him stories of those early times, when Danny and the twins had been babies. She tells of dragging a wagon loaded with three toddlers to town, because a stroller held two at the most, and, of course, a second car had been out of the question. She tells of struggling to create a meal for five out of a single can of tuna, of learning to fold a coffee filter from a paper towel. These are mere crumbs, of course, tidbits to divert him with. And so what if her stories spotlight her part in their survival? It's all she has to go on because during those early days Frank had rationed out his communication with her, as if words cost money. Why had he never talked about working two or three jobs at once, and going to school at night? She still hasn't a clue about how he'd felt.

But she will never describe to Danny the strata of despair that underlay those days, the impenetrable bedrock of boredom, fatigue, and self-doubt. Or of the mealtime messes, the diapers, bottles, the earaches, the battles with mysterious allergies. Let alone her anger at the doctor who'd bandaged Danny's left hand when he'd shown signs of being a southpaw, like she was herself; or of her rage at the school counselor who'd put Danny in the same class with the twins, so that BACK TO SCHOOL nights turned into ruthless displays of Danny's D's next to the girls' A's. Nor will she ever mention the YMCA leader who'd let team captains choose up their friends, in front of bleachers of parents, until no one was left but Danny, poor weird little Danny, the leftover, the outcast. No, she'll never bring up these horrors, ever.

"A baby!" Danny says, his voice full of disbelief.

"A baby," she mutters. To think of Danny with a baby...Sonya admits she is shocked and appalled. He had always seemed the least likely of her three to reproduce. For some time she has thought all of them sterile: mules, products of Frank the horse and herself the donkey. Ill-starred, mismatched...

True, Vera had once written, asking if Sonya had fallen or been injured when pregnant with the twins. There was some sort of a problem, and Vera's doctor was puzzled. Well, of course Sonya had smoked, and drunk alcohol through both pregnancies. Everybody did back then. They just hadn't known. Nobody knew, back then.

Danny with a baby! Sonya also admits she sees him as inept, as somehow flawed. She visualizes Danny at the crib bars, his hand raised to smack a screaming drooling child. She is suddenly so tired, she wonders how she will manage the walk home. But she says, her eyes down, "Just think, Danny, a baby...this time next year there will be a new set of prints in this sand."

"Ha! Unless he's as slow as I was and doesn't walk until he's old enough to vote. In which case I'll be carrying him."

Him! It's to be a boy, a little blond boy, so fragile, so vulnerable, with only Danny and this Diane, and who is that? with only them to fend for it! Sonya straightens her shoulders. "Well, so what if he doesn't walk till he's two? Children mature at varying rates," she hears herself pronounce, feeling suddenly so wise, so seasoned.

A mission is stirring in her. She must have a hand in the raising of this child! Her mind spins wildly on cookie-baking, quilt-making, song-singing. She will become an empowered grandma. She will resubscribe to *Sunset*, she will read Dr. Spock, and *Highlights for Children*. She will trade the recliner in for a rocker. She will do it right, this time.

Now she can hardly wait to get home, to get started. She almost sprints down the beach, thinking of lullabies and walks on the beach and trips to the park. And stories to tell about the grandpa this baby never had a chance to meet. She trembles on the edge of tears and/or a fit of the giggles, recalling funny odd moments with Frank. That year she took up tennis (due to her crush on the instructor), and dragged Frank down to the courts for practice. He'd always been a natural athlete, could beat her at anything no matter how many lessons she took. So he'd loved it, had fired at her unreturnable serve after serve spinning with English, until he'd gotten his feet crossed and had fallen flat on his back. Oh, how she'd laughed, what wicked glee! The people in the next court had raced over to help him up—while she whooped with laughter. Served him right! Showing off like that.

And the Year of the Boat, that awful fishing boat he'd foisted on them. As captain, how bossy and belligerent he'd gotten, barking orders, do this, do that...and then he'd thrown out the anchor without first securing it, and they'd sat there watching the "bitter end" of the line disappear into the murky waters of the bay. How she'd enjoyed that, how she'd laughed at poor Frank's expense! Now she does giggle, and Danny turns to give her a quizzical look.

"Nothing, dear, just thinking of your dad," she murmurs.

"What?" he asks. "What about Dad?"

"Just stories, dear." She's suddenly aware that these tales are unsuitable to his mood, not the kind he wants to hear. Well, there must be some warm fuzzies...but what? She thumbs through her memories as if turning pages in a book.

Oh, yes, Danny's birthday bicycle from a Western Auto sale. They'd gone all the way to Salem for it, brought it home in a crate, and that night Frank had assembled it. It had taken him all night because the directions had been in Chinese. But Frank had hung in there because it was for Danny, and all Danny had wanted that year was a bicycle.

The next day Frank had run up and down the street beside Danny, trying to teach him to balance on his new bicycle. Up and down, up and down, panting, exasperated, until he finally gave up. Then when Frank had gone into the house to complain to Sonya about how uncoordinated Danny was, they'd looked out into the street just in time to see him proudly sail by on his shiny Chinese bike. How that had irked Frank! As if Danny had been stalling, waiting for Frank to turn his back before succeeding.

Sonya stifles another giggle—this story isn't suitable either. What in hell can she pass along to this grandbaby?

But she smiles at Danny who's giving her that look again. "I'm thinking of the legend we'll create about your dad," she says. "Well, not legend, exactly. True stories with a little spin on them. Never mind, Danny," she adds when he frowns. "Never mind. Think what a time we'll have next Christmas with a new little one. For once, we'll do it right."

She lofts down the beach toward home, full of ideas for an aggrandizement of Frank. The family badly needs a hero; moreover, it needs her to create it. She can do this for Danny, do it the way he wants it done. Maybe there's a workshop somewhere, it's the kind of thing in vogue now...but she must hurry, there is much to do, not a moment to spare.

For right behind them, the ebb and flow, the wash of the surf is erasing their footsteps almost before they pass.

ACKNOWLEDGMENTS

Lupta derit apel event, conecto tatio. Nam dit quia non-sectori saped que pro et volor simost et esequia ndamus do-lessed quodiatur? Qui volorem recaecae doles debit omnihil eria dellam lam expliamusda velecerum rerferum eum volore, qui alignis sunturit, corrum, eum iuntibeate commolo riassum, nescian dipisit eseribus apient.

Ci diatectur acium voluptaquas aborro magnihilibus nit eicto tem quas andem netur as consernam, voluptur? Quibus velibus, erem erchillaut vellatus quam evelecae odit ant delen-dae ommos et fugit explab intiunt acia voluptatur? Quidusdae et ommo est distiae nis vollam, illupta volupie nihicia nimi, ulparia ipitibusam quost, sum hiciis que occum int liquas re-pellori apiet endus sum et que ipsandipiet quia quo ea dolupta dipsa aut eum nobit repedigni consequatur molores remos do-lescid et verferitati te deles eos et oditiis de et quam fuga.